Helen McClory is the   *Edges
of Vision* (Queen's Ferry Press),   ...tire First Book
of the Year award, and *Mayhem* c   ...04 Ink), as well as a
novel, *Flesh of the Peach* (Freight, 2017). *The Goldblum Variations* –
a collection of experimental micro-fictions – was published by
404 Ink (2018), and Penguin (2019). Her short stories have been
listed for distinction in *The Best of British Fantasy* (2018), The Best
of British and Irish Flash Fictions (2018/19), and nominated for
the Pushcart prize. Helen is a part-time lecturer at the University
of Glasgow and co-founder of writing retreat Write Toscana.

BITTERHALL

A Novel

by

Helen McClory

First published in Great Britain in 2021 by Polygon,
an imprint of Birlinn Ltd

West Newington House
10 Newington Road
Edinburgh
EH9 1QS

9 8 7 6 5 4 3 2 1

www.polygonbooks.co.uk

This is a work of fiction. Names, characters, businesses, places,
events and incidents are either the products of the author's imagination
or used in a fictitious manner. Any resemblance to actual persons,
living or dead, or actual events is purely coincidental.

The excerpt on page v is taken from *Stigmata* (1998) by Hélène Cixous.
Printed with permission.

ISBN 978 1 84697 549 3
eBook ISBN 978 1 78885 375 0

The publisher gratefully acknowledges investment from
Creative Scotland towards the publication of this book.

ALBA | CHRUTHACHAIL

British Library Cataloguing in Publication Data
A catalogue record for this book is available on request
from the British Library.

Typeset by 3btype.com
Printed and bound in Great Britain by Clays Ltd, Elcograf S.p.A.

And to think that there will be readers of our book. They will open it. And they'll make fun of the murkiness of our night. Says the author - We, for so many years, see them, trying to find themselves, get lost, a hundred times on the point of finding themselves, seeing themselves, looking at themselves, recognizing themselves; finally tearing away the lovely, thin veil that blurs their vision, the guardian of truth, and thus living for years, on the edge, quivering with desire, that is, fear, that is, desire.

Hélène Cixous, *Stigmata*

Daniel Lightfoot

Autumn Soft

I am on the swing in the garden, under the oak bough, late August night, a couple of beers tipped over beside me in the short mossy grass and my heart is a neat bundle of sticks in love with the dead and the unreachable. Up in the house a single light shines; first floor, the bedroom, my bedroom, so it looks like there's somebody up there. And I, hazy, imagine them looking down on me, and at the same time down on the whole of this city, with some dispassionate warmth, like a God.

My head lies against the swing chain, the fabric of my scarf at my throat grey in this light, blue indoors, I'd grabbed it on leaving the new housemate and his girlfriend at a strange moment all together in the kitchen. I think how he, Tom, is legendarily good looking. Only later will I see Tom unravel and almost fall, and I will catch him.

Work is just beginning to launch itself to its full purpose, and I think of the objects I will handle, which I have seen in the catalogue or taken out of packaging and put into the safe, so frail in my careful hands; I think of the monumental paperwork, the email chains to and from absent bosses mostly floors above my soundproofed basement room.

I feel for the metal chain of the swing and kick off again, a gentle sway, a little more, wind in the face, cold, and the ground makes a good sound when I kick it. I don't think about the thing I am trying not to think about. Shhhh. I think for a while about this ground, leafy, dirt in footprints, old scuff-mark furrows from swing-riders, and of the tensile strength of the chains, and of the cold of the seat. All I can think, just for a moment, is: Just be calm. Bed soon. Back up to the diary I am reading and I do not yet know of everything wild that waits above us to kick off, with my housemate, his girlfriend and me.

I want *you* to love me, if I'm being honest. That's why I start so gently, in the garden, in the present tense. A good story begins tipsily in a garden, and carries on through well-proportioned rooms in the past tense in which blood is being spilled and was spilled, is measured out already, and the possessors of that blood were embarrassed at its spilling, and hold their hands over the wounds, pretending everything was fine. When exactly is this happening, and to whom is it happening, and who is making it happen? We begin to become tricky, don't we, when I write in the first person. What tense do my intrusive thoughts manifest in? Somewhere between the first and second, like a harsh note in a piano recital, a piece so often played it should be clean of errors, yet here and here again the wrong note spikes in the same predictable, always jarring way, repeating itself, a bad inorganic refrain.

Intent is the issue, too. It's a holiday to take up a different tense, a different perspective. But I'll let you decide who is who, who is not who, who is real (real enough, then?). For a clue (as much as I've got), there is a centre to this whole thing. It's up to you to mark it.

Aside – everything is an aside. Except the centre. That is the centre. Find it. Come along and around me. Us. Fill the edges of this thing.

The Self

In the garden at night, opening my eyes after closing them over, and keeping the drunkenness and feeling all in, and trying not to let it out I take a swig from one of the beers. It's flat and stale and tastes of my own mouth. I click tongue against teeth and think good, the taste of it, think of that. A small body flashes on the old stone wall, moonlight white. The new housemate's cat prowling. I let it go without trying to get it to come to me. That morning it had looked orange saucers at me from the housemate's – Tom's – briefly open door as the housemate – Tom – made a cup of tea and yawned good morning at me in his boxers in the kitchen, while I held my robe – Christmas present ten years ago from a long-gone boyfriend – tight around me, not knowing where to look. Knowing exactly where to look, I had thought, that bulge, the trail of hairs blond but still there. And people think I'm a prude. I shake my head. Cat's going over the old stone wall. A little bell sound. A bell on its collar. Then she's crouching to leap down the other side, her white tail there a moment and gone. Silent snow, I think. Without the bell she would catch everything and sink her teeth in. But she can't. So she will go through all the gardens of this part of town causing no harm at all. The cat is called Mrs Boobs, Tom told me.

'Was fucked when I named her,' he had said, in his English voice – sounding to me like a crisp, low round of applause in a half-empty theatre – as he smiled into his tea, and raised his eyes to mine, 'and somehow it stuck.'

'It's pretty memorable,' I had said, politely, lost in his wide, shimmering blues. It mattered not a bit what he had said, but everything around it: cool, brilliant, probably brutish, seen across some distant ground from my own poor territory, my peripheral beinghood – Midlothian, adenoidal, not, as I am constantly made aware, aesthetically gifted in the face or body. Tom is aesthetically gifted. I could almost hate him, I think, but I know it would merely make me an idiot if I don't wait to see what he is; all his sticky, tender layers, underneath, outwith and beyond me.

Tonight is okay; tonight it's early autumn and a few stars, and no one about, everyone passed out – or busy – in their own beds. You are loved, Daniel, I tell myself, with a slight, drunken kind of sincerity that is also unstable. You are stable. Neither of these are true things, I know, I know, but it is something I am now saying to myself, a different kind of repetition. From today onwards. Only when I'm not likely to blurt it out and have other people hear, and look at me with confusion and pity. New housemate, new housemate's new girlfriend – Órla – neither of whom love me, no one has ever wanted to stay with me for long. They know, I think each time a loved one, a friend, a lover, dumps me, they know the kind of terrible person I am.

'You are loved, Daniel,' I say out loud, but softly. No one, not even the cat, hears me, thank God. I am trying to make it happen, cringing at trying, and though powerless not to try, at least, through the small degrees I am capable of believing it. It's all been done so many times before. Swing, I think instead, and feel the wind lift my hair. All the stakes, for this moment, are small. My life, my body moving in the dark against all the other darkness, moving, swells of small life, cats creeping over many walls, their teeth unable to clamp down on throats, because a little bell declares their sublimated intentions. I am loved. The world loves all in it. A man long dead is the current target of my affections.

Pathetic Fallacy

I found the diary in a friend's house three days before Tom moved in and I stole it and ran away. It was the handwriting that made me do it; I would say, if asked, I'm a sucker for gorgeous handwriting. That is, not handwriting that is perfect, but which seems to exude a quality of welcome dalliance across the page, an open pleasure in the act of writing down just exactly what you wish and at your own pace, directed at no one and in private. James Lennoxlove of Bitterhall has just this kind of quality in his writing, which is all that is left of him, the man himself being dust. I even liked how our names might look together, that juvenile of me: Lennoxlove and Lightfoot. The great tall L of Lennoxlove with the loop through the top, full of air, finding its twin in my L, if he, Lennoxlove, wrote it out by its side.

It wasn't clear how Mark came to be in possession of the diary, an accident of boxes from his mother's and uncle's merging households. How I decided to take it is simple impulsiveness. Mark, the kind of rich boy who found me amusing and so, in a moment of spurred viciousness, I stole this diary. Vicious to me, I knew Mark wouldn't care. Would laugh. Would say, Oh Daniel, in a way that would madden and wind me for days. Because I was all reactions, as I often told myself. Easily wound up. I put the brown-red clothbound book down the front of my trousers and let my bulky jumper and nervous smile conceal it. I gave a hurried excuse about being home for breakfast with my mum.

But I didn't go home to mum. I went to the place I live, the

7

eternal non-home of my generation, the rental house where I and my two housemates have our various lives, decently set out so that they do not overlap or hurt one another too much. All strangers, yes, because I have never been able to find anyone who would request to live with me.

I went up the stairs to the room in the place in which I live and set the stolen diary square on my table and read it from start to one quarter or so through in two sittings (break for tea, taken in a dwam, a cup of tea and some bread, chewed slowly and carefully while eyeing but not reading the diary, so the crumbs didn't get near). It was easy enough to read it, that flowing handwriting, welcoming me in. It felt like being plunged into a warm bath after a long time standing naked. What a beautiful pink there was in the sky when I came to and the great garden trees blue-black against it, my face mushed and hot where the heels of my hands had been pressed against the temples. I was crying. Relief I thought. Not a whole life, this one being gifted to me, or that I had more rightly stolen, not even that. I wondered if I could ever be loved like Lennoxlove loved the world.

I decided not to read any more for a little while.

Fixes

A good day looked like this – nothing. A good and bad day looked like – I went into work early and down into the basement of the university, stopping in on my boss, Dr Glaister, who understood budgets and all warm palms needing shaken and the requirement too for staff morale and so for her to be at a kindly remove, providing a good email promptly, cakes on staff birthdays, plants in every space that could take a plant. Stopping in to say things were going well – they must always be going well, the personal is professional, and there to the staff room – kitchen, low calm lighting – to deposit my noodle box by the kettle and swipe for coffee and consume this, consume moments of amiability any passing colleagues might have to offer and proffer my own, and after that to disappear into my project; the blessed calm of it in a room padded and soft with no sound but me and my machine, everything smooth if it was to be running that day, and to my small side office, easily answered courteous emails, emerging for lunch and if no one about, then, then, the slip into thinking, gulping down a bottle of water while the kettle steamed up the glass cabinets, and pouring hot water into my desiccated meal, staring in wait at the staff kitchen table at my noodles swelling and pieces of carrot thinking of anything else I could; someone might come in and make small talk and I'd smile easily and make it back. I'd eat and they'd eat, and always the smile, it faltered as their fork approached their lips and I'd keep steadily thinking to myself, talking politely, meanwhile imagining certain images

I find soothing, such as picking several daisies, say, or imagining myself on a calm fogbound lake with everything cool and my raft perfectly sanded and smooth, standing in soft clothes. Back to work. Finish work. Walk home, sometimes the pace of my thoughts keeping up with me, over even the blast of classical music in my headphones, until home, and sometimes too much breath too little chest and fragile bones and I might just shake myself apart and so I would go, if it was really bad, up to my room and curl up in a ball hugging a pillow and gasping until I relaxed, slept, woke up a little better or rather more resolved to be better. There were no really bad days then, only my hands got so tired of holding myself up. It was natural. I forgave myself that. And began each day knowing I would survive it, and hoping for normal if at all possible, and never expectant, like a disciple awaiting the descent of the most holy all the days of their life, in some desert cave, getting to know it well, stones are peaceful, the heavy, reassuring grace that any day can be broken down into measurable portions, toil preferable to the works of the devil that swings and slithers up to them at night, whispering their doubt that any such an end will come.

Men of the House

It was the day before Tom moved in. My heart throbbed in my wrists as I went downstairs after that first reading session, as I tried to recover my decorum, such as it was. I tapped my fingers on descent. I wasn't sure yet if I had experienced a change in my life, as happened at times, from one Daniel to another, before-Daniel being somehow brimmed up and spilt over by Lennoxlove's writing to be mingled with it, to become something else – I hoped not more tender, Christ, possibly not more tender than I was already, I might actually die from that, or disappear up my own fundament to nevermore emerge.

The kitchen empty as it usually was around that time and pleasantly dirty in its pre-Badr state. Badr came in from work around seven. Minto was about, surely, in his room, sometimes his little white face and beard and twittering eyes as he slipped out to his toilet. Owner of the house Minto, the recluse, the hermit. One time only I was in there and saw the faded armchair, striped wallpaper-like pyjamas, damp spot and the bed. And. All. Those. Books. Minto fumbling but charismatic too, a deposed king of somewhere whose borders were now shrunk to this. The smell of the place, not awful but certainly lodged in the back of my head, so that when the door opened, as it infrequently did, I remembered the foost of it rather before I smelled it. One time only I'd been in there was the day I'd moved in, and handing Minto – tremulous red hands stuffy with arthritis – an antique cheque; after that, envelopes in the postal nook at the hallway. One waved hand, kindly enough to bid me leave his presence.

Badr, the final and most normal flatmate: friendliest man ever, made good dishes that filled the kitchen with rolling saffron waves of scent. Insisted on mostly eating these meals on the sofa – blackbeetle-coloured, pvc – and playing videos of this singing contest show from Russia he was obsessed with. Cat-singing, huge roof of mouth singing, that was what he liked to accompany eating. Badr was careful and obnoxiously, to my tastes, clean, liked spritzes of bleach after every use of the sink or shower. I had yet to learn much about him beyond these facts in the nine months we had been living together.

I had heard from a colleague in archives that Dr Minto was more than a widower, cast out from the university under a cloud – of rumour, but more, of toothy suspicion – but I, not wishing to know, had waved my hand, kindly enough, and got on with the prep for the intricate digital transfer process for which I had been employed. Half a year ago? More.

The Annunciation

Badr wasn't home quite, no bleach or high cheer, so I made myself tomato soup from a can with a twist – the twist being lemon rind, grated a little, and a splash of vodka, and yes I hated myself even for the idea of this being a twist or any kind of innovation, but it really was quite tasty. I checked my emails as I sat listening to the microwave. Nothing important. The door rattled, and Badr was now coming through.

'Are you there, Danny boy?'

'Yes, Badr,' I said, smiling. Badr came in the room like a jolly sun in a cartoon with his shopping and rolled about putting things correctly away. I took the soup out of the microwave and sat back down, braced for a moment. I felt like screaming oh for fucks sake in the middle of the room, which was a kind of posturing idea, since I could quite well manage screaming anguished obscenities from my seat while I ate the soup. And I'd have to live with Badr after that.

'I have a good lead on a housemate,' said Badr, 'potentially.'

'Oh, that's good, someone from work?'

'Someone from my gym actually.'

I ate half my soup, washed out the bowl and poured a glass of water.

'He's coming to look at the place,' said Badr, folding his bag-for-life under the sink.

'Oh?'

'In half an hour. Can you help me clean?'

'Oh.'

Himself

Badr got it. In came the stranger filling the whole space. Dark blond, slightly out of breath. Black coat like something professional, black jeans, tight, muscle tee under, the wrong thing for the weather and for the other gear, these being some clothes cobbled together in a rush. Black Converse. Younger than me by a good few years I thought, though this based only on his look of unlined confidence. Touch of a tan on his face. Freckles. Unruined, possibly vain. Bigger than both Badr and I. His balance, the way he stood and moved through the spaces suggested the grace of a larger animal, predatorial, a creature that could leap and pounce, but could let you know, in subtle ways that it would not. Fuck me, I thought.

The Tour

I got myself up and smiled and shook the offered hand – handshake just as expected. Badr took the lead and guided him around the communal spaces, the living room first, the kitchen, the halls, then his room – if he wanted it, on the ground floor, view of the garden.

'The garden is communal too, and you'll have a key to the shed.'

The stranger stood in the centre of the room and stretched out his arms as if to try and touch both walls, though they were many more metres apart than he could touch, it was some kind of gym move, I guessed, an exercise he might like to do in his new space. When he wasn't wearing a coat, presumably. 'Yeah, looks great. Listen – are pets okay? If I'm interested.'

'Pets are okay,' said Badr, 'like, one pet.' Minto wouldn't notice an animal if it pissed on his lap. Maybe then.

'Okay cool, cool. I have a cat.'

'I like cats,' I said, 'always adds something to a house.'

I wanted, after my cringe, for him to look at me like a predator would, turn those eyes on me, scoff, scorn.

'Yes absolutely,' was all he said, with a slightly odd smile – he turned his face from me quickly and took a breath, and my thought was that he hates me, it can't be that he's shy – 'Well. Looks good. Listen – any chance I could move in tomorrow?' He was saying, 'I know, short notice, but my old lease is up, I have the day off, and like I was saying, Badr, I can't stay another month . . .'

He looked around proprietorial but also preparing to leave, to be gone. If he moves in he won't stay, I thought. Also: he looks like a celebrity, not one I know, but one who hasn't become famous yet, but is marked to, a celebrity in waiting.

'Oh yeah, of course,' said Badr, 'we need the room filled. Sooner works for us.'

'Cool, thank you. Good meeting you both.'

And then the door was slammed shut, the walls reverbing, and Badr and I were looking out the lease to copy and show Minto, well, leave for him in the cubby.

'Seems all right, eh?' said Badr.

'Yes,' I said, too firmly. But Badr, if he knew, never spoke with me about my desires, what general part of the population I fancied, nor anything of himself on that matter. I went up to my room to worry about other people, other scenarios.

The next day Tom moved in with Mrs Boobs, and unofficially, his girlfriend.

Herself

Órla was just about the strangest person I had met apart from myself. She came the night of the housewarming, she was late, and the men of the house were tipsy, and rapidly it seemed that she was in some parallel universe way a kind of version of myself, though, as far as she let on, without the hampering awfulness that at all times I have to fight back from my brain. Mind, how would I know such things? Battlefields are sometimes as smooth as a spring meadow to look at, the terror subcutaneous, twisting roots and expanding sinkholes at the biological level. Maybe atomical.

She resembled me physically as well, to my eye, and that was encouraging. She was exactly my height, and had grey eyes – to my brown – of the same long shape and heavy lashes, and brown hair a shade lighter than mine, thick and shiny and unruly. The hair that as a child your mother frets over with the brush and dabs of spit. Stupidly, dimly encouraging it seemed. Daniel . . . I told myself, as I handed her a beer from the fridge, exchanging it for the wine she had brought.

'So,' said Órla. 'Thanks. I got it at lunch so it needs to cool down.'

Irish. I couldn't tell where from. I shied away from looking at her, as I always did, getting overwhelmed with the contact, the contract, of shared human gazes, taking the time instead to scope out the fruit situation, still five bananas in a bowl on the table. Away elsewhere in the house the macho bonding hour was long in its cups. It seemed the godlike Tom liked to laugh about bad reality TV as much as the others in the living room, and I didn't need to be in that or any other conversation such a crowd might have.

Órla stood there in the kitchen in her blood-red coat, alert, waiting for something.

At last, I tried to zero in on her face, thinking it was about time I said something, looked at her. Something welcoming, but all I could manage, the eyes too much, a clever, crackling lively stare, was to attempt a deeper picture of this enviable stranger from her atmospherics. Then she seemed like me and also like an open vista of the sea with a high wind blowing, like a glimpse of the shore below cliffs, and the white water and somewhere seagulls crying. Eyes grey but flashing. There was a depth, is what I'm saying. This impression is of course coloured by all that came after it.

But that night: Órla's blue scarf covering all of her neck and that dark red coat, something I would wear if I was her, because it looked excellent, made her pale face shine and that red lipstick contrasted well with all. I was somewhat awed by the moment, you can tell. Standing together we both looked good, like conspirator siblings, full of health. All that lent strength by her clever way of dressing. I made a note to get myself some oxblood cardigan at some point in the future. Órla cracked the beer, made a face drinking. 'Nice coat,' I said. Her eyes sought me out again, and I looked down and away again like always.

'You're wondering the why, aren't you?' said Órla, 'I hate beer, I always drink it and hate it. Does the job, but.'

'Not really,' I said, opening a bottle of bitter lemon, fingering the bottles on the counter for the right one. Basic gin.

'Oh look at you, like you know what I was going to say,' said Órla. 'No "why what" from you. And thanks, it's from a charity shop.'

We sat down at the kitchen table, her trying not to break eye contact, but me, the expert at breaking it, slippery, the kind of person a security guard in a shop tries to keep in view, but who always vanishes behind the stacks. I began to wish, despite myself, that I could stop being that way. It was because of her; she was offering me something, I thought. Was it more her almost tangible mood I found so distinctive, rather than what she actually said? From the living room, the throb of music. Badr had a few friends from way back and a few friends from his office, I'd met them and felt the need to be evasive, and Tom had himself, and that was enough. His laughter came often. A pang struck me, a deep ringing sound in my chest.

'Don't tease,' I said, looking at her at last, 'I know what you mean with your "why".'

'Oh aye?'

'Tom, right? You're asking me if I wonder why you're with Tom. Instantly, like that, you've asked me a question to be the judge of you and him. But you phrase it or believe it – just in this instant you think I've come up in my mind first with the question – dilemma – of why you are together. Which is quite presumptuous of you, or—'

'That I'd be thinking it was a preoccupation of yours?'

'Just that,' I answered.

Already

Órla looked at my drink, 'Is it good, bitter lemon? I've never had it.'

'Try some, I don't have a cold.'

Órla raised the glass up to her lips. She would get red on the glass. She drank daintily. The bands on her throat moving, shadow and limn. I turned away—

'Ah, how'd you like it?' I said, thinking, already?

Órla wrinkled her nose, 'It's bitter.'

'It is bitter,' I said, looking at my finger swirling a circle on the table. Smiling.

'I like it. Pour me some.'

I handed her a fresh glass. 'I feel like I know you,' said Órla, 'isn't it weird?'

'Do you?'

Órla didn't say anything for a while. Then – 'You're not – flirting with me?'

'A moment. Could easily be confused for flirting,' I said. 'No, I'm not, I don't think so anyway.'

'You have one of those faces,' said Órla, 'the way you move about. Avoiding my eye. Smiling a lot.'

'Does Tom have one of those faces?'

'Is it nerves?'

We both laughed.

'Sorry,' I said. 'This conversation's all weird, isn't it. Started the wrong way round.'

'I like talking to you,' said Órla. 'Let's talk about some big topic for a while.'

'I think we were, obliquely,' I said.

Órla shrugged. 'Tom – do you think he'll settle in well?'

'You sound like his mum,' I said. But Órla laughed.

'We're not, like— I think this could be good for him,' she said. 'Are you getting warm? Can I take your coat?'

'Aye, you could put it in Tom's room,'

'I suppose you – might – be here a bit . . .'

'I promise not to become one of those live-in girlfriends, not paying any rent, eating all your cheese on the sly.'

'I wouldn't mind,' I said. I picked up the bundle of her coat and walked into Tom's room. The first time I had been in it as Tom's room. I stood for a second. Boxes. A strange smell, Tom's cologne, I supposed, obliterating what it had smelled like before, of vapourised weed; I sniffed, trying to be subtle. It smelled now like white light, you must know what I mean; like light on snow, like green branches, broken. The cat absent but there in its white-haired blanket on the chair. The sound of Órla's chair scraping on the floor. I put down the coat and I thumped my heart with the flat of my hand, just once.

'He likes that poster a lot,' she said. Silent feet. She was standing beside me, we were both facing the same direction.

'"Reach to your dream by the beautiful ocean." Very motivational.'

'It's Japanese. And ironic,' said Órla, 'at least, so he says.'

There was laughter from the other room, at which the two of us laughed.

'Do you love him?' I asked. I had meant to ask, how long have you been going out, but it amounted to the same thing. Órla breathed in a little bit, then went to the hair-strewn blanket and stroked it.

21

'I was there when he rescued the cat,' she said, 'he was drunk but he wanted to help her. She was in an abandoned building. He broke a window, lifted her out. And when he came out his knuckles were all messed up, looked like he had been fighting. That's what he told people. Fighting a building to rescue a cat.'

A pause.

'God it's weird, isn't it? To talk so quick like this. He's – anyway, more than he seems.'

I made approving sounds; I didn't know quite what to think about where she had come from, what world we had grown up together on, quite apart from this one we now found ourselves in.

Órla and I left Tom's room and went to sit on the stairs.

'Will we wake the old guy?'

'No,' I said, 'I don't know if he sleeps anyway.'

'What, he's in there, reading from the stack, keeping up on how to be immortal?'

'Badr told you about the books, hey? Immortal old man with a bookish tendency. Yes. He'll outlive all of us. It's his house. We're just perching in it.'

'You'd be what bird, exactly?'

I sipped my drink, 'Parrot.'

'I had you for a crow myself. And so— Hey, do you think people who have houses get to live longer? Live more real lives than renters?' said Órla.

'Ouch,' I said. I smiled in the way we always do, those of us who will never have money or a place in the world – two unconnected things. 'Ehhh,' I said.

'Me too,' she said, conceding.

Pale Like Grass Dead Almost

Somehow the hours had passed and I and Órla had spoken it all away learning tilted grand things about each other – and then we were making a snack. Tom got sleepy, he came into the kitchen – Badr upstairs to sleep, the guests away home – billows of colder air, we had moved on to get sustenance, now so had this new third. He looked into the fridge with drunken sincerity.

'Toastie?' I offered the plate.

'Mmm,' said Tom, putting it up to his mouth, closing his eyes, bit down. Órla, perched on the countertop, already to the crusts and talking away with her mouth full about an old cookbook of her grandmother's, lies in it, stolen recipes, then on to a child who had been born, his father a priest, and given away to a cousin of the family.

'I'm off to bed,' said Tom.

'Oh, is that how it is,' said Órla, lifting one tight-covered leg to point in his direction. Now, this late, her top sliding off her shoulder. I all still in a marvel at her. This twin I'd never had. This lucky one.

Tom moved in smoothly and picked her up in his arms. Órla wiped her fingers on his sleeve.

'And you're coming with me,' he said in a low voice. I found myself opening the window, just cracking it for the air. The air was good outside, I envied those who had left. I was going to go outside, after they'd gone. To bed. When I turned round however Tom had dropped Órla back on the counter and was kissing her, his thumbs running up her thighs, her arms around his shoulders. I turned, hesitated, picked up a beer, a second one. Then I looked back. Órla had her eyes open, kissing Tom, and she looked at me, directly.

Lights

I left by the kitchen door, closed it firmly behind me, and sat on the swing, feeling vaguely... Disgusted? No. Turned on? Ah, I wasn't sure. Yes a little, and much else besides going on. Women were not so much a source of this kind of thing. Displacement, then. But in any case it's a fool's errand to try to lay it all out clearly in taxonomy. Emotions have granularity: they respond and evolve to each contrasting situation you find yourself in, so rich is life, so much verve and pounding – texture, and poignancy. Look at yourself, Daniel, I thought. The way she knows and looks at me so quickly, this is some kind of message passing between us. She loves him and she doesn't know it herself, so my job, eventually, will be the noble route to help her hash that out, and move myself on to fantasising about another dumb straight boy. These and such other types of indulgent late evening shit, in the garden, with the lights going out in the house, with everyone casting themselves adrift into the booze-eased night but me. Here we return, almost, to where it begins.

I like that she is not a stranger to me, I thought. Flashing eyes that lay herself open, scrutinising me at the same time, that's a bit of a gift. No one wants to be seen more than me. I drank more of the beer and felt cold creeping up my legs. I thought that I would learn more about her and what she wanted; what's with her and Tom – what does Tom want? He's the one. To get fucked. She's going back with him into that room. They are fucking on his bed. It's not his doing, it's hers. Her desire, getting him to – I winced at this thought as if it were one of the intrusive ones. But it was all me, and did not really hurt. Two people were together and I was left out, and that was just the world being the world. I meant no sabotage or creep, I had nothing in my heart, other than the violence and infinite loop of violent acts, dulled at present, thank God. Nothing, I thought, outside, to do with them inside.

But Not Yet

It was later. Foxes crying outside, huffing, foxes in the lanes behind the houses. I was awake for the hour when the bakers and the delivery men, now up and dressed in the dark, are leaving in the dark. A neighbour was rolling the bins to the kerb. A rumble felt in the teeth.

It was later, time flickering. This was habit: sleeping all right, shadowy terrible violences as usual and Badr's roast chicken, occasionally looking at that stolen book, not reading it so much as acknowledging it for a future time, at fallow then, and Tom was a late riser, I supposed, as I hardly ever saw him. Stayed out longer too, I hardly ever went out after coming in from work but he never seemed to come back. It had been a few weeks. Just a glimpse would do me, then. Foxes crying, shortcut through the lanes to the library, to the rattling carts and typing, or down to my place of work in the digital archive. I was given nothing to go on. And Órla, I hadn't seen her at all, and missed her the more, even, than my crush, the way that if you woke to realise mirrors all were without your reflection you'd wonder what was going on with your being in the world.

Call me Daniel the monk: for those new weeks, at least where it counted, mostly sexual and socially inactive in the world, though my thoughts I confess were not pure. But I was strong. And so I worked. And to do so, this task of surviving and life's work, kept out of everything's way, and outside of it, hands in my back pockets, scarf soft at my neck as I breathed into it. The rain, wind. Books arriving for Minto. Minto asking me via note to sell some read ones. The printer was almost ready to go into use. I had to get the room fitted out for perfect storage. Badr got a pay rise. I got a cold and recovered binge-watching a comedy series on Netflix. Not miserable. At night the sounds of sex in the house. At night Lemsip and gin, mixed together. No word from Mark for a while, perhaps he knew about the diary, perhaps, perhaps. Perhaps Mark, after a lifetime, had decided he hated me, and was letting me out of his life this way, by silence. Just the usual myself, my only always reality of dreadful things.

James

I was reading another segment of the diary one day at the kitchen table, like I wanted to be caught at it. I had questions I needed other people to ask me before I could collect my answers from the floor of my understanding. The diary started in at a nameless period when James Lennoxlove was twenty, with entries about once or twice a year, until it stopped, without reason, as diaries often do, because the unreason is death, or a feeling like words are insufficient.

James Lennoxlove of Bitterhall was alive in the early nineteenth century. He talked often about going to India, and primarily of his great passion for all things, particularly the Northern Lights, which he saw one day riding home from his 'natural' brother's household. I was re-reading this passage at my table – *a marvellous fabric high in the evening sky like fairies dancing in luminous green skirts, here now there, and the horse not frightened at all, which made me think she could not see it, for even a dumb beast would shourly surely be stricken with wonder and awe* – James wrote as if for publication, but I doubted he'd achieved it. He'd been quite upfront about his brother being illegitimate, and the fact that they had both had to struggle in the wake of his father's poor handling of family affairs and subsequent death. The illegitimate brother was a Catholic, a fact that worried James deep in his soul, and far older than James, which seemed to raise questions about inheritance. The father left James the big house and Mungo the business interests, though it was Mungo who had a huge

29

family and James no prospects of employment and no wisdom for managing estates. Both brothers only knew of each other's existence after the death. In fragments I saw it, through James' descriptions and offhand notes of account. It was a difficult relationship between two essentially kind people who wanted to like one another, the hospitality of Mungo's wife Mary over a Christmas that James attended at their home, excruciating. (A priest housed up, who he had glimpsed walking blackly about the frosty grounds between the pigpen and the chapel, giving him a mortal fear of papist attempts at surveillance or general menace against All Good Scots.) James' continual befuddlement at what to do with the crumbling house he had been given evident, wanting as a young man to put on dances but finding his efforts at enticing guests fall flat on each turn, as the details of small scandals emerged from his family's past and present. Oh James, I thought, I knew his loneliness, this man who was long-dead, and stung for him, and imagined being him, holding out for RSVPs to my party, so lovingly planned, for the barrels of drink to get in and the food and the extra servants, and the date on the calendar drawing ever near, and all in place, and no one coming.

He Sees Me

I was finishing the Northern Lights moment – James was talking about how he had arrived home and tried to stable his horse but had felt such awe (his favourite word) and woe in his heart that he forgot to lock the stable doors, only to rush down, in the middle of writing the entry, to find the horses were quite calmly sleeping, the gate rattling open but no temptation at all, for the country was dark and cold, though the world above it brilliantly dancing still like a ballroom full of swirling bodies to which he below a single mortal was witness – when Tom came in from the outside world, sweat-drenched in his workout gear and clinked about loudly in the fridge.

'What're you reading?'

'A diary,' I said, without looking up. My whole body was ringing with lights too, first from the passage and now from this entrance, two different kind of stirrings.

'Cool,' said Tom.

'How was work?' So far our conversations had been this slender and polite, and it made me wonder if there was any way we could build a bridge between us that might hold a more meaningful weight. I had managed so effortlessly that first night with Órla, who was at that minute working on her PhD thesis (the human detail in medieval manuscripts, 'meaningful errata and doodles through the ages, basically') at the university library. I thought she had the right idea, looking to the trivial for something greater, but it was hard to see in the scribbles, asides about the weather, bickering complaints, anything more than a human mind slouching in the face of the great overwhelming questions of their age, peacing-out rather than engaging. But that was what we do, was Órla's argument, but even as we seem to disengage we can't help but be doing the opposite.

Tom was eating something he had pulled out of the fridge, and drinking a glass of juice. I saw him move about on the periphery as I remained bent over the diary, reading the same passage over and over, catching the flow of the letters, their sense long discarded. He came up behind me, and stared down at the page. I made no move to cover the diary, assuming he would quickly lose interest. He did not display any sort of response to it.

'Yeah,' he said with a sigh, 'work's all right, same as always.'

'Do you like working there?' I had not grasped exactly where 'there' was, or the nature of the work Tom did there beyond 'marketing . . . ish'. He often did late shifts, and came home in casual or dressy clothes, carrying boxes of leftovers from events, mostly creamy sorts of booze or prepacked products unavailable in local shops, wildly flavoured crisps with Korean labelling, lolli-pops with animals wholesale preserved inside. These he donated to the household, though I was not in a rush to try any of them.

Tom made a disdainful noise, 'Pays the bills. I'm going to find something else soon though.'

'Oh?'

'Don't worry, I won't just quit and leave you hanging for the rent.'

'No, not worried about that. Just wondering, if you were to leave, where would you like to work?'

Tom swung round in front of me into a seat. I was startled by the intensity of Tom's look, but then, I was always startled by anyone's eyes, should they be aimed right at me, and not some-where in the region of me, or behind me, looking at someone else.

He had his office bag on the table and was pulling out – a small furry thing. A soft toy horse. A horse with a fish tail, iridescent.

'A kelpie,' I said.

'No,' Tom said, snorting, 'it's like, a horse-mermaid. Listen.'

He pressed its sides. A muffled, crackling whinny ruckled out, turning into a kind of song at the end, upbeat, repetitive. I reached out for it and stared at its eyes, which were heavy and large and full of shimmering particles that swirled around as I moved it about to the sound of the tune.

'Who's marketing this?'

'Uff, vodka-type company. It's like, not quite vodka, it's their special recipe from this old source, made of grasses. The company was purveyor to a tsar, or something. Not a tsar, cos it's Estonian. You won't have heard of them.'

'No, probably not,' I said.

'Check this out though. This button here,' said Tom, reaching, pushing it, 'is wifi enabled. It's listening now . . .'

'Listening?' I leaned in. Tom leaned also, both of us holding the toy. Sandbaggy body with something firm inside, the soundbox and the internet enabling device. I noticed Tom's fingernails ragged and his fingers not nearly as blocky as I had expected.

'It's like a marketing thing.'

'Gross,' I said. 'What a piece of shit thing to do.'

'What a piece of fucking shit,' said Tom, almost laughing.

'Listening to us? To everything we say? Not another one. It should probably be illegal, companies monitoring us for nefarious marketing information.' I leaned further forward, almost pressing my mouth on the body of the thing. 'Hey, if you are listening, Fuck. You.'

'This kind of shit is exactly why I want out,' Tom said. 'You can't even bring up, like, the moral implications of this, people just look at you. Dead silence.'

'Oh, I have an idea,' I said, illuminated by swirling internal lights. 'Yes, okay. Yes. No one should be in right now. You up for coming to see where I work? And playing with one of the new toys?'

We Have the Room

We walked quickly; shortcut between the lanes. No foxes. Leaves in great piles between parked cars. Tom had stuffed the thing in a plastic bag, I carried my lanyard. Up the steps and into the low grey university building, swipe, no guard, never any guard, down one flight of stairs. The narrow corridor of the basement stretched away, lighting up as we walked.

'It's spooky here.'

'It's mostly boring,' I answered, stopping beside the door humbly marked 'copier'. 'Here's where I spend most of my time.'

First the antechamber, coat hooks and gloves and the over-the-foot socks, which always gave me a sting of aftermath, bloodied footprints, police tape, though this quickly left as I keyed in the code and opened the second door, and let Tom go in ahead, let him work out the purpose of the place. Long rows of shelves retreating in parallel lines, like in a library, but each shelf empty, set deep and padded with black foam, cradles for what was to be put there.

'Looks like – a Bond film,' said Tom, in a whisper. This place was conducive to quietness. We walked to the end of the room, a strange act divorced from sound barring the click and hum of lights blinking on again with us as we advanced, the floor of the room being padded too. At the end of the wall, taking up a good chunk of the space was the specialist 3D scanner and printer. Beside it stood, tall and thick, the big grey safe containing those objects I was to begin copying in the morning.

'Pass me that,' I said, reaching for the bag in Tom's hands. The crackling of the bag a disproportionately ugly sound and unnaturally loud. I pulled out one of the deeper scanner trays and plopped the kelpie inside, taking a moment to adjust it manually, before moving to the controls to see via the camera that it was correctly positioned.

Tom watched silently. I murmured to myself and touched the screen and stood back. 'Bear with me, it takes some time for it to get things calibrated.'

'What's it doing?'

'It's scanning the shape and weight of the object, then it scans for materials. It can recognise some things easier than others; plastic, of course. Paper, leather, wood. To my knowledge no one has used it to scan a cuddly toy. Then it attempts to see if it can recreate it,' I pointed a foot towards one of the canisters under the printer, 'with the raw materials it has available, using its clever little robot fingers.' I tapped at the next part, the grey square where, in other printers, a simple jet could make an object out of liquid plastic, but here, a number of needly fingers could spurt and sew together, in theory, anything of anything we could give it that it recognised how to use.

'The loom of all things,' I said. Ah, was I proud, those days, a show-off caretaker.

'I always thought the advanced scanners replicated stuff out of . . . I don't know, rearranged atoms,' said Tom.

'Maybe one day.'

'So what's in the trays?'

'Cellulose, ink of course – though here we have some special ink canisters that we mix to recreate the exact types used in the object we want to replicate. Inks from medieval Europe, Japan, and so on. A heavy resin that resembles ceramic. We can also do a good approximation of specific glazes and ceramics, though that one hasn't really been tested. When it gets particular, it's a laborious process, but there's Jenny down the hall who tests for composition in the objects and June who specialises in proprietary blending of the inks and glazes, all on site, unless it proves really tricky to source . . .'

'What kind of things do you copy?'

'We haven't copied much yet, three things successfully, so far. It's taken a year to get the room set up and the machine ordered, installed and working up to standard. There's a box full of dud test subjects somewhere around here.'

'But, like, what kinds of things?'

Lights flashed in the scanner tray. I rechecked the controls. It was at seven per cent physical, two per cent material.

'The aim is to copy important rare objects from all over the world to create replicas, mostly for museums – and, if some here have their way, for some private collectors who will pretend they have a real Ming vase or whatever to impress their friends. Lots of money in that,' I said looking at the trays. 'Though it would have to be a medium sized Ming vase.'

'Why?'

'What do you mean, why?'

'I mean, why do you need to do that?' Tom said, looking at me. I pretended to re-examine the controls, though the percentages had not changed.

'Why do you need to do anything? So that we can have a record. So that things won't be irretrievably lost. There are bibles that are nine hundred years old that exist in libraries, where a single frayed bit of wiring could seal their immolation. We can copy them, allow the real one to be put in permanent storage, and have the copies available to be touched, to actually be leafed through. Delicately of course – the copying is so good it can replicate the fragility of the pages. We're working on how to finesse that. It's a library of Alexandria, with more politely asking for things, rather than just pulling them out of passing ships. And we can take pretty much anything deemed worthy of copying. The downside is it takes months to do the process properly. Paperwork, permissions. For books, every single page has to be individually scanned on each side to allow replication. Objects are faster. So with this one, we're just copying in the outside. There won't be any devices inside this.'

'Okay, good.'

'Yes, good. Sorry for the screed. I just get – excited.'

'No, you should. It's pretty cool. What do you think will be inside our copy?'

'Well, it can't do working machinery that well from just scanning. You have to upload a programme for that, with full outlines for moving parts.'

'So no wifi. What will it have then?'

'The best estimate of the machine,' I said.

In Silence

Tom wandered off to look at the empty shelves. I monitored the progress of the scanner. Technically I wasn't allowed to leave the room while it was scanning, but technically I wasn't even allowed to be there, wasting materials like this – I would write it off as another dud though, I had decided, having earlier made a mistake in overestimating duds, it would be easy enough.

'There's a coffee machine just outside the kitchen,' I said.

'Replicant coffee?'

But he went anyway, leaving the doors open so he could let himself back in. In the silence, I stared at the machine. It began beeping. I had expected this. It frequently hit up against a materials issue and now it was beeping, but even the beep I enjoyed, pitched as it was, a low pleasant noise, something akin to bleeps from old space films; the only small reprove I would give it was the lack of colourful pastel lighty-upness from the console. The codes described a need for a particular filler and some liquid plastic. I had to refill the trays, and walked to the concealed cupboard in the wood-effect wall, tapped the pad embedded in the door, which always gave me a small thrill: the future here, right here, at my fingertips, even if the wooden look was more something from a seventies den room. I walked into the cupboard and stared at the grey bins of stuff. I was thinking that my favourite was the wool, my least favourite, the leather, which came also in a liquid form for the jets, and sloshed about, ominous, stinking. I was thinking, perhaps I don't hate the smell of it, if I think of it every time I come in here, obsessed with its disgusting potency perhaps. All was still.

Epiphany of the Copied Good

Tom appeared at the doorway of the cupboard, holding two cups.

'I got you milk in yours.'

'Cheers, thanks.' Not moving, staring, as Tom filled the entranceway, positively dewy, interested, wondered, turning his head around to take it all in, but also – discomforted, perhaps by the narrow space of the cupboard, or the closeness between them, or my darting eyes, their avoidance, which I knew annoyed some people, and couldn't help, especially this close. I leaned over and dragged out the trays, and merrily said, 'Needs a refill . . .' and Tom and I moved some ballet of clumsy feet and coffee – thankfully unsloshed – and trays lifted and fitted one by one, and somehow we were both back in the cupboard again, with the pretext of – showing the trays, and their contents.

I took off the lid on the leather refill to display it, and Tom winced and covered his nose.

'Smells like a dead hamburger. You know what I mean.'

'There's also the gilt bottle, up there, smaller. Real gold. There's an idea that we might make a dirt bottle too one of these days, refilled to correct environmental sources for each object.'

'That way you'd be really able to fool people.'

'No, that's not it at all,' I said. 'Well, now you've said it. Maybe. Okay. But it's more – verisimilitude. And excessive pushing at the limit of what we can do, how far we can go.'

'Dirt would convince. Get the right patina on it, and it's like, why even have the real thing?'

'You're testing me, Tom.'

Tom leaned in to read the label on a proprietary ink, 'Kells blue 0004. That Kells?'

'That Kells,' I said. 'You don't really think this is—'

'No, no, sorry. I think it's amazing. Just, has to be in the right hands. Otherwise the world would be overrun with fakes.'

'It's still hideously expensive to do, and there's a lot of paperwork around to prevent forging.'

'Unlicensed forging.'

'I just want to keep the old things safe, Tom, that's all I want to do. And I get to do that here, in a very regulated environment where everyone is working incredibly hard to do it, together. To save the past, but let people in. To touch it. To understand. To be allowed closer – to never let it be lost. No more things lost through human carelessness. Everything right here, on these shelves, and out in the world, and the originals kept in the perfect preserving conditions.'

'I don't think it can possibly do what you want it to do, Daniel,' said Tom.

And I felt my heart lurch, felt dizzy almost, at the tender reproachfulness in the other man's voice, Tom's hair shining in the soft light. And I thought, I thought to myself, small urgent ideas of movement, of rushing up and taking him by the shoulders and kissing him softly at first and then harder, more hungry – but I hesitated, and ran my finger along the trays, making a hollow sound. Not that I cared if Tom did not want me, that I might be rejected – but Tom *might* want; there was a charge in the air, no falsifying that, either Tom's great dislike of the whole mission of this place, its solemnness, made him want something else, escape, a fight, or, or, and I looked for his eyes, as if that would help, Tom having, I saw now, more to him than was visible, smooth and bold like a ship with half of it passing beneath the waves –

something else then. Stopping me. Órla? Regretfully no, I was not so considerate, and anyway what, just over a month together, I wouldn't be the wronging one, I thought, but an early disruption for what might not justly last. The room then; yes, I thought that was it, I leaned back on the trays and looked heavenward, or at the narrow quadrangle of the ceiling, the room, cupboard and greater part, held sanctuary, quiet space. Not like a church but anyway still calm air that if broken by my passion in this way would never be the same again. I saw it quite clearly, every time I returned to the cupboard as I must almost every day of my work here, it would be the cupboard where I kissed Tom (and where either Tom kissed me back, or Tom pulled back shocked a little, or Tom reacted badly – this I did not think would be likely) and forever after I would lose my peace in here, lose the tranquil security, lose the absence, utterly, of violent images. It might already be too late for that, even the idea of a sexual frisson was sharp to the touch, and I moved as if frightened of the space suddenly sidestepping out into the room, which was equally calmer than me in its inhuman, padded way but more space and the instance between the two of us, whatever it was, was –

'Oh good, it's finished scanning the object, nearly there on the materials,' I said.

'Does it take long after that?' said Tom, looking around.

'A little bit, it's not a speedy process, it's an accurate one,' I said.

Quietness, the supreme quietness of a soundproofed room, only with two of us in it, firmly apart, waiting for a device to finish processing.

'Are you willing to give your life to this?' said Tom.

'What a strange question . . .' Though it was not phrased as a question. I tried to keep querulousness out of my voice. The proof was coming, soon, though, the thing that would make Tom realise. The epiphany of the copied good.

Not the Thing Itself

After a while the printer made the sequence of beeps that meant it was done and to take the replicated object out of the creation tray and put it into the finisher, which generally snipped around and freshened edges that needed freshening. I made sure to do this so that Tom did not see the slightly ugly object before it was truly done.

Then the process was finished.

'There,' I said putting the replicant into his hand. 'Tell me if you can see a difference,' I said, passing him the original.

'No soundbox inside, though it almost feels like it tried to make that, since it's the same weight,' he said, holding them one in each hand, judging, 'I can't see anything else.'

I took the copy and looked into its eyes. The glitter swirled; the printer had even added a liquid into the cavity of the eye so that it would do so, judging how to do it I did not know – from some minute motion of the original during the scanning process? If the printer made a copy of a clock it would not be expected to keep time, the mechanics all being on the inside, and beyond the knowledge of the scanners, beyond the power, but this, it could do, it could try to get the slightest movement on the surface to run true. I felt a thrill – some hidden ability in my machine had revealed itself, late at night during this illicit use, as if it only would under these circumstances. I thought of a copied clock with hands that moved by some impossible means, though they wouldn't, there had to be something. Then of the Northern Lights moving like fairy skirts, something I dimly understood as beams moving sinuously along unseen currents, and then of clocks with little spirits inside, turning the pieces. Fey magic. In short I did not think of Tom at all, until he clapped me on the back and said we needed to get home.

The Sky Falls and My Heart Is Glad

Up the stairs and down the front steps of the drab university building, crossing the small square and turning down the back alley where the leaves lay in their long piles, perfect for kicking – I was so elated, I didn't care what Tom thought, I launched myself at the leaves and kicked them, though they were damp and fluttered down in an unsatisfying way. I had clapped the copied kelpie under my armpit, while Tom had the original – I noticed him holding it in one hand by the head, and tried hard not to work this into some symbol of Tom's mood as it pertained to myself, instead to be carefree, to kick another big mouldy clag of leaf litter, while all we passed through was flattened to a dingy orange in the street lights. We travelled in our strange moods through first the alley and the back lanes running homewards, until we reached the start of the area of town were we lived, where it was partially student-stuffed tenement flats, then opening up into elegant roads, single family occupancy almost-mansions, or offices or nurseries. We chose the mews streets, the dimmer parts, as if still moving towards a secret plot, needing to go unseen.

'It's hailing,' said Tom, holding out one hand. The hail came in a sudden rattle down upon us a second later.

'I didn't think it'd be cold enough,' I said, having to raise my voice. A piece hit Tom in the eye.

'Ow, fuck!'

'Oh, quick, in here, there'll be shelter,' I opened a garden gate.

Huge trees here in a garden backing a grand house not yet broken up, I think. We sheltered under the thick arms of a beech and listened to the din. The hail danced off the branches and landed around us, the ground quickly turning white, there were so many of them, small though, the size, when I stooped to pick one up, of nothing comparable. Buckshot, though what did I know what buckshot looked like? Certainly not small and whitely melting. Larger hailstones were cracking off the cars parked in the lanes. I wondered if they would break a windscreen.

'Do you think it'll break the windscreens?' asked Tom.

'Wouldn't that be amazing,' I said, looking at him. Tom laughed.

'All right,' he said. A pause. Quiet rattling sounds. 'You know, I feel like I know you a little better now. I hadn't – before.'

Fuck, I thought, that pause between hadn't and before, amid the gravelly sounds of the hail falling. I stood in silence, let my gaze go lax. Then Tom crouched and scooped a handful of the stuff, now in a layer an inch thick, and put it in his mouth, and crunched on it.

'Ehhh!' I said.

'It just came right out of the sky, didn't it?'

I laughed. We stood for a minute more; the din began to lessen, and stopped all together. We walked back, almost grabbing each other for balance, rolling on marbles, homeward to the house on the not especially notable street, the place where we lived, darting through dark shadows sharpened by everything streetlit around them, and, ahead, Tom's little rescue on her haunches under the shelter of the entranceway yowling to get in.

'There we go,' said Tom to Mrs Boobs, letting her go ahead, and I on the step feeling in need of rescue myself, of something to brace against, attempted to stuff back inside myself all the feelings, hopping, roiling about in me, a man of autumn weather

47

suddenly, fallen leaves, a ragged and chilled end to decadence, with hope and desire the last indulgences to go – great blocks or sometimes little falling pieces hard and pure, watching Tom go in ahead, following his pet, into the smells – foost, bodies, bleach, popcorn, tonight – and the closeness of this place. I shut the door promptly behind me, and hurried into the kitchen to make tea.

Reckon

'How will we tell them apart?' asked Tom.

'Put them on either side of the fridge,' I said. 'What do you think?'

'I like it,' said Tom. 'Listen – I kind of like them. I mean, the fact you can do that. I didn't give it enough credit before. What you do, I might not fully grasp the technology or the point, but I like that we did this.'

'Why, I asked, 'why do you like it?'

'Because it's your thing,' said Tom, looking around, 'Your – passion. You've got a life's work, a mission. Who has that? I don't.' He picked up the toy, the copy, and held it against his head, as if trying to read its mind or perhaps wipe his face with it.

'You didn't like the copier room,' I said.

'No.'

'I can see why people might think it's oppressive.'

'But you don't feel like that. Too used to it.'

'From the minute I first walked in, when we'd just fitted the flooring and the shelves weren't in, I was happy there. To be in that place, it's just – calm.'

'I think the copy's better than the original,' Tom said, staring out now at the garden, replica in hand, cat weaving around his legs.

'Why'd you say that?'

'Well, because it doesn't have the wifi device spying on us. It's just a lump.' He placed the object back on the fridge and looked between them both. 'Yeah, life is weird,' he said, 'I think I'll be thinking about your room for a while, trying to get my head around it, before I can have an opinion. I normally know right away, if something's right or wrong.'

'You have a strong moral compass?'

Tom nodded, and looked at me. Silence. The fridge hummed. Looked at me.

'Think we could burn the original?' he said. 'I think we should burn it.'

'Yes. Outside, or on the stove, or . . .'

We settled on lighting it on the stove then carrying it outside to smoke and crackle on one of the paving slabs just beyond the back door. The fur caught quickly.

'No EU standards here,' I said, wincing.

When the fire got down to the soundbox, it began to sing. The normal grating jingle it had given out before; only our listening to it in the circumstances we had set in motion gave it a kind of poignancy, a feeling immediately unrooted by my thinking that it was poignant. The two of us stood around the tiny fire, staring down. Cheap sentiment, I thought. Chemical smoke poured out of it, and incongruous sounds. Tom poked it with a stick. I looked up at the woolly sky, trying not to cough.

'It's going to a better place, the world of silence,' I said.

'You're so weird, Daniel.'

'You're the one that wanted to set fire to the original.'

'No, I like it. It's like, we made the better version, now we can rid the world of this menace,' he said, 'one of them, anyway. I think there are a few more. It's just a prototype though.'

'You didn't say that. A prototype! Oh well, there it goes. Try not to breathe in the toxic shit.'

The singing continued longer than you might expect. I hoped the neighbours heard, and wondered about it, as the plastic of the soundbox melted off, as the wires sparked, and the sound died away. In the hush I felt empty. And then, standing there looking at the smoke severing from the burnt body and going skywards on its lonesome, I began to feel good.

Reckoning

Inside I washed my face and neck at the sink, and stripped to my boxers and with urgent disgust threw my clothes immediately in the washing machine. Tom washed his hands at the sink. 'Good idea, can I chuck my stuff in?' he said. Tom stripped. Bent a little loading his clothes. The dimples on his back, straightening up again. I methodically got out the detergent and poured out a measure and set the machine, and stood back, watching. Tom would move away soon. And I wobbled my head. He would go to the small ground floor shower and close the door, and steam would come out from under the door. And I wondered.

'You okay?' said Tom. 'I hope smoke didn't get in your lungs.'

I looked around. Tom's body beside me, larger and stronger than mine, breathing in and out, hair dishevelled.

'Ah, no, nothing. Just – what a night, eh?'

Tom in his boxers. Tom next to me, hairs rising on the side of my arm, Tom looking concerned, perhaps, or just puzzled, so hard it is to know beyond the small expressions that our faces can make, have learned how to make, what huge swath of self there is at work in this moment, and the next. The gears of the mind that we suppose are at work, but have only some control over. Against the horrors I wanted, but I had already said something flippant enough to let the other man leave, *coward*, and there he was going, just as I had guessed and maybe even wanted. Tom shook his head; the last few pieces of hail, miraculously unmelted in his golden hair, were unseated and scattered across the linoleum.

'Well, off to the shower,' he said.

But he waited. I said 'I'm going too. Uh, upstairs,' I added, with a little nervous laugh. Tom looked at me, again a beat too long, smiled slowly, and left the room.

Entry, Entrances

At Twelfth Night in the year 18— James Lennoxlove went to a ball at a neighbour's house and saw a murder. This is how I was drawn back into the diary, which had languished on my table overwhelmed by the lives of living people and more incarnate crushes. But after idly reading the first line of that entry, I could not help but pursue, falling heavily into my chair to read on.

> At Twelfth Night I went to a ball at Gilmour's house and came away at midnight in mortal terror and shaking all over after seeing the murder of a maid, committed by if I am correct a groomsman of another guest, the Duke of H—. Even tho I have no thought that anyone should read this, I do not wish to share his name here, in case it is read. The Duke is a powerful man, and I do not know what his feelings might be on the matter, whether it would inconvenience him or cause him some other pains to have the crime come to attention though I know what is right is justice. I have not been well in my mind all night and it is now the morning and I must face the day, but first I give this account. I pray for everyone and the murdered girl most of all, and to know what I must do now.

In Lennoxlove's telling, unusually disordered as it was, I could see it all: the darkness of the courtyard, back from the fires at the entranceway, the cold mire of horseshit and straw, the stable door open, him looking for something he had left in the saddlebag of his horse, and spying the terrible act, and leaping on the horse, a kick, riding it roughly away without a word to his hosts, and how he thought he heard a shout behind him, though it could have been merrymaking, or someone asking where he was off to in such a hurry. The only thing I did not know was what Lennoxlove looked like, to better imagine his look of fear, his body in the saddle as he gripped the reins and steered the spooked animal down the dark frosty lanes towards his home five miles away. He had never described himself, only other people, which he clearly enjoyed. The neighbour, Gilmour, had 'a high forehead and nervous complexion, a kind mouth, a rag of handshake', his wife 'comely like a calm goose, and I suppose such a thing exists'. So for expediency I imagined Tom in his place.

Lennoxlove wrote in great excitement and despair at what he had seen, and I wondered how I would have responded, if I'd have gone to pieces, rushed in to stop the murder or apprehend the killer, stormed into the great hall – I presumed, the great hall, shining with candelabra – to yell out for all to come and witness what had been done. I played these scenarios and variations in my mind, skirting each time around the act itself, as Lennoxlove had done, sparingly, only giving the detail that it was 'done with a knife' and that the groom 'looked very ill about it, like he was going to faint with the horror, but he was also laughing in bursts, like a mare', all of which clearly had distressed Lennoxlove and caused his terrible fear and flight.

After reading this entry, I took a short break and opened the bedroom window. It was blue outside. Cold, though never as cold as the cold of my childhood, and probably never would be again, barring freak weather. A cold pale hand on a hot knife, I thought, and shuddered. I stared out at the houses opposite, stolid in the falling, grainy blue, almost all divided like this one, though with more expense and formality, upgraded flats instead of single high-ceilinged loose floorboarded rooms with locks on the doors.

Their large stately gardens being either left to gentle neglect – red and yellow trees grown wildly too large, shedding leaves that someone or other might scrape up, eventually – or divided into purse-mouthed squares of gravel or patio paving. A single star caught my attention winking in the slowly vanishing distance between a branch and part of a rooftop. I wondered at the lives being lived at this present moment in this district of the city, somewhere between affluent and haphazard like my own, not thinking overly complex thoughts about them in case I should imagine them knifing each other on mezzanines or by floor-length windows, fresh corpses slithering wetly down the panes like large, clothed slugs – I turned my head, wiped it, turned back – then thought about the lives of those for whom the houses had been built, roughly around the time of Lennoxlove's day, a much easier idea unaffected by the account I had just read, sanitised by images taken from various TV miniseries: pristine cuffs, beautiful flowers in small china vases, writing sets, turns about a room that was this one, but repurposed, for use by a plucky young man with a dramatic and love-filled future just waiting to be entered.

But I'm young yet, I thought. Ish. And though James is dead, who's to say it wasn't like that for him, just as perfect and beautifully framed? Aside from that one aberration.

Gnaw

My poor heart and all its tangents: I put my fingers through the narrow gap of my window and tapped that way to be heard by something, or someone, or nothing as chance or the rules beyond me allowed. In the next section of Lennoxlove's diary a year had elapsed. James was twenty-two and it was spring. He talked of how it had been a long time since his last entry, without giving reasons why. He never said what had come of what he had seen, what decision he had made, if justice was served, what form justice took back then.

James Lennoxlove was alive in his fragments and chose to use the next particular span of writing (a single page) to talk about the oncoming of the future and his tailored suit ordered from Edinburgh, and, at last, in strangely oblique language, the person he was in love with. 'Person', that was how he put it. My eyes widened. I switched on the reading light, prepared, with a thread of excitement, to read a little further on, but tentatively, and for some reason my eyesight blurred; outside the world was closed down to a few frames of light, and I could smell woodsmoke from some chimney, which is a disaster for the kind of mood I was in, and I rolled my eyes and got up, went downstairs and sat in the living room on the sofa with Badr and watched whatever it was he was watching, until normal life blunted me the right amount. Badr made popcorn, and laughed loudly, and turned his head to comment on this or that, or to ask me to pass the bowl. Maybe I wouldn't know Badr in a few years; maybe Badr would move in with someone, or move out to his own space, and in a few years we would be nothing to each other but casual former flatmates, figments on whatever social media site would be popular then, seeing each other once in five years at a meetup in some pub. Maybe is a word to soften; it was going to happen. And Badr would have a whole other life, and eventually or sooner than hoped would die, and be buried, and I would die and be buried. I gnawed on my popcorn.

Be Well

Just as I was in this pit of myself Tom passed by the living room on his way out, grabbed the top edge of the doorway, hung there, 'I am going out tonight,' he said, 'to the – gym, yes. The gym. Anyway. Take care,' he dropped down again.

'All right, man, be well,' Badr said.

There was a sheen already on Tom's face, a flicker of alarm that transformed itself into a smile, and from this to a wink at me. I looked at the TV, too flooded by the stupendous or stress-drenched possibilities present in that wink, in my interpretation of the wink, and also by the idea of Tom in all his health coming to dust one day, and no more gym for him, or any autumn nights, to address my flatmate in any kind of an acceptable way beyond a mutter. And by that time Tom was out the house, and the hallway was shuddering at the violent close of the front door.

I wanted to get up off the sofa and run after Tom, jog out to him and accompany him down the street towards the gym in the crisp, cool air, asking, as if it were that easy, what was wrong, if anything was, whether a momentary pain or a great unbearable one, or a desire, a momentary one or a great unbearable desire, that I might, just maybe, be able bodily to fulfil.

It would be nice not to have to think such large ungainly things while watching a historic rerun of *Whose Line is it Anyway?*, but if I had thought with frantic morbidity since childhood about the passing of all people, their various destinies and pains, mostly inaccessible and forbidden to me to aid, awkward as I am, frightened as I am, closed off and cowardly and dealing too poorly with my own shit as I was, particularly then, then the thoughts had become habitual, nothing to be done, not so much a train of thought as a permanent line. It cannot be helped. People die, people go, nothing is permanent, and I make eternal return to this idea, for fuck's sake, Daniel, people try to say what they mean in small ways and large and sometimes are misunderstood, or cannot bring themselves to complete a thought, or are at cross-purposes, everything is euphemism to hide various taboos, so what? It's not so difficult. We are permitted our troubles and privacy as much as our desires. Some things are unutterable, and that allows them a certain fullness of being. Or else they are too trivial to mention. If Tom is troubled, it's the kind of trouble he can fix with a workout, or if not then he will try another method. No terrible pain everywhere in everyone, maybe just a little pain they want to keep to themselves and for themselves, see, these people on the TV have quite enough energy to make jokes despite what burdens they may have, what madness they might similarly be wracked by. Be well. Badr had a shit day at work, and here he is, quietly eating popcorn and making sure you're doing all right, in his own way. So all will be well.

A Seed

That evening Órla came in and sat herself down in the living room, and Badr went off and made her tea 'and a biscuit, if there are any!', and Tom was not home.

'Have you noticed Tom's been . . .' she began. Hurriedly, offhand.

'What? Is something wrong? Are you . . .' I said. Órla flapped a hand at me,

'Oh it's nothing like that, what you're thinking, disaster-man.'

'No, seriously. Órla. You look rattled.'

Órla turned in her seat. We sat close together. I thought of two people on a dinghy in the sea, and the sofa squeaked in just such a way.

'He's – oh this is going to sound fucking stupid. He's been – his speech is different. Have you noticed?'

'I think he forgot the word gym earlier, if that counts.'

'Hmm,' said Órla.

'What do you think's up?'

Badr came in the room, put mugs down, little plates and forks and pieces of kitchen roll.

Órla looked down, 'Nothing, probably,' she said. I prodded the side of the sofa, felt its squeaky hollow give, and someone laughed on the TV, and an angel passed over the room.

Come to the House

At Mark's mother's place, the last weekend of October, there was a Hallowe'en party I had gone to since I was an adolescent, though I had known Mark since we were both little. This year I invited Órla and Tom. And Badr, but Badr didn't care for fancy schmancy dress-up parties, he said. The MacAshfall house was on a slight hill in the north of the town. Three storeys tall, modernist, with lots of glass and flat concrete slabs at angles, a garden – great square concrete-sided pond, huge rectangular foliage beds – that merged into the home via the giant glossy Swiss cheese plants set against the glossy wooden panels and spartan concrete of the interior, and at night through gentle reflections of those inside appeared as if they were outside in the garden, which was, so late, long gone to seed.

Mark's uncle welcomed us in, taking Órla's coat first, with gleaming eyes. He always looked, to me, like Mark's future self, large in the face, bald, shiny, settled in comforts, but good hearted, except for the times he was not; he had a blunt streak, not cruel but thoughtless sometimes. Mark and his uncle. Who was, as no one was saying, now Mark's stepfather. Who was, as Mark had confessed to me once while stoned, probably his dad. Not that he gave a shit, except it all had to be a great secret. Mark was alluring in that way and in that way only, in his witty charming spoiled rich family intrigues, and that he had known me since we were both four, and had managed not to give up on me despite my issues. In my worst moments, I thought this was down to too much ego on Mark's part in concealing other people's varieties of faults unless they happened to pertain to or interrupt the smooth and daily happiness of Mark himself. It was so easy to be friends with him, it made me feel almost young to be with him, with so many years held up by the two of us like it was no weight at all. And Mark had, still, all this cool stuff in his attic and I was always perfectly willing to be his pet, so long as we both knew it and drew attention to it. As we did. Everyone in the MacAshfall household found me lightly, artificially hilarious. You're like a little cat, Daniel, come and go as you want, take anything from the fridge. Daniel, if you fail your exams I'll tip you down the stairs, so don't. You're my lucky charm, so if you pass I will too, and if you fail that's me done. What does this mean, here, chapter twelve, the company's let me go, the latest girlfriend's dumped me – and so on, and Hallowe'en, and the MacAshfalls' wistfully beautiful party.

Blithe Spirit

Mark's tall, angular and terrifying mother – always Mrs MacAshfall, 'call me Maggie' as she might – had set up the turntable, with Mark choosing the records. She had a considerable collection from many past MacAshfalls and her own curation. This night, all songs selected were from the twenties and thirties – the ambience was right, the crackle of haunting, between-wars voices turning in the air of the study as guests got into this year's theme in ivory and sooty satin.

Órla had chosen the top hat and tails route – with some considerable help from Quick Zip Alterations, who were, she said, amused at her need for considerable darting, and the trousers having to be from a separate set entirely, made for her hips. She gave a sharp, quick turn on her bright black heels to show off, after which Tom swept her to the dancefloor – the parquet space between the turntable on the sideboard and the grey blocky fainting couch, space in which no one else but the two of them danced an improvisational twirling dance.

Mark said, 'Well.'

Mrs MacAshfall said, 'Look how beautiful they both are!' And then, to me, 'You've chosen well.'

I said, 'Thank you for having us, here's some wine. Is the punch ready?' and to myself, and a little to Mark, in white coat tails, 'I've been ready for the punch all month long.'

It was known as Blithe Spirit and always served in crystal Marie-Antoinette glasses: frothy, liquid, white, with an impossibly delicate perfume, a silken kick, and acting upon the whole tussle with great adept fingers was something that seemed derived from the bodily, something sleazy and worrying, but quickly buried under a sudden jolt of lime. Of course it was Mark's uncle's favourite drink to make, but was undeniably the pleasure of the year as well. Mark and Mark's uncle and I stood in a line by the punchbowl watching Órla and Tom dance, and took short sharp gulps of the drink, making such conversation as needed to be made. Other guests danced. Mark and I whispered, Mark's uncle drifted away. Órla came in for a drink, dragging Tom with her. He looked dazed, and hearty. Mark handed them both a punch with a knowing look, which was the look Mark strove to project whenever he was playing host in a house that did not belong to him, and wouldn't until both his mother and his uncle died.

'Maybe I could replicate the house for you,' I said.

'Maybe you could replicate my uncle and we could push the fake body off a bridge? Or the real one. The fake would be much preferable. We could prop him up in the corner, rewire him as a lampshade.'

'What about your mum?'

'Spanner in the works. I love her too much to fake her death.'

Decadent Loss

Later Órla, tired of dancing, came to the sofa and flopped down beside us. Tom had vanished.

'You've known each other for a long time,' she said.

'Oh an absolute age now,' said Mark.

Something was unsaid. Órla's eyes were vivid and glassy.

We moved on to talk of Mark's life, and of his last girlfriend, and of Órla's last boyfriend, and, at Mrs MacAshfall's insistence, the dooking for apples began while some terribly sad singer crooned across the years about meeting once again in Berkeley Square. Several of Mark's mother and uncle's friends got sloppy drunk, white-haired and young alike, and danced, and the room was loud. I felt myself begin to disappear. Smokers traipsed outside, Tom among them, just drunk enough to start begging for spares. Tom like a ghost all night, flitting about, never stopping to talk, not even to Órla, after that first dance. I had a glimpse of him from the hall, a strange sight of this appallingly handsome man in antique formal wear, standing talking earnestly with a slight, clever-looking hedge-fund type from London disguised as Fred Astaire about – something muffled – while the man lit his cigarette with the end of his own, and I jolted just a little at the way they almost touched. Cupped hands, breath steaming – Tom's brilliant dark blond head in the spilled light pulling back, and his laughter. Stamping feet from the cold. The way a smoker blows upwards, hissing through his teeth, while he does a shuffle from the chill. With a sigh, I went to the kitchen and praised

Mrs MacAshfall on her canapés, which were cheap pre-bought and heated sausage rolls – my favourite, and provided especially for me alongside the finer snacks she had for everybody else.

Thematic Continuity

It was later.

I perched on the great central wooden stairs, watching the drift of people around the features of the house I knew so well. By candlelight it was all different, by Hallowe'en graces it was too, the veil thinning, but not at its thinnest yet, too many people milling, too much braying and the smallest, most soothing small talk going about in the air as if they needed cushioning, as if they knew what was coming, soon. I had been drinking steadily but my mouth was always dry. I had vanished, I had let the night strip away the others and time in the way parties could, a little mournful before it had already ended. Órla caught sight of me and handed me something dark bronze in a glass, and sat on my step, arranging herself carefully, the staircase wide enough that there was a lot of space between us. Through the stairs, the floor below. It was dim, with slants of light.

'Shh,' she said, and so I was quiet.

Then she said, 'How old are you?'

Startled, I said, 'Tinder age, or real age?'

'Tinder? Old school. You've never been on Tinder in your life.'

'I have, you know. Once. It was intimidating.'

'I'll bet,' she said, lying.

'I'm thirty-six,' I said, 'same age as Mark.'

'No way! You don't look it,' she said, 'no grey at all, and you don't have the kind of – the kind of look people have. Old and tired like. You look young.'

'Wow,' I said.

'I'm twenty-eight. Sorry.'

'My anxiety makes me look younger I think. Don't apologise for not having existed as long as me.' I looked down at my drink. I was holding it strangely, at an angle. The darkness on the stairs made my hand seem alien. I wondered if I might ever see Tom again. You will, I told myself, what a thing to think. Morbid. He's probably in the kitchen, Mark's probably clapping him on the back. Contacts everywhere. Or telling him – no, I wouldn't believe Mark was telling Tom.

'Can you tell me something else, about yourself?' asked Órla.

I got myself more comfortably situated. I looked up at the ceiling.

'I've been coming to this house for thirty years and I always love it. There's always something new to find. Mr MacAshfall was a collector of antique books. When he died Mrs MacAshfall sold most of them off, but there are boxes in the attic that have treasure in them. Gilt-edged books, singular editions, personal memoirs, hand written, letterplates of extinct birds.'

'I suppose that tells me something about you,' said Órla.

'I could tell you more personal things,' I said, 'but I'm not nearly drunk enough.'

'Let's sort that,' she said, and pulled herself up, bringing back from the kitchen a whole bottle of bourbon, and sloshed out two glasses full.

'Loose lips sink ships,' I said.

'They don't tonight. Early nineteen-thirties, everything still to be lost.' She said.

And sipped, and waited.

Open Books

'How long have you and Tom been together?' I asked.

'It was about a month when he moved into yours, so . . . nearly two months?'

'Going all right?'

'Nosy! And also, I'd imagine you might notice if it is.'

'What do you mean?'

Órla nudged me. 'You know . . . I'm there a lot. You can probably read the room.'

'All right, I can. And . . .'

'And?'

'I've asked already if you love him. Rudely early, I know. It's just, the other day I felt you were going to tell me something. About him and you.'

'I feel like you have an interest that goes beyond the polite,' she said. 'Forget it. No. Don't forget it. I brought it up then, stupid, just something I felt. A passing – thing. Just why are you asking now?'

I looked over at the bottle, clumsily grabbed it from her hand, my fingers sliding over hers. Warning alarms in my head. I wanted to talk about Tom. I wanted to talk about James Lennoxlove. I knocked back a quarter glass. Only half of the bottle remaining. Was it full, before? She probably despised the intrusion. Loved and despised it. People like to be seen, but I was dancing on a line between reaching out and overreaching.

'I'm so rude,' I said, 'so invasive with you, I'm very sorry,'

I wanted to call out to Órla. I wanted to ask if she didn't love

Tom, could I have him? And also did she have an idea if Tom might like me, even a little faint hint of liking, be honest, desire, like a trail of smoke rising like a miracle into some still sky, something to guide me hopeful onwards. It was too dark now, it was too glimmering. Where was Tom? I longed to see him, his muscular figure, dashing in a suit, sharp collared, come leaning up on the bannister, and say to me, 'Let's go'. Anywhere, the garden, the hedges, press up against me, smoky, and heavily, while I, my head spinning, pushed back.

'I like your outfit by the way,' I said.

'Ah, I don't love him,' said Órla, with a small flourish of her glass-holding hand, 'I don't think I do, anyway. He's been very good to me though, except lately I wonder what he's thinking. He's speaking strangely. He's a tiny bit – distracted. By his own business I imagine.'

'You sound like a Victorian woman of few means.'

'Oh my God, what did I say? Why'd I say? You know I mean something better than that.'

Silence.

'I mean there's something wrong with him, a little.'

'I always feel like I've known you forever,' I said, 'I am sorry, if I push you.'

'Do you think I should love Tom?' Órla said, suddenly shifting along the stair to lean on me, 'Ah shite, I've had too much to drink now for sure.'

I felt her weight pleasantly on me. But again, a sting of worry. I knocked it off with another drink, burning my lips. My vision had begun to swing about.

'I am the worst person to ask,' I said.

Órla pulled herself back up to sitting; she looked over at me. In the dark her eyes gleamed. Her lipstick was a little blurred. She opened her mouth, and closed it again, and laughed.

'Oh I know that,' she said. 'Ah well!'

And with that, she stood and went downstairs. I stared after her, then drank the rest of the bottle, only a glug, from the tilted end. She'll be off to find Tom I suppose, I thought. To find him and take him to the garden, to the hedge, to press herself against his smoky mouth, to let him push his hands over her body, shivering cold though it might be, with the luxuriousness of the other who wants you, drunk and uprooted and starry. And I imagined looking on, and her eyes on me. Tom oblivious, and then she would say, Daniel wants you. Daniel, come and take him, if you want.

'I would take him by the hand,' I said quietly to myself.

In the Kitchen

'I could, you know.' said Mark,

'Mark, Jesus. Don't, Mark,' I said, grabbing him by the arm. We sat on the floor of the kitchen. I remember I couldn't remember why we were sitting on the floor.

'She's a good looking woman. You know I'm willing to do this. For you, brother.'

'I need more to drink!' I said, and got up too quickly to my feet, the room rebounding, spinning, aggressive. 'Is your mum in bed?'

'What, I think so?' said Mark, passing his uncertain gaze across the room, 'she's not in here.'

'Are Órla and Tom still here?'

'Yes, Daniel, remember? I told them to use the guest room,'

'One of the guest rooms,'

'One of them, yep.'

'I feel like I knew that already,' I cast about with my hands, 'Oh . . . I want to sleep with him,' I said balefully. 'She knows I do, and it's like a joke to her. I feel like a teenager or something. Fuck.' I knocked over the glass I was trying to fill with whatever liquid was in the tall shaker jar jostling in my hands. It was white and smelled like feet.

'Is this the punch? Man it does not keep well. I don't want to be selfish, though, I don't want to hurt Órla. I love her.'

Tender.

I sank back down to the floor. Floor was safe. Cool.

'You know I like you best of all when you're drunk, Daniel,' said Mark, 'You love everyone. Drunk, not drunk. You're a blinkered blethering prick but you love everyone with all your fucking heart. Don't drink that shit, come on. It's time for – hot chocolate.'

'Alcohol in the hot chocolate?' I said.

'Alcohol. In the hot chocolate,' Mark said, hammering about in the cupboards. 'Found it. And look! The guest star – marshmallows!'

'Looks stale. Is it stale marshmallows now? In the MacAshfall residence?'

'Does the job though,' said Mark, stirring the mixture, 'like me. You know I'm the man for it. Did you see the way she looked at me? Yeah. Fucking . . . get in there. Whisk her away. Leave Tom. To your tender ministrations.'

'I already told you,' I said, 'it's not good to try and steal anyone away from anybody.'

'Hmm, learned your lesson then?'

'What do you mean?'

'No more stealing?'

'Come on man, what stealing? Stealing what?'

Mark pressed buttons on the microwave, sounding them out as he did so. After a moment he spun on his heels 'You! Stole! My! Diary! Well, not my diary. My ancestor's diary. My. Ancestor!'

I scoffed. Forgive me, Mark.

'I thought you weren't going to steal ever again after that policeman caught you with *Out.*' He said, 'Juvenile delinquent. But here we are, promises, piecrusts.' He ripped open the marshmallows. Several dropped into my lap and I found them on the floor underneath my legs and put them in my mouth. I hated the cloying sweetness, sudden and inhabiting my whole mouth, but the texture was enjoyable. It took a lot of concentration to chew and finally swallow. Refocus. Mark was sitting next to me again. Hot chocolate. Stinging smell under the sweetness.

'Do you ever feel like you're permanently missing the important things, the fulsomeness, like all the facts are not available to you, and so you'll make an error, a stupid one, one that other people would easily see?' I said.

There was a silence.

'Fuck sweet things,' I said, 'I think I came here to get something.'

'Hmm,' said Mark, 'that's life. Oh,' he sang, then, 'you're talking about the hunt for clues that you don't even know are clues, in order to solve the mystery of how someone mysterious feels about someone else, or how anyone, even yourself thinks about anything in general? The impossibility of knowing, a person, a situation, this,' He opened his arms and gestured at the room.

'Yes!'

'No. Drink your hot chocolate before it gets a skin on it.'

A Glass of Water,
an Open Invitation

I blinked. I remembered at last why I had come downstairs.

'You sidetracked me!' I said to Mark, and got to my feet. I felt less drunk than I had done just a second before – as if a window had just been pulled open and fresh wholesome sobriety came blustering in. I wouldn't have wanted to test my chances behind the wheel or anything, but I was happy to remember my purpose.

'I was supposed to get some water for Tom,'

'Didn't you just ask me where Tom was?' Mark asked.

'Yes. I forgot,' I said, getting up.

'In the joy of my company.'

'No. I hate you,' I said to him, patting him on the arm.

'I hate you too,' he said, smiling and handing me a glass of water.

Meanwhile in other rooms there were people waltzing still. They had been waltzing for hours, though now in candle light, the music soft, the people drooping like dancers in a competitive marathon, but still, when I walked between them, carrying my water glass close to my chest, smiling, they moved around me with sleepy flickering grace, they did not look as if they would stop until the sun came up, and the sun might never come up; such was the power of this house.

I climbed the stairs and went to the guest room. Órla grabbed the water and said she did not need it, even as she was giving some to Tom and drinking the rest herself. In her left hand an empty toothglass. She went to fill them both in the en suite. I sat down on the bed next to Tom.

As I sat, the frame of the bed rattled. The room rattled, and I rubbed my face. The party, downstairs, I thought. A quake in the house from merrymaking.

Tom gave me an oorie look. By that I mean, like something coming forward into his expression, slowly and strangely, like a large horse coming forward to you in snow and fog. Perhaps this had as much to do with my drunken eyes struggling to pull into focus as the man himself. He had taken off his jacket some time ago, and his shirt was open. The hair on his chest was light and there was a scar, horizontal in the flesh, like the mark of a pocket cut above his heart. I had not seen that scar before, but it looked old. As I looked, the scar undid itself and became wet with blood – I flinched back; the scar vanished.

'Hello,' he said, leaning forward, for me retreating. And kissed me.

I pulled back again. His lips had been very cold. There were faint shadows under his eyes, delicate purples in the tanned skin. I meant to get out of the bed and back away, but I was drunk and he was lovely, and he was weird and something was happening, now, so I held him by the shoulders and looked him in the eye, though he would not focus and nothing made sense. When someone is not themselves, what does that mean? Beyond the usual, more understandable outer states of, for example, broaching on the overly drunk and raving mad. But Tom was not more drunk than me and he was not mad, but. What boundaries arise and how do we negotiate them in our hunger and need? Tom and Órla . . . But I was thinking more of what I should do or not do, with my body, with my need. I felt his pull; he was pulling me. He was something else. I was a shiver. I was hard. I unbuttoned my shirt and threw it away. Then I kissed him back and we both merged together in the oorie warmth of our mouths.

There has been a lot of pain in my life, I was thinking, rationalising; I see pain in my head, I have a pain, a madness of a particularly personal sort, even in our impersonal, public days, a vivid made-up repeating suffering that is embedded in the drab fabric of my days like a stain I fixed with hot water long before I even knew what I was doing, and all of what I try to do I have to do around that pain. I was near sobbing at this point, only a few seconds having passed, Tom still letting himself be held by me, his mouth open a little, his eyes someone else's – so I should just accept what is not pain, and that I can, and not overthink.

'Are you Tom?' I asked.

He smiled at me, in a kind of condescending way.

'What does it matter? I want this,' he said. His voice was unlike himself; softer. Even the accent was different. A thrill ran through me, up the back of my body. I was alarmed and I was hungry. I launched myself again at his face, the room blurred, vision shrank and all was touch, strokes, kisses, hot tongues. Above it my mind always threatening the tip into disgust, or worse the harm. But I closed my eyes and I let myself be carried by the trembling oddness of what was happening.

Hangover Deluxe

Bees were buzzing somewhere. I could feel the heat of the sun through closed eyelids. Kept them closed because I was, I knew, on a precipice – if I opened my eyes I would be awake. It would be, as you know, a bad thing to be awake after drinking quite as much as I had. I took some measured breaths. So far so okay, so . . . open. I cracked my eyes. Whiteness. I wrinkled up my face. It's easy enough if you do it all at once, I thought, and forced myself to, sitting upright with my eyes open, and my body was only marginally upset with me. I laid my hands on the red cover. Still wearing at least the upper part of my suit, then. My hands interested me as something slightly alienated from the rest of the scene, aching, an echo of something last night, and now it was black suit fabric against red duvet fabric, then my hands, which had pulled back the covers and helped me into bed the night before, during a period when my mind was, at least it seemed to me at that moment, away from the controls. Piloting blind.

I was in one of the guest rooms, the slope of the ceiling high up like a church. Me in bed in a church. In a big red bed. And in the bed, more than me. Visible one – by arms over the edge of one side and two – by a pair of feet on the pillow next to me. I saw part of a black suit on the floor. Tom's white suit was nowhere to be seen. Oh, I thought, that doesn't seem right, and scrunching up my face again, got out of bed to deal with direct matters and rehydration before all of this. No trousers on. Boxers on. Socks on. Whatever I had done, I had done with my socks on. I went mechanically towards the en suite, barely seeing, I stuck my hands under the tap, drank from them salty sweet and cold, used the toilet, washed up, ran water over my eyes, came shuffling back out across a vast carpeted floor the exact same sanguineous colour as the walls.

The great red bed was installed in the massive high-ceilinged room. Light from the big window, white woolly-sky light, still too much. Who on earth had decided to make the room this way? Who wanted their guests to be struck in awe at atmospherics, acoustics, an assault of one single lurid colour, to think what, first thing, when they woke to face whatever the day would bring them? I stood and stared at the bed. It really was large enough to fit three adults quite comfortably, without them even having to touch in that space, even if they were journeying sleepers who rolled about and kicked. It could not, I thought, fulfil its place in the narrative of sacrifice, suffering, grand rites, that the room suggested for it; ludicrous to think so.

The way rich people live. I would suggest to Mark they changed the sheets to something a little less satanic.

I contemplated going over to the bed to pull back the covers to see who it was.

I knew though, of course, for the moment I was too stunned to let myself know, to remember all that I remembered, saving myself from myself.

I decided, for self-care, to reconstruct my memories of the night after coffee. I recovered my trousers, changed my mind and pulled off a long dressing gown from the back of the door. The MacAshfalls provided gowns for their guests. They were, yes, an incredible lot of people, I thought, admiring the jade-green silk and the tiger stitched across the back.

Too Much of a Body
and Things Done With It

Down the great planks of the staircase, right at the bottom and into the kitchen, large and mild and elegant and familiar – I reached out my hands and grabbed hold of the counter in the centre of the room, bent over, sucked in air, and let out a long gasp.

'There is a woman in my bed.'

'Melodramatic as usual,' said Mark, coming out from the pantry. 'I'm making some food for the masses. Sit down, and I will tend to you.'

'Thanks,' I said, and immediately rubbed my throat. Prickly skin. Grimy, 'Christ,' I said.

'Sinner,' said Mark, looking amused. I threw up my hands.

'Seriously though, Danny, you have a good time last night?'

'You sound extra posh and atrocious when you're angling for details,' I said, 'Danny. Echh.'

'Nothing wrong with Danny,' he said, putting down a cup of tea and a plate of reheated sausage rolls in front of me. 'This now, fruit later.'

'Fruit, oh no. No.'

'Fruit, you idiot. I'm just letting you know, you're getting an apple after you eat this muck. How do you survive?'

'With an unexpected grace.'

'And how are you feeling anyway?' said Mark.

I looked over at him. It was not a Mark sort of question. I bit into the pastry of the sausage roll and felt my stomach rumble awkwardly. Margarine and meaty blandness. If Mrs MacAshfall had made this, or Mark, I felt sure it would have alcohol in it. And some type of fruit. Meat and fruit together. I shuddered involuntarily. Through the window I could see a willow swaying. Curious thing.

'Did Tom . . . uh . . . last night?' I asked.

'Use your words, Daniel.' Mark's big, smirking, kindly face.

'What . . . ?'

'Because, well. I confess I heard *something*.'

I put my hand over my head, 'Yes, I remember it a bit. No I mean, was there any kind of fuss?'

Mark shrugged. 'Only when he left. Almost broke the door slamming it. Almost knocked my mother into the Noguchi table on the way out.' I sighed. I drank my tea loudly. I remembered.

Baited

After breakfast I went into the garden. No neighbours close enough to peer over the high hedges and see me (bare feet on the cold slabs and wet ground, wrapped in only half a suit and a green silk robe) and my deep obsessive thinking. Not of the night – time enough later for the night, faces to meet, stilted speech and recovery; oh that kind of proximity and flatmates, such ill-advisedness – but I was thinking instead of a way to get back from a sudden onslaught of hard sharp edges and images coming on, not with me yet, but which I could sense like a tide drawn out and waiting to rush over me. I could almost see these images, hatefully overdone, before seeing them directly. It was the knowledge that I would be mentally unwell soon. Like, I imagined, epileptics know with their auras. A different kind of experience entirely, I'm sure, nothing changed in my vision, no pain in my head beyond the hangover stuff, just a sense. Of crouching. That I would like to start running, like a dog, before the tsunami comes sweeping detritus, grey water and – no. I would not begin to catalogue dangers. That would lead me down to thinking again.

It is always this repetitive. To understand it also takes repetition. To speak it to myself to position myself and try to fight the vertigo of unseen horrors was also to engage in it, engage it. The enemy that makes itself by being looked at. But which cannot entirely be quashed by not looking either.

There were no bees outside.

Reconstitutional

Órla came up to me as I stood by the pond. Lipstick-haunted lips, weary, smiling face, those wide, clear, arresting eyes. She printed a kiss on my cheek. Though later when I looked it was not there. We began, piecemeal, to put our stories together.

'You all right?' she said,

'Is there a bruise?' I touched my face, suddenly realising there was indeed a bruise there, under my eye.

'More than one, I'll bet.'

We walked around the pond, looking in. At some point it had been a swimming pool. Now it was a stretch of dark water, ligatured with die-back rushes.

'How'd it get started?' I asked.

'I came in from the toilet, and saw you kissing. I thought he had passed out. Then you saw me – you don't remember? It had been weird before though, so weird. I don't mean to make an accusation with any of this. You were snogging. Tearing each others faces off,' she said, and I swore I could see a smile play over her face.

'You don't mind then? You aren't hurt?'

She pursed her lips and shook her head, 'No, um. That part – after we kissed. Well, it was all of us in it together. But that part's not really the issue. That night was something strange, Daniel.'

'Tell me how it was,' I said.

He Kissed Me

'Tell me how he was.'

'I was with him in the bedroom, while you were off somewhere, before all of what happened – he'd been missing in action most of the evening. Then he just walked in from somewhere and he was – different. His eyes were glassy, like he was drugged. He was cold, in his hands and feet and also in the way he moved. I'd never seen him like that,' Órla said. 'Well, a little bit. He hides it under affability.'

'He was frightened of something.'

'Yes, he was. He has been frightened. For a while, I think. Of something. I didn't realise it at the time, brushed him off. What of it though?'

'Then what . . . ?' I said.

'He stood at the window – the reflection there.' She shuddered. 'I don't know. I don't know what. I was drunk too. But I think I saw something there.'

'What?'

Órla swallowed. We stopped by a bank of dead flowers, pale as a spring sky with patches of brown, we were moving further from the house and closer to the night before by moving away. I could feel the awful images just waiting to get me. I rubbed my temples.

'A different man,' she said, in a dreamy voice. 'I backed away. The moment passed. I feel like I failed some kind of test. When you came in, I pretended I wanted you to get water. I needed a moment.'

'We were all far gone by then.'

'No, it wasn't that. And not Tom. I think he was nearly sober. You don't believe me, do you?'

'I don't know what you want me to believe. He did whisper something to me, after we—' I said, 'but I didn't want to even try to relay what he had said. Because it barely made sense, even through the drink. His sibilant, hot voice in my ear. Lennoxlove's diary, of all things. He had said something obscured and anxiously fast about Lennoxlove, and himself, speaking of seeing a groom in a dark barn, but in a cupboard somehow, of being a witness, but I just put a hand up. And without pausing a fist hit my face. I made the choice that I would not alarm Órla with partial information. I would wait.

Órla walked on a few steps. I tried to feel if my body had been through something. All I felt was an ache a few degrees left of my shabby corporeal form.

Narrative

'I came back in the room, ah, after washing up' she said, 'and you were on your feet, looking fucked and dizzy, and he just punched you. To be fair, you did get him right back. I thought you might knock him down. That laugh he gave. I'm amazed we got him calm again so quick. What was any of it about?'

'I can't say I know. I think you'd have strange ideas about it. A haunting.'

'A haunting,' said Órla.

The pool lay black between us and the house. Through the glass we could see Mark moving about, in and out of the kitchen, Mark's mother sitting on the fainting couch with a paper, a group of three freshly-washed strangers standing, looking back at us between the huge houseplants. We could see our reflections in the glass, and the reflection of the water.

'I have to say, I don't know him all that well – how well do you know anyone?' Órla said, 'I don't mean to make anything of it, but that night, with you – it was not . . . entirely Tom.'

'Mmm.' Thinking I believed her, and I didn't believe her, but I only said, 'Do you remember what we talked about, after he left?'

'He begged us both to stay near him. He was frightened.'

'Are you worried where he might have gone off to?'

Then, when she didn't say anything, I asked, 'Do you love him now?'

'That's not a very helpful question,' she said, touching my hand.

'I think . . . I think he's become obsessed with something, a book of mine . . .' I said.

'A novel?'

'A diary.'

I couldn't feel my toes. He had kissed me. More than that, grabbed me, stroked me, illuminated me. And everything with Órla too. And he'd hit me, and gone off somewhere which was something else to think about and understand. Later. Probably he'd a lot to sort out in his mind. My own head was thudding and yet I had never been happier to be where I was, or more physically strained by it, a disturbance below the surface of the body, which meant below the surface of the mind. It was clear to me, even then, that morning, that Tom was rolling off the edge of something. Órla walked in step with me, our arms interlinked. We did not have to say anything. Tom was a large figure floating over us like in that one Chagall painting, *The Kiss*. I felt the silk on my arm meet the wool of her coat. Tom was becoming our project together. He was in development and we must understand through observation, nothing further. I was loved, I thought, all of a sudden, that was why I was so happy, despite the fragmentation and the aches. Tom gone, hopefully to the flat, to his own bed and a comforting shower and second sleep, Órla at my side. And that morning I knew that I loved her, even with so little to go on I knew that she loved me, because, and through which, we had become conspirators, earnest ones, and we would always work for good together – or what we thought was good.

'Shall we go in?' I asked.

A fat wood pigeon burst out of a hedge and flew over the house. There was no such thing as always.

Resolving

Órla and I left in a taxi, and resolved to plan what to do in a few hours. I needed to excuse myself and go lie down in my room. She came back later in the evening, and we kept a vigil waiting for Tom to show. Only around one a.m. did she receive a text from him, a little star, no words. He did not come home that day, nor for three more days, but he sent cryptic messages. Órla responded with screeds of words, and each reply was an emoji, nothing else. A star, a moon, a hill, a horse, the sea. I tried to remember what we had done the day we knew he had vanished, and then a little bit before the party, when Órla and I had gone on a walk together and talked about everything else besides Tom. If we had neglected to realise how severe this problem was, then it was understandable, but perhaps not forgiveable, not redeemable, unless we did something to recover him.

The fourth day brought a texted photo of a Highland cow, apricot coloured, standing beside a telephone box, looking as Highland cows do, nonchalant and charismatic. I began looking for photos that looked similar online – it turned out there were lots, but only of a handful of places. Órla texted back instead of words, a globe and a question mark. Finally an answer came – a list of numbers, coordinates.

I packed and ran for Badr's car – left, with instructions to use it any way we needed to recover him – while Órla stayed behind in case he should wander in, our ghost boy, our prodigal love. 'Swear you'll not start sending me emojis, by fucking Christ,' she said.

I smiled and touched her shoulder lightly. And headed north.

Órla McLeod

Between Dog and Wolf

When I was a girl, I wanted to be exorcised. I liked the idea of possession and of some priest bending over me muttering the right prayers to rip the demons out. Speaking from my adult mind I think it was that I craved to be so open to the world as to take within my body something huge and lurid and melodramatically evil, to be utterly defiled and then – to be cured of that. To become again only a girl, bruised but ultimately just as I had been. Or to be killed by this expansive suffering, and to be through the other side and heaven-bound after the purgatory of my short life. Sometimes no one is around when you're eight and you're watching telly late at night. You see what you shouldn't and it becomes a part of you. I wanted to be a nun too. A possessed nun seemed to me the pinnacle of career ambitions. I wanted to be pure and heaving with violence. At the same time godly, meek and being rent apart.

What has this to do with anything? Tom. Daniel. See, I've always had the attraction to the splintering, inhabitational and polluting. Or at least to a cultural idea of pollution and plurality and its holy cure. The idea that someone skilled, a person with a vocational calling but in all other ways normal, can scoop a body out from its demons. And now the one is split from the many and made quite confounded. Possession – symptomatic of a cultural overspill and tainting. The patriarchy perhaps. You have to have an idea of property and who a body belongs to, to have possession. You know that what it must be most of the time in recorded cases is severe mental illness clashing against religiosity and fear of the dissolution of the self as a realm of contagion/corruption. But *some* of the rest of the time it might not be. It gets to be demons, sometimes. There's a margin for error. There's a margin for anything. I love margins. Being reductive we might argue, for a moment, just for fun, that's where the true faith and selfhood lives – that's a part of my thesis: marginalia and doodles are where the action happen, the moments of truth set not even against but *below* or *aside* the TRUTH of the text in handmade books. The self constructed in multiple tiny wonky lines, often curses and pictures of fantastical horses. Or dicks. Of course faith and the self, they live nowhere; constructed like the recursive heads of mushrooms in that forest of consciousness that is all of us alive. I get notions too about how margins mangle and complicate the divine and allow room for the glorious catastrophe of bodies inhabited and the concurrent spin out of the self. Messing up the greater body with other seeming rowdy parts. Let me be clear: I don't think sexuality has anything to do with the devil or the angels. But the self, yes, and its plurality.

This is a long introduction to me.

When I first met Tom I was drunk and high, and he was sweating in a work shirt clutching a pint of cider. He seemed hale and dubious. Didn't speak much, but what he said he said close and simple. Seduction by agreement. I led him away from his friends; we snogged by the stairs in the club. I was too old for that kind of thing but the blue and pink neon lighting hid that fact under its own issues. Between the dog and the wolf, the hour of evening howls, we stepped close and pressed bodies. Around about the time Tom became dispossessed of himself I was my worst self, irritable with him, like I might be at a child who was not mine but was foisted on me. But then, in that first moment with thrumming bass and our lips meeting and his hand on my back still holding his cold pint glass there against my spine, I considered myself smitten, though distinctly aware I was so. Tom was wildly handsome. In a domesticated way like a wolf raised by English Labradors. Like something confused but living the life it knows.

You could see the effect of him entering a room, hackles going up on the other lesser dogs, hairs on the backs of necks. A communal desire that stands between wanting to have or harm – dangerous that. He could not be anything else. Not until he met Daniel, and read the book, and let a certain split work through him – the devil's split – muckily creating a space where his scrawling footnotes could begin.

Tom Decays

That book, that diary, drab red-covered handwritten relic on the kitchen table in the Minto house, contained its own world – not for expanding upon yet. I want to step back a moment here and think of texts, generally. It's significant, but not unexpected, the role which texts have played in our assumption of madness. Our reading of them – I mean, mine and Daniel's – the fact I think of 'reading' Tom and his decay at all.

We're both big into our texts. I'm the academic who foregrounds the text within its book – the vessel that survives to pass a book down through the years to us, the text only a passenger (and one of many passengers if we're talking about a book of any age). Daniel's the one who for a living replicates books. Who knows a book's physical specificity is utterly upended in our age. There's a kind of sadness in that which cries to him to value the uniqueness of a thing at the very same time he is destroying that uniqueness. So he's tormented and I am practical. I've talked to Daniel about the pleasant balance in our tendencies; it's why we are writing this book together. But in deference to an idea of reality we're doing it separately so that stories that emerge are individual readings, not conjoined.

There's a poem I found once that I've never managed to remember enough details from to locate again. I had memorised a few lines of it – I had a few lines memorise themselves – while it hovered before me on some site:

> I have a kind of appalling tenderness in my head
> A bruise from a fall in childhood

I know, stupid. An obvious tablecloth escapade, a literary trick whisking the reader from the expectation of one state (mental tenderness) to another (physical damage). I know poems are famous for doing this. But it's still funny to me. Give me a break, because of my studies I mostly encounter old and middle English poems on stolid religious themes. There was another bit:

> And so I hear them run their nails against the binding of my skull
> And so I let them in. And in the letting in
> something gush out.

'Gush' is one of those words underrated for its awfulness. Gush, like the sound a tongue makes when you've been smacked in the face and your mouth is filling up with blood. I can't remember who or what 'them' is. What's important is they are plural. I've been thinking of this unsettling fragment of poem – which let's be honest isn't that good but got itself stuck fast in my head through a mix of repulsion and chancing on my pet obsession – in how it relates to Tom and the diary that he became obsessed with.

Tom is a book that did not want to be a book. He's populated by characters he has no say in. He's marked by our hands holding onto his edges and wearing him away. He's a book with something like that poem in it – content not worth the pages it is written on and not needing the pages to be written on since now we're taking it out to put it in another place. I think that's what the internet does to texts. See John Berger. Or any other theorist. But stamped or scribed indelibly in its original setting, anyway there is a split from the text-Tom and the form-Tom. From his inner content and his being. A proliferation maybe rather than a split. Let me be clear – this is not about mental illness. Don't be tender yourself. This is not about mental ill health. This is about plurality and possession. He's both the story Daniel and I tell of him here - inevitable errata, derivations, blah blah blah - and the body he has and the inner life he has, which Daniel and I are trying our best to give lines to. He's the diary. He's the diary's omissions. He's the ghost. He has succeeded where I haven't in becoming plural. And it's not just down to me it happened - he split himself. He was split. Something clawed at him and he let it in and in the process let himself out. Selfletting, like bloodletting. Each red bead of him a letter and some of it captured here.

Distraction/Decoction

To get to it: I was late for the housewarming. Tom went ahead of me from his work while I scrambled to finish a bit more research – there was always a bit more to do before I felt like I could afford to quit for the night – and got myself to Tesco for a wine – under six quid with a non-cringey label – I could give to the hosts. I was glad Tom was moving in somewhere new without me, that he hadn't even thought to ask if I'd move in with him. Took the pressure off us for a while. Let me say again at that point Tom was not more than he was. I still didn't have a clear idea whether he knew how to clean up after himself and wouldn't want me for a combination housecleaner and sexual services provider as some had before. Likewise I had flaws I wasn't ready to inflict on him yet. Relationships tended not to survive the full onslaught of me in one of my righteous, didactic moods.

When I got into the house I saw how things had been tidied away not just stuffed behind things as I'd have done. One person at least was house-proud. Or maybe the lads were just better at hiding the evidence of a rush clean. Tom let me in; he introduced me to Badr, and some of his workmates, and some of Badr's work-mates. The first group had dim faces I remembered from the club. All men. Badr had a couple of female colleagues. They gave small tight waves and hellos. My stomach dropped. I would have nothing to say to any of these people. After a while I got myself out on the pretext of opening the bottle. In the kitchen was another housemate. He introduced himself as Daniel. How shall

I say Daniel looked? First impressions: He stood in the light of the refrigerator, slight, soft. His fluffy brown hair a little too long on his head – later I learned there was a small bald patch back there – and he was swaying as if he was listening to some music playing in another room. He talked very softly but in a way that enticed one to lean in to listen. He gave the impression also of not wishing to be overheard by someone listening in the wings, and along with that had a slightly surly, distracted air that made it seem that this someone was waiting on him, and if he did not go soon he would be late, suffer some kind of ticking off. But here he stayed because he did not want to let you down either and was as generous as he could be with it. He was, I saw, a man of interior ambiguities and the whispers of the fairies in his ear. He looked like he slept in his socks.

'Nice coat,' he said, then lightly flinched as I looked at him. A tricksy man then to like right away but he had enough going on that I somehow did.

'Here,' I said, handing him the wine, 'I don't want it. I don't even know why I brought it.'

'Beer?' he offered me a cold can.

'I hate beer, I always drink it and hate it. Does the job, but . . .' I said. We sat down at the kitchen table and I was about to ask all the usual who are yous. Then something strange in his look stopped me. The way I found myself looking back. It was kinship, there in our glances performing itself, hard to put into words without sounding trite. And I said instead, 'You're wondering why, aren't you?'

'Why what?' he said. 'Not really,' he poured himself some bitter lemon, and made me a glass too, with vodka. I tried some. Not bad. Laughter came from the living room. While Tom sat on his throne, easy monarch of any place. He told stories, then, if you can believe it. He had anecdotes and courtiers fanning themselves. And I was irked at my jealousy and tried to outrun it with this strange man there whose manner intrigued and who, so quickly, was vitally connected.

'Oh look at you, like you know,' I said, 'no "why what" from you. I got the coat from a charity shop, by the way.'

'Don't tease,' he said, 'I know what you mean.'

'Oh you do, eh?'

'Tom, right? You're asking me if I know why you're with Tom. You want me to be the judge of you and him. But you phrase it or believe it like you think I've come up in my mind first with the question – the dilemma – of why you are together. Which is quite presumptuous of you.'

'That I'd be thinking it was a preoccupation of yours?'

'Just that,' he said. We both took a breath.

I saw how clever he was even for all the distraction. I saw something bright and dark in his eyes. I determined we'd get drunk and have a grand time and I'd go home without saying bye to Tom and probably never have a conversation as meaningful with this stranger again. Petty, yes. But forgive me; I'd forgive you for it. I didn't know what the substance Tom and I had was yet, or what Daniel and I'd come to have, or Tom and Daniel. It seems so tangled now, but then it was a matter of talk. Talk gets to be tangles, later, and we were bound up in words long before we were in bodies. And I love it for that, too.

Speech as Union

We stayed up late in the cave of our new friendship, covenous in the kitchen while the others socialised in the merry light of banality. It turned out Daniel and I had studied partially the same things at our universities, with codicology being the common passion. Daniel had turned himself to digital replication – I knew of the basement lab, the work they were doing there in general if not specifics, because I'd seen the applications to copy out manuscripts on my supervisor's desk and been along to conferences on digital humanities where they discussed the university's investment in the new setup. In my mind a copied thing was a brilliant idea, faster than a facsimile and almost impossible to tell apart from the original. But I wasn't sure how that fidelity – I wanted to say, uncanny fidelity – might recontextualise the thing itself in ways I didn't like, and if I didn't like it, what cause I might have to feel so, whether it was merely kneejerk or in fact valid. I wanted to press to see if he loved the physicality of old manuscripts, as I did. Surely. The fullness of a book that's really a thousand years old and how delicate and indomitable it is.

'I love how many lives a manuscript has lived in those years,' I said. 'How people change it with drawings or marks of wear, defacements.'

Daniel looked sad. 'But every time we touch a book, violently or even gently, with the tips of our fingers, we're wearing it down and away.'

'Oh no, I don't think of it like that. We have to be careful, yes, but the book tells us in the handling what it can take. I turn the pages with clean fingers, I listen to the pages crackling gently, and the spine. I go with purpose, and both I and the book are working together, in revelation of its contents. What else is the technology of a book for but to be touched and interacted with?'

'My work is to help lift those interactions into another space, and let the old book live a new life. I know some people might say, oh well you just make facsimiles, how is this special? But I make copies indistinguishable on the molecular level, really that close in, to the originals, so that people can touch those instead. So that they can keep learning. So that—'

'So that nothing is lost,' I said, 'I don't believe that's possible. But good effort, anyway. Good use of the 3D printer, rather than to make tat we don't need. Worthy. Though I'm yet to be convinced it can replicate something so well that *nothing* is lost in the translation from original to copy.'

There was a pause in which we hunted for something to say, our abashed silence colouring the air. I knew I hadn't offended him, though it might have a lesser man. There, I was already admiring him. He caught my eye and smiled, at last. A blink and you'd miss it, I thought, and smiled back at his turned-away face.

'I feel like I know you, already, from so little,' I blurted. 'Isn't it weird?'

'Do you?' He said. For a moment I wondered the deviousness or depth of the question – was he hinting that he and I had met? It struck me as not at all unlikely and I thought of him stepping off from the otherworld in which he clearly dwelled, the world of doubles, ascending into my dreams. His passive figure peering at me from behind a distorting toadstool, or drifting next to me as we went over a city, chatting sinuously, quietly, about the Rutland Psalter. And then another, more base, startling thought.

'You're not flirting with me I hope,' I said.

'No, I'm not,' he said, looking aghast, before his face settled into calmness again. 'I don't think so anyway.'

He seemed like he might flirt without knowing himself for it.

'You have one of those faces,' I said, 'the way you move about. Avoiding my eye. Smiling a lot.'

'Does Tom have one of those faces?' he said.

'Is it nerves—' I began to say. Our words clattered together. And we got up a little while later and did stuff to get away from these questions for now.

Performative Utterance

I kept thinking, you will never touch me. Only by accident will we ever touch. I poured wine. This was another day, when for some reason the two of us were alone. I can't remember now, why. We began to talk about art. The point of art and artists we loved – Daniel almost always giving me a male name – a must-see somewhere in a country neither of us had ever visited. We talked about the psychic toll of working with objects that will outlive us – obviously Daniel did not feel the same way, since he had agency over these objects, since he was the transformer, the source of continuity. And I was only the witness, even if an educated one. Half-way into the second bottle we began talking about desire.

'Desire is the main concern of art,' he said, 'all art comes from the need for something. There's never a moral side to art because of that. When artists create something they sometimes push into the grey zones of their own morality, and on past that, because the art allows for it, and one must self-define.'

'Okay, but my work brings me into contact primarily with moral art. Hyper-moral: guides for the good life, prayers begging God through various intercessors for them to be cleansed of sin. All the high beautiful words, the illustrations, the body of the book submit to this. It's not desire in the carnal sense, it's not need in the need for hungers of the body. It's spiritual clamour. To call it desire is to reduce a great thing into a lesser thing.'

'You think bodily need is lesser than spiritual need? You think they aren't connected?'

I sat up straighter and nudged the bottle with my glass until he poured me some.

'Uh, well.'

He smiled, 'they are both equals. We have our bodies and we have – don't have – our selves. You know what I mean.'

'What even is desire?'

'Nothing should ever be denied. No desire should be rejected.' He told me who had said that, but I forgot instantly in the haze of the wine. It wasn't Blake, though I'm sure Blake said something like it. The room seemed lit with a rosy glow. Every object in it, even the light, had been placed there to make up the scene in which we now sat. I pictured Tom's muscular back against the toiling sunbeams of a Blake illustration. I tried to see into the depths of myself and wondered if I desired something in this moment that could be understood in the regular terms that I knew. And what I would do with that knowledge. Nothing, I supposed. I glanced at his face. His eyes were squinted with drink, he kept pulling small thoughtful faces, as he tried to address my glib questions. We talked and tipped back the wine. Badr came and went, never stopping to chat, but looking on us fondly as we drank, like a mother whose benevolence is secure even in the most foolish of moments.

'Do you ever get touch starvation?' I asked.

He looked up, startled. 'It's all I know. I think,' he said, 'if I were to be touched, I think I would jump out of my skin,'

I thought of my books in the archive, lying, waiting to be touched. I thought of a skinless Daniel. In my mind he resembled uncooked sausage meat, his delicate skin laid aside like clingfilm. I pushed my hand over the table very lightly, a little above it, as if pushing a glass for a ouija board. I pushed until my fingers were hovering just over his hand on the desk.

'And if I touched you now?'

Daniel looked slightly left. I lowered my index finger. The gap between us was only a few millimetres. Voices from the otherworld addressed him from stage left. He raised his eyes to meet my eyes. That was about the whole of it.

Dim Spaces

Tom's room. Dark and dingy, covered in cat hair. I would spend most of the early autumn nights lying in that bed with Tom, us fucking, touching. At first. Then later lying awake pretending to sleep as Tom lay awake pretending to sleep. Something had come to lie between us shining and sharp and his, not mine. He slept so little and try as I might to boldly ignore it each shift in the bed clapped me out of my chance at sleep, and I couldn't figure out how best to start on it without the situation degenerating into a blowup. I might strike you as the kind who batters her way through life but I have at least an idea when not to push. I suddenly switch to a tread with a delicacy you'd scoff at. Socialisation as a woman, you might say. I'd say I saw, as through a glass darkly, the vastness of what had got into him, and wide-eyed lay watching for it to emerge. Though that might be hindsight's untruthfulness casting me as wiser than I was.

But anyway, before all that, that night of the housewarming, I watched Daniel covertly as he stood looking about at Tom's room. Him commenting and prying without trying to look like he was meaning too much by it. Stop it, I wanted to say, just come out and make your move, if you're going to. But of course, he wasn't.

Standing in the room I was burdened by the overwhelming stink of Lynx (I would buy Tom a nicer cologne as soon as I felt able to) but nearer, I got a waft of Daniel's scent. I moved a little closer. Not flirting. He smelled of old books. Chewed wood. Bitter lemon on his breath. He seemed to know things and I was

108

hunting to know. He did not move away. Something else. I couldn't place him. I didn't want him. I was deciding. Handsome, or not handsome? Friend or foe? Too soft, or pliant and supple? Straight or gay, or in between? The light from the hall outside shone on the side of his face as he looked about saying meaningless things. I wanted him in that way of wanting to know in the non-biblical sense. I wanted to unscrew my hair out of its bun and hug the Daniel right out of him, absorb him through my lips and eyes and skin before he was called away by whatever called to him. Yes, that much.

We just left the room. We drank, we talked, I learned that his mother lived alone, sold done-up furniture online, and that his best friend was called Mark and lived in the most fabulous house – they'd known each other since childhood. He'd had a cat that had died and his mother said it haunted her for a year and a day. He didn't believe in ghosts. Of course, I said. He told me more about the job at the university copying objects of infinite preciousness, which was at the planning and implementation stage, but also about some books he liked, which diverged wildly from the canon of the venerably old. I sat next to him. I listened to the scent of him. I felt his strangely soft voice. I searched out his dashing eyes and wondered if behind the shell a boldness lay. I did not wonder, then, why I wanted him to have that quality inside. Outside of our conversation the house bustled with other bodies who drank and laughed and began to depart. The last guest went, bar me. Daniel and I went into the kitchen and made food. There came Tom, stumbling. I got up on the counter, kissed him deeply, his arms got up around me. I saw Daniel watching us.

'Goodnight, Daniel,' said Tom.

The shining end of a sentence.

Captain Panic

We went to see a superhero film. Tom's idea. This was our first proper going-out date. He was on time at the cinema, driving up in the dusky light in a silver car I realised later was Badr's. I'd got the tickets, he'd get the meal at the fast food place afterwards. He seemed excited by the prospect of the film like a small kid might be. Faffed between what sweet to get then ordered the biggest bucket of popcorn and mashed it into his face by the handful before we even sat down, while I had roasted almonds and water. There is too much sugar in our lives anyway, and not always of our volition.

In the coolish dark we sat watching adverts with our heads pressed against the seatbacks from the push of the giant screen. I wondered if we'd hold hands like tweens. The film started, and the big explosions were so loud I had to cover my ears. The scene was a humanitarian disaster, but what was really awful was that one superhero didn't trust another one and was rude. Who cares if I'd seen this kind of thing a dozen times already; I pulled out my hipflask and unscrewed the top. The contents smelled of the warm tinny whisky that had been in there since the year before, the last time I'd gone to see a superhero film. That time with a bunch of us from the bubble tea shop. I sloshed a bit down and resumed watching.

It was probably due to the clamour that I didn't notice Tom's behaviour until about two hours in when the inevitable flirtations of lead hero and lady hero got really egregious. I glanced aside to make a joke to him and saw he was staring down the rows at an empty gap. It was unusual right enough given the film had just come out and should have been packed at that showing. Someone had booked and not shown, I guessed. I glanced over at Tom. Bored? His eyes, in the flashes between car crashes, were glazy and rolling. I leaned to his ear.

'You all right?' I whispered. He didn't answer me, or move his gaze. It was warm in there. I wondered if he was getting panicked by the environment and needed some air. I took his arm.

'Let's get a refill,' I said, pointing to the popcorn. He rose obediently and we went into the foyer.

'I should have expected it,' he said, wiping his eyes.

'Are you okay?' I asked again. He didn't seem to be responding to my words, but to his own.

'I knew it. Where was it - another film I think. He went into the cinema and he saw a ghost there too. Not a ghost. A demon. An it—'

'Here,' I said, leading him towards the empty concessions area. I bought a bottle of water and broke the seal and put it up to his mouth, and he drank it down greedily.

'Sorry, I—' he said.

'Feeling any better?'

'God, how embarrassing,' he said, putting the bottle up to his forehead, 'I just overheated, I think.' He straightened his back, 'Shall we go back in then? Up for that?'

As if it had been me who had felt like shit. He even rubbed my arm. It took all I had not to snap at him. But what would I have said? Admit your weakness, man! Or, it's okay, for fuck's sake, you felt rubbish and we needed to leave and I got you out! All things that don't require an angry tone of voice to say.

Swallowing Tree

You too might contemplate why I was with him, and you'd know to ask it aside from the obvious 'just look at him' response. So it was, Tom in the morning as the alarm went off pulling the covers off me to sleep a little longer. Under an umbrella that tilted to reveal the Tomness of him waiting for me outside of the library. Tom sullen when I didn't give him the right response. Tom at my place pulling on his jeans, then his tee-shirt, then leather jacket. His back to me the whole time, the texture of different fabrics and skin. But also, everything around Tom. The emptiness of my bedroom after he'd left. The solid feel of it right before I brought him in again. The maleness of his room. His white cat, wandering around or watching with her beautiful hypnotic eyes. The candle I set alight while I studied, cedar scented, that I'd never light with Tom around. Without him, Effie and Anna with me in the living room of our place choosing what film to go out and see, what drinks we could make from the leftovers we had. The sound of the post through the letterbox. Picking up the post and sorting it. The sound of buttering toast, phone notifications buzzing beside the plate. Going out to work in the blue light. Leaves coming off the trees like yellow letters. The moments before I went in to see my supervisor, looking down at my phone with veiled desperation. The weekly skype call to mam and da. The twice-weekly text to Stephanie. The weekly argument with Effie about the dishes. The twice-weekly trip to the big supermarket – with Anna sometimes since we got out around the same time of day. Waiting at the bus stop. Walking through the park. Dogs spotted. Cats peeped. And all the while yearning for Tom, a pure, scalding need, which is only really possible in the absence. I know well enough that the tender, careful, early stage of love is a momentary thing so desperately wanted to enjoy it, though I was struggling with how.

What else is passion, but suffering – we all have the dictionary definition in mind. That which is in the old Christian sense suffering in the body and mind, and in the old romantic a gilding tawdry swoosh of feelings and fluids. At heart both types of passion are a disruption to the norm, the norms of the body and the norms of routine. And so old fashioned as to be kind of arcane, but then, I had a proclivity to that. Visionary stressors at least half cliché, with all cliché's specificity and audacity. Tom, present or absent, was my feint at an opulent, medieval disruption. I so rarely have it, in my life. There's too many of us on this planet to have any of the wild agonies of spirit and love from those old near hallucinatory lapis lazuli and vellum eras, was my thinking, so I had unconsciously always tried to be sensible in my desire, to keep it level, to never overstep my portion. I didn't go looking for medieval levels of desire, just as I only took a scholarly interest in magic-as-science and science-as-morality, funny little asides as currency or full unhinging and holy suffering there. No. Like a tree whose bark calmly swallows whatever presses against it, takes it, rust and all and never begs, so were my life and my days. Some other time I'll talk about how desire is a punishment, for a woman. It is terrible to want in this way. So we do, and it wrecks us. So then, I was hungry for the passion of him while carefully aware of his everything else and his expiry date, and trying to keep my head up. And there, Tom pushing me against the wall and tonguing me, hand on my tit. And elsewhere, Tom slighting me by turning away and a drawn out bray in front of his office mates as I came up to greet him. Singular Tom in his healthy uninterrupted incarnation. I thought I knew that was all the passion in him. What a charming uninkling, then.

Repeat

In the kitchen at Tom's house there appeared a toy on the top of the fridge. It caught my eye because of how ugly it was – a white and neon Eeyore with pervert's eyes. We were making dinner. It was one of the few times I was outside of his room those early days, though right enough I was sore, sawing into a loaf for garlic bread. Standing stirring an orange stew Tom was talking away, and music was playing on speakers, the kind of thing that can stand to be ignored.

'What the fuck is that thing?' I said.

'The song?'

'No that,' I pointed with the knife. The beast sat icy white, flopped over on one side.

'Funny story,' Tom said.

'Is it.'

'Actually, yes. That, babe, is a clone.'

I looked at the thing again, got up close, 'I don't like it, it's looking at me. A clone?'

'Daniel made it. At his lab.'

'Christ almighty, kill it.' I had it by the throat and pretended to stab at it in the belly. 'It's heavier than it looks. Deeply suspicious.'

He left his stew and took the thing from me. I noted a look of fondness in his eyes.

'Ah but it took a lot to make this one.'

'What happened to the original if this is the clone?'

'We burned it,' Tom said, and in his voice a distinct pride, and a smiling, abashed look, which he covered up with a quick tonal shift. 'The original was a thing from work. A promo thing. It had spyware in it. For a vodka company.'

'Sure, sure.'

'I came back and Daniel said, "Look we can do something with this." And he wanted to show me where he worked anyway.'

I resumed my bread duties. 'What's it like then, his work?'

'What's he told you?'

'Nothing,' I said, which was a strange lie to give. 'I can't remember that he'd mentioned much at all beyond saying he worked in archives. But here it's clones? 3D printing then. That would be for copying rare objects, mm? For museums and stuff?'

'Yes, that's it' said Tom. 'We went over there and he unlocked the lab and fired out a copy of the original promo thing.'

I saw two shadows entering a deserted building, walking downstairs, their faces swept clean of any feeling. I got back to sawing the bread a while. Broke the silence at last to say, 'So then you came back and you burnt the original. Where, outside?'

'It took ages to make the copy. We had coffee. It hailed on the way back.'

'But where did you burn it?' I said. I was suddenly keen to move us on to the actual burning which was, it seemed, a kind of ceremonial act. Something itched at me, let it be said. His look. He was still holding the beast.

'Must have smoked a lot with the electronics.'

'Oh, it did,' Tom said.

'And does this—' I moved closer to him to take it, 'does this have bits in it? Is it watching us. Seems like it could be.'

'No,' he said. He hadn't let it go. He took a little breath and shifted it. There was a small sound of objects moving. 'It's solid inside, mostly solid, see.' He pinched it, and the fabric moved around. 'The machine couldn't scan inside, so it just filled it with little bearings, I think. Anyway, I like it. This one.'

'You like the copy? You seem like the kind of person who'd only like the real thing.' I said, for something to say. I was standing close to him, but he wasn't standing close to me. He took a breath in.

'Who's to say it isn't real? I'm holding it, it's real to me.' He said. Then with a funny look on his face he went by me to put it back on the fridge. Devotional site. I returned a second time to the bread, and found myself mashing butter into it with my fingers, pushing yellow into the gaps I had driven into the loaf, seeing only the yellow, inhaling it, smelling it on myself afterwards for hours. I thought to myself, how strange. It was just a stupid toy. You never know what'll bother you always, what can turn a relationship off on tilt.

Invitation

When I wasn't at the university either in the library looking at scans of marginalia in codicology databases and taking notes or playing hunt-the-supervisor or drinking coffee, I was at work. Work then was a frozen yoghurt and bubble tea shop a street over from the main part of the campus, a small street-front room with white moulded seating, unhinged pink mural and toppings with the look of inedible plastic.

One day Daniel walked by the shop and saw me, came on in.

'What'll it be?' I said, pretending I didn't know him. He blinked, played along.

'Uhm. What – is it?' he asked, pointing at the big board.

'You've never seen this before? Well – we've a treat for you. It's a kind of tea, I mean, you know that. Says it right there. You can have it hot or cold. The milk teas we have are plain, taro, matcha latte, caramel latte, chocolate, coconut, honey. The others are black tea, peach tea, jasmine tea, raspberry tea, nettle, white tea, green tea, lemon and green tea and blackberry tea. It comes with tapioca balls or jelly. The jelly comes in lychee, grass, pineapple, apple, banana – disgusting – aloe, strawberry, peach and winter melon.'

'What about the tapioca?'

'It comes in tapioca flavour.'

'Will I die of the sugar?' he said, smiling shyly.

'Yes. Definitely yes.'

'Order for me. Your favourite.'

'Okay. A cold taro milk tea with tapioca. Li'l bit less ice so you get your money's worth. Normal sweetness.'

'Yes, that's right.'

I turned and began the process. Daniel stood at the counter. I could feel him there, exploring the shop with diffuse grace and a few twitches of his hands and shoulders. I hadn't seen him since we'd first met and that had been weeks. Perhaps he thought I had forgotten him – a twinge of pity, then. I was in the blissful honeymoon of me and Tom, Tom and me. My flatmates were sick of hearing about it. But the girls at work only knew of the relationship slightly. From the afterglow when I ran in late.

'Are you Tom?' Jen asked him, smirking, 'Órla said you were handsome. Is he handsome, d'ya think, Anj?'

'I dunno, I dunno,' said Anj in her gruff voice.

Kids. Daniel was dying.

'Leave him be,' I said. I handed him the drink, 'On the house. In case you die.'

He took it and hesitated.

'Haven't seen you about.'

'Shh. Loose lips sink ships,' I said. The girls giggled as they pretended to clean up. I went round the counter and we sat in the window watching people queuing at the bus stop pretending to be in control of their lives.

'I've missed you,' he said, playfully.

'I'm easily missed for all that.'

'Oh yes. Climbing out the bedroom window before the house awakes, lest we accuse you of living there. I wouldn't mind you around more, you know. Badr wouldn't notice, he's out most of the time.'

'And old Minto?'

'I've heard a rumour Minto has left the house on important business in Nicaragua,' he said.

'A drug deal, eh?'

'Oh definitely.'

'Funny that I've never seen you by here before now.'

'My routes don't take me this way much. I'm in George Square, most of the time. Or in the house.'

'So you came here on purpose. Did Tom tell you where I worked?'

'I think you've put a spell on Tom. Or maybe he was always that way.'

And that was how it began. Of course Daniel spoke about it first. For all his elusiveness he had things gripped between his two hands, he could talk his way around to the pertinent parts.

'Oh?' I said.

'We'll go into it later. For now – listen. Mark, you remember I told you about Mark, well, he's having a Hallowe'en party. He has one every year. It's lavish, costumes, booze flowing, at that house I told you about. I wanted to invite you. You and Tom, but I didn't want you thinking I think of you as a set.'

'So far as you know that's what we are.'

He stared at me a moment, 'I hoped – never mind.'

'Never mind it.' I said. Feelings inhabited me, too slippery and confused to speak on. I looked at him as he turned and sucked on the giant purple bubble tea straw. No one ever looks anything but cute doing that. Even harsh ugly people are given a wisp of adorability. Not that Daniel was ugly. It's this glimpse into their childhood selves. I grabbed the cup from him and took a long sook myself. Lips over where his hand been. The balls rolled up the straw and into my mouth, black, and I chewed against my back teeth. Swallowed them, down my throat they went, into the pit of me, feelings, acids, sugar, thoughts, cells, all.

'I'm there,' I said. 'Consider me there.'

'I'll send you the theme later.' He said. We stood. He hugged me, gave a surprised look, then was gone.

Skin

A book of religious poems is made; it begins with skin. In the meadow a thousand years ago, a herd of nine red yearlings are drawn away from their mothers by a man in a smock, calling, bearing an armful of sweet hay. Tails beat the air as they trot. It's raining lightly on another island; the rain will be on this one soon. The drover lures his nine red cows over the meadow to a low stone-ringed field. His youngest, a girl, slaps their flanks – dusty with pollen, the soft red fur quivers – through the gate one by one, towards the cutting stone. His eldest boy looks up, just a moment, from sharpening the knife on a long black strop. The clouds come in. His sister wipes her wet hands on her own sides, and looks about for how to begin.

The vellum is cured at the hands of skilled workers on the sacred island from the raw calf skin, which is of high quality, and soft. The book is one made to order, Old English text copied from Old English text, illustrations chosen by the buyer and inserted as miniatures, ornate with pleasing details of flowers or fruits common to this area of the world. It takes a team of scribes and illustrators working together for months to make it as perfect as they are, in their effort, able to. One side of the vellum was the outer-facing part, where the hairs grew on the body of the calf. The other side faced inwards, against the flesh of an animal that once fed and walked, lived. It is high quality; nevertheless there are imperfections, raised veins, a stippledness on a few parts. They write on this skin, dead skin, the scribes and illustrators, the edges of their hands rest on it, skin against skin, the points of their tools mark where the borders within which the writing or pictures must lie. They tire; they rub their faces and touch this dead skin, which doesn't feel them back. The penmanship is beautiful, showing only small variations between the characters of the men who write it, their moods for the day, the light they had to see by, the temperature that cramped a finger or caused a momentary distraction in the line. Behind the flyleaf are hidden little ink marks made by one writer or another, testing out a new quill, writing their initials or a corded flower on a stem. Such small things to last so long in secret. The flyleaf is sealed away against the leather binding, until such time as the method of sealing fails.

The book is finished and the buyer takes it home. The buyer's family cherish it, then, over generations, slowly forget it. A candle burning too closely to a library shelf smokes a line across the cover. Its spine crackles like a fire when opened. Fashions change; the buyer's entire family are killed on the wrong side of a war. There are innumerable wars, it is a miracle it has stayed so long in the one family, until now. The book goes to a soldier's house. The soldier's son practices his letters under the image of the Virgin, piety towards her belonging to the old religion. He draws a horse shitting and a portrait of himself as a soldier. His brother draws a boat. The soldier's grandson, hard up, sells the book. The buyer sells it on. The buyer sells it on. The buyer dies and his estate sells it on. The book is lost, recovered, sold on. No one has opened the book to read its poems with the devotional attention for which it was made in five hundred years, though by now the book is much older than that.

The book does not remember how old it is and no one is asking it to tell. A small private museum holds the book in a box in its storage area, until a university buys the book, and takes it to where other books are, to cherish what the book is, what

122

great vessel it has become. It begins to be read in a new way. New hands gently touch its skin, its dead skin, try to understand the marks left on it by the hands that made them, now lying much reduced in vanished graves in graveyards full of their narrow like, once living, cautious, skilled, near what once were tall, steady collections of buildings, hubs where beautiful books were written for export or to be stored in libraries, places where page lay open next to page on huge tables in the light, text to text, illustration to illustration, scribe to scribe, on islands tiny, now out-of-the-way places of half-fallen stones and blackberry vines. The graves of the calves that made the pages that make up this book are not known, and neither are those of the drover and his family, nor the people who made the vellum that made the pages, nor the grasses that the calves ate, nor the flowers.

This is the book that I, a thousand years after its birth, wanted to know. By touch. By sight of course, but I could see that in the database, online, all scanned in and correct. I wanted to touch it. I did, with my bare hands – the white glove thing is a lie. I had been taken in to see it years before and watched the archivist open the book in its foam cradle, I had listened to it creaking open and smelled the mustiness of its pages. Some sweet note in there, grassy. I had been shown the horse shitting and the boat. I had looked at the drawing of a boy, funny long body and big head, and the sword he seemed to be holding in his big old spiky hand. Later I had copied out a poem from the scan of a page, learning how to read the old language there, in the old hand. *This* was the book I wanted to write something meaningful on. Cheek of me. It was much older than I was, and surely everything that could be was known about it. I was determined to come right up in my mortal body and lean in, find out the right question to ask of it that it had not been asked before. So that I would have permission to touch it again.

Some Quiet Hour

Tom began to be haunted; this was a week or so before the party. It began with a sigh in his sleep late at night or early in the morning. I lay awake with the cat up on my chest vibrating with purrs. Then she stopped purring and I heard him mumble, *Not like that*. I reached out a hand to stroke his hair. He turned over and curled up into a kind of hunch, muttering louder. *No*, he said. *In the throat*. By his tone it was hard to say if he was afraid of the action he was seeing, or instructing on it. I pulled my hand away and he groaned, the cat leapt.

Some moments let anything in, wonder and fury and the devil, all without much movement at all, breathless and gentle on the surface.

I got out of bed and went to the dark kitchen for water. I peered back across into his room and saw his big shape on the bed and decided I couldn't sleep and I couldn't wake him. I'd wake him and he'd have the misfortune of remembering what dream it was. Where if I let him sleep it would pass on by in the next REM cycle into the abyss where dreams go to drain away. The house was quiet. Mrs Boobs came in and mewed at me, and I let her out the back door. Then a creak from upstairs. A series of creaks. Daniel.

'Oh, hullo,' he whispered from the stair, 'just came down for something.' I sat. He was fabulously layered in his dress. The slippers on his feet, in an almost but not quite matching shade to the thick, red terry robe swishing about his knees and letting out glimpses of striped pyjamas. Topping the robe was a long, old kind of dust-grey velvet smoking jacket, and that scarf he was always wearing wrapped double round. His tortoise-shell glasses were on his face crooked. True the heating was never on in this place so he might well have been cold, but he looked too like a Victorian body, sans little sleeping cap. If those were in any place available and the cap slightly less ridiculous in the general fashion he'd have been right on the purchase. His hair was all up as if he'd run his hands through it repeatedly, which I was to learn later was a thing sure enough he did when distracted. As he looked about I had the sense he hadn't been sleeping, that for all the associated garments sleep was the furthest thing from him and so was company and that my presence was unwelcome. He found his way to the table, and put his hands on the chair nearest mine. I could have easily leaned over and righted his glasses on his prickled pinched face. Imagine.

'Ah, right,' I said.

'You didn't happen to see a book in here, earlier? Clothbound, old? I was reading it.'

'Not sleeping, then?'

'I keep odd hours,' he said.

'I'll bet. I see you as a Minto type, you know. In future years you'll be the owner of this house, a cryptid to the other occupants.'

'Christ,' he said, rubbing his eye. 'That's grim. You haven't seen it then?'

'A book? No,' I said. 'Sorry if I upset you. Wait—'

'Don't worry about it. I didn't expect anyone to be up. I feel a bit underdressed.'

At this I laughed. He looked hurt a second and then smiled. I made a note not to tease after midnight, unless we were both in the clear mood.

'The book though. I saw it earlier,' I said.

'Where?'

'In Tom's room—'

That clattering intimacy of talking over one another.

'Oh,' he said.

'D'you want me to get it?'

He shrugged. 'Don't want to wake him.'

'Oh, he's not sleeping well,' I said. 'Could stand to be woken.'

And I tapped Daniel on the shoulder and tugged him towards Tom's room. Something fun about the idea of sneaking in there together. And Tom talking in his sleep. What secrets he might spill, and Daniel to work them out with later.

Formal Settings

I remember Tom coming up to my flat just the once, early on. Sure he came loads of times but the only instant I can remember is in the light of everything after it. Late night, following drinks after his work. Him sullen and large on the bar's low stool, hunched shoulders. Not responding to probes about what his job entailed. 'Everyone's a wanker there,' he said, staring off at the wall of gins, 'shallow bastards looking to get ahead. No need to ruin a good night,' he said. I hopped up for beer, a juniper IPA for him, some local porter for myself. I felt like he'd respect that. Beer but fancy. The right level of risk, something to talk about or reject. I suspected Tom cared deeply about the taxonomy of crafted objects, consumable or otherwise, or would, if pressed in just the right way to explain his feelings on the subject.

He took a sip. Fuck that perfect pre-Raphaelite mouth, that caught the eye from the other side of any room like the sight of a bruise on an eyesocket. I wonder if that tender side to his features made him this solid and blank as defence. I wondered about his childhood. Around us the wide space of the pub buzzed thickly, Friday bodies shifted uncomplaining to make room, to move forward and closer to one another and cried with laughter and the barstaff poured shots in lighting rich with shadows so that the drink gleamed as it fell.

'I love this,' I said, meaninglessly, and knocked back as much of my beer as I could without drawing attention. We hadn't had sex yet. No, I know, almost on the first night, after the club. But we were having it that night and the knowledge of that hung awkwardly between us. We drank our drinks and went back too early to mine, with the light still up. The excuse was to show him something on Netflix. Two of us walking against a stream of folk going out. I wanted to be past this, at the point where holding his hand would be as natural as breathing, before the point handholding gets dropped. As it was we walked close, by necessity. The air between us was blue and sharp and the hairs on my arm were up.

'You're so close to the park,' he said, and I wanted to die, on his behalf I wanted to shove us both into neural oblivion, I wanted to skip all steps to the aftermath, in bed, sweaty and fulfilled preferably. There was my doorway, like a bad joke. I stood next to him hunting for my keys, trying not to make the bad joke. Up the three flights. I'd never noticed before how cathedral-like the staircase was, how like a cathedral or an ancient nunnery in some old film, all shadows and echoes and tight steps. I see shadows everywhere, you'll say. Like granting the thing that was watching us a space to watch us from.

'Fancy a drink?' I said, hustling far away from him in the kitchenette that connected to the living room, which had fairy lights and pink candles belonging to Vee, and photos he could look at while I cracked a beer. It's always this way. I sighed, regretting, wanting. The blank of him and the bulk of him. Then he looked at me. And he had that hallowed desire there, that's not pretence, that's not pushing itself. That's almost a tremulous thing. The warm domestic air of the room did nothing to diminish it. I touched the counter with my fingers, picked an earring out, and another.

'Nah,' he said. 'Come here.' So I did.

Tell me, is it ever how it is in the films, when they slam in through the door and spill their passion everywhere bright and assured? But this was close. We stood together. 'Oh,' he said, 'I want to kiss you, is that all right?' and I responded by kissing, and the human-electrical storm that had been gathering and setting my teeth on edge just cracked open the sky.

What was he like, in bed? Like any man who cares what his partner wants to feel. Generous. Quick to respond. Quiet, which I wished he wasn't – so much. He slept and I joined him, knackered both. My flatmates came back in the small hours. Tom was still there, asleep. I touched him with my foot, and he woke. His face close again in the dark. Better that way, when I couldn't see it all.

'You hungry?' I said.

'Fucking starving,' he answered.

Hours later, I stood in the kitchen, drowning in apprehension, throwing out wax cheese wrappers and an emptied biscuit box. My fucking heart was going to get broken. It signalled very clearly and from a long way off. But, I told myself, better just relax into it, for now.

The Person Asleep Is With Many Others

The body sleeping didn't stir when we first tiptoed in but did a little when we began rummaging. It was true I had seen the book in there earlier. Tom had been reading it before bed. Not the first time. I'd seen Tom with it several times over the course of the weeks he'd been living there. I hadn't asked about it and it only held slight professional interest in that it was handwritten and a little old, but Tom was so engrossed I didn't want to pry. Anyway, nineteenth century, outwith my remit. I'd thought at first he owned it, only he'd usually put it back outside on the kitchen table or the living room. It appeared to move without much human intervention between the two places and nowhere, sometimes gone for days, sometimes popping up on the counter or on the stand by the door where the keys and post hung out. That Tom read at all surprised me. I'd decided it was some book the house kept in common. And so it was, kind of, though Badr didn't bother with it.

There in the dim room Daniel put his hands on the top of the chest of drawers and I opened Tom's bag.

'Will he mind?' Daniel whispered. He stood there, looking at Tom. I looked at them both and tried not to allow myself much room for speculation. As you can imagine, I speculate wildly. It's almost something I can taste. I didn't answer Daniel because I didn't know. I found the book with my fingers. Rough cloth. I took it gently out the bag.

'We've disturbed him,' said Daniel.

'Anyway, it's your book, right? Don't worry about it.'

Tom was moving about on the bed. A stripe of light over him. His sleeping face frowning, and then, a slow inward breath switching, to *hhhhhahhhhhhhuuh*, the eeriest noise. Daniel and I straightened and stood watching, frozen, unsure of our mission then, the easy centre suddenly dropped. We waited. I passed Daniel the book and at this, Tom shifted violently, throwing one shoulder, hands in the sheets.

'No!' he cried out. 'Give it here!' but he was still asleep. He made the noise again, then rose into a seated position, stiff upright and opened his eyes, which were blankly blue and staring. He made fists with the duvet, and his face contorted with anguish – I don't like to use such words, but that was all I could call it.

'The knife,' he said, in a strange strangulated voice, 'get it in her!'

Then he dropped his head and breathed out in a long shuddering sigh and fell back down onto the pillow. Curled himself up, fists to head and legs up to his chin. His breathing was coming in feverish judders. Little whispers emitted between gritted teeth could have been speech or release. As I was making to leave, the pressure in the room seemed to drop. That's how I'd describe it. I felt my throat tighten, and I swear I saw bright blotches gathering, the kind you see when you get lightheaded. Slowly and slightly at first, window panes began rattling. The bed Tom was lying on began rattling too. It rattled up and down, against the wall, scraping, in a way that it would do if someone was shaking it, or fucking in it to a really weird pattern of motion. Tom, to my eyes, did not appear to move. He was solid as a stone in his curled position. I got closer. His eyes were open, and unmoving, his mouth a little open, his bottom teeth showing. Daniel came up too, reached out a hand as if to pull the blanket back or up, and the rattling intensified. He whipped his hand away as if burned.

'What the fuck . . . ?' he whispered.

The rattling went fainter. It stopped. Tom lay there in his strange sleep, twisting himself. A small still *gleeful* voice in my head said, 'Oho, look at this now.'

Folie à Deux a Real Risk

Daniel and I sat in the kitchen, the book on the table in front of us. A neat, slightly scuffed rectangle bound in reddish cloth. It looked reassuringly placeable by age and classification. On the first page was the name of the writer and his place of address, in big swirling inky loops. Ostentatious, I thought.

'Could it have been some kind of fit?' Daniel said.

'He was just dreaming. The rattling, though . . .'

'If you're sure,' he said. 'Dreams are strange things, you know. I'm sure he didn't mean anything by what he said.'

'Maybe the "her" wasn't me,' I said, 'when we sleep we go to be with the mass of human subconsciousness. It could be anyone at all he wants to stab, living, dead, made up.'

'Houses have funny settling floors. When we stood on it together, that probably explains the rattling.'

I nodded, like I believed him.

'Have you read any of this?' he said then, and he reached over and tapped the book with two fingers. A strange motion, I thought. Like knocking on wood.

We made coffee, heavily sugared. I wasn't going to sleep again. I could have – I'm not so easily shaken. But I am easily intrigued by psychodrama and Daniel is easily led into telling stories, and even before he began on the story of this particular book, well, I think a part of me was lit up wanting this to be the moment when I saw a possession come on before me.

'This diary isn't mine, by the way,' he began, still whispering as if Tom might hear us from the next room. I settled in. Let me say again I am not that fanciful. I knew logically it was Tom just having a nightmare that was shaking the bed and us probably making it worse by blundering about; his some human fear, present even in sleep, of moving predation in the dark. But I also felt excited by that girlish wish for this, this overwhelm by malign forces stealing into a body that couldn't really take its strength. It didn't really matter if this was caused by fictional sources of torment, by dreams only. The overspill, oh that was it. I was ready.

'Where does it come from?' I said.

There's a kind of intimacy in sharing a foolish idea, in the middle of the night with both of you in your pyjamas, fretting up a storm of possibility.

'My friend Mark. It was his – I stole it. I've been reading it, and, you know, it's fascinating. James Lennoxlove, intermittent stories of his life and his days, from about age nineteen up until thirty or so, I think. I thought Tom was reading it casually. I noticed it had been moved about. But I think now something about it may have unsettled him, I mean in a profound, lasting way.'

'It's a young man's diary, right?' I said, nodding at it. 'Anything in it beyond the usual sordid stuff?'

'Yes, actually. As a younger man, James Lennoxlove was witness to a murder, one night before a party at a neighbour's house. It's not much, just a few pages of description, then he drops the subject. The next entry is over a year later, and he doesn't reference what he saw at all. I haven't closely read the whole thing, so my thinking is he must reference it later, and in more detail.'

'A murder?'

'Yes, of a maid by a groom. In the stable.'

'With the candlestick?'

'No,' he said, laughing, 'with a knife, as you've already guessed.'

I picked at the book and opened it to a page and read,

I am so much happier than I could have imagined with this
new person in my life. We have gone to track the deer in the
Bitterrave forest of an idle afternoon though not to hunt them
but to sketch, because art is this person's great love. Not me,
but that I can accept, because—

'Person,' I said, 'here, about going sketching deer. He seems to
go a long way to avoid saying the gender.'

'I noticed that, too,' said Daniel.

'It could be nothing. I mean, what Tom was doing. Disrupted
sleep.'

'You'd noticed he's been stressed lately though.'

'Could be work. Could be any number of things,' I said, my
mind glowing so brightly I imagined Daniel could see right into
my head, see the red and orange lava slopping about in there.

'Spooked. No, you're right,' Daniel said. He sipped on his
coffee for a moment. We both sat not saying. It hung around us.
You want to grasp and to know the thing, get it named. To have it
and to that way disarm. As if a named bomb won't go off in your
hand. But even speaking of the thing obliquely, as we were doing,
is itself sometimes impossibly hard.

'I don't think there's anything we can do,' Daniel said.

'Keep an eye on him,' I said, 'make sure he gets enough sleep.
Rests and relaxes enough.'

I looked at the window. There we sat in the reflection, in the
glass all hollow. Stillness. Daniel, in his reflection, took off his
glasses and put them on the table. He looked very different, less
pinched. But then much the same, unmovingly agitated, like a
pool of water into which some current is pouring, churning. But
likely this was my projection onto him, and he was still to his

depths, calm in a way I would never be. I felt the cold and damp of the old room then, even with a jumper. I wished we had a fire, something to gather ourselves around.

'I didn't realise you wore glasses,' I said.

'Yeah, only if I'm reading,' he said. 'I have – I have a really bad feeling,' he said, 'like I'm sitting in a fog. And something is coming through it, towards us. Sorry. Probably sounds—'

I had no idea what he was talking about. I sat for a moment. 'Oh, fog. You really do have trouble seeing then. The glasses make sense now,' I paused. 'No, I know what you mean,' I said. 'It's like there is something coming through the fog, *through Tom.*'

Lennoxlove

I read: *I am a young man in love with someone beneath my station but also so far beyond it that such strictures cannot be placed on us, only rank disgust.* My eyes glazed over. Oh a scandal of love, huh. I flipped through a few pages more. More hunting, more talk of society, a trip to the city. Vain, rich boy who goes where he wants and gossips and has the occasional epiphany about something everyone knows. Here he orders the beech wood cut down and new farmland ploughed. Here he orders a black jacket and considers his brother's coolness towards him as evidence of their parallel and untouching lives. Here he admires a woman at a party, only to be told that she is some kind of upperclass hussy of no repute. I rub my eyes and do not care. What does Tom find to care about? I flip backwards, forwards. A scattering of words catch my eye, make me itch. Then I notice it: the dates. Under each entry James Lennoxlove writes a date (without year), but they don't make sense. He writes about the love in June, but describes falling leaves. The party with the socially-disparaged woman appears to be for the new year, as he mentions resolutions and forward-looking games, but the party is placed before his birthday – which he previously says is in November, so must either be a year on from, or in reference to the party he ran out of, where the murder happened. Winter appears after summer, autumn is whenever, the leaves constantly drifting in the woods that are never cut down. The diary is out of order, or the order he has imposed on it is not true. In this light the gossip reads as carrying a sly red line through it, untruthfulness. I read again. There, something too polished, too playful in the way he says, in the forestry entry, 'like all good men must I improve my lot.' And belying this, a handwriting that just feels slightly off – slants a little too rough, or too hasty. I can't speak on the matter, since it's not my century, my area of study. I sat back from the book and there it sat, all edges and disquiet.

'What did you like about this text?' I asked Daniel.

'Oh, I think it's his attention to scenic detail. He makes a lot of beautiful observations about the natural world.'

'Not much to go on for an obsession,' I said.

'Tom probably saw other things in it that he liked. The secret love, the sense of isolation – the, ah, historic details?'

'See, I don't think that meshes with him, who he is. Unlike us, he doesn't have an academic interest in minutia and proof.'

'How much do you really know of him?' Daniel asked.

'I know *that* much,' I said. 'He's a man who likes the real, the now. He likes beer, working out. Women. He's not a stupid or a shallow person, but I think that he wouldn't or shouldn't get interested in something as mundane as this record of a life.'

'You don't know that,' said Daniel, peevish.

'But,' I said, holding up a hand, 'did you notice this?' I pointed out what I had noticed.

'It's not right,' I said. 'There's something almost forced in it.'

'Ehh,' he said, 'can't say I saw any of this. On the other hand, if Tom's the way you think he is he wouldn't have noticed either. Would he?'

'And what would it mean to him if he did?'

'Obsession?'

I ran my finger around the lower edge of the book. It was

scuffed and my nail caught on something. I picked it up and examined it. You find hidden latches that open the world that way. But there was just a wrinkle in the fabric. I let the book fall to the table, sinner that I am. And clapped my hands.

Morning

Tom wouldn't remember, of course he wouldn't. He'd slept the whole night, felt well rested. He got up and hugged me when he came into the kitchen.

'You're up early, for the weekend,' he said. Raspy, seductive voice.

'Mm,' I said. Daniel put on some tea and opened the back door. The air outside rushed in violet grey light and I took some slow deep breaths of the dry air and potting mulch smells and listened to the birdsong.

'We should have a barbeque sometime, if the weather stays dry,' I said to myself.

Tom buttered his toast and sat looking at it on his plate.

'Not hungry?' I asked.

He lifted his food and began eating it. Not totally mechanically – he did smile when I spoke, nodded a few times. It was morning, that was normal. Daniel did the same, though he talked, too, small passing things, through his hands. The book was still on the table. We had taken turns to read it all the way through last night. And now it was there, and no less conquered for our going through it. I wanted to look at my phone, do something normal and distracting but it was in Tom's room and I couldn't make myself go back in. Not until the curtains were open and the day was better established.

'Birdie,' Tom muttered, 'that was her name.'

'What?' said Daniel, but he saw Tom's face and turning to me, said, 'Oh, you know, I need to get out to post something. I wonder if you're up for a walk to the shops?'

'Me? Sure. Tom, uh—'

Tom was staring at the book on the table, holding a crust of bread against the table, butter side down. I took in what he had just said. I felt a stab of horror at it, but so vague and plunging it was hard to stanch, hard to locate the source. Birdie, is what he had said. I scratched my fingers through my hair; it was knotted and needed brushed. Tom sat staring at the book. What if I grabbed it and threw it away? But the thought of touching it gave me unholy discomfort. I'd have crossed myself, if I still did that. Delays of gesture and sloping feelings all about me. Chilled, I felt. The men in the room moved about, or didn't move at all.

'Go on without me,' Tom said. 'I'm just going to do some reading I think.'

Neck of the Woods

We went on a walk. There was a place I liked to go. I'd found it years before, in my first year in the city, following a bus route looking for adventures. Some pathways wound through a wood up to a hill, hardly a unique thing, but this place I liked for its atmosphere. First we had to get there. After breakfast I told Tom I was leaving for home. Daniel had to make a run to the post office, we'd walk out together, he'd come back maybe after the library. We went quickly round the corner.

'How does he seem to you?' Daniel asked.

'Spacey. But, like, he'd had bad dreams so it was understandable.'

'He ate his breakfast okay.'

'I don't think Tom's ever skipped a meal,' I said. 'Anyway, it was just toast. You can eat toast at any time. It'd be the meal for the end of days.'

Daniel nodded.

We walked not saying much. We boarded the bus heading generally south, keeping silent there as well. We needed to be somewhere no one from our regular lives would chance to come across us. It was like going off to an anonymous hotel together. Daniel, sitting in the seat diagonally in front of me was wringing his hands. I leaned forward and tapped him, but he didn't notice and kept going. Wash wash wash. I moved to sit beside him, and pried his hands gently apart, and let them drop. I think that was it, the first time we'd touched, and I could tell it did something to him. All I tried to think was, the walk would calm him down. I looked at the passing world with glittering eyes.

We got off in suburbia and walked to a pathway beginning at a doorway in a high wall. The track went through hill woodland. It ran alongside where part of a university campus had once been, and before that, a sanatorium for shell-shocked soldiers of their War to End All Wars, and before that, I'm guessing some nobleman's house in woods that were at that time far away from the city. The woods belonged to the people now. Just in balance, the buildings that once housed the university, the old lecture rooms and admin' and that, were now the demesne of wealthy residents who could pay for the idea of the permanent view. Can't leave it to the students, after all, and have us hoping for too much. But I'd found it years before. And it was still in that way mine.

We set off into the woods with the sunlight streaming, followed the trail up, hardly speaking at first. It felt weird to be in nature. Everything had an edge to it. Trees massing, dropping their leaves around us in slow flashes of yellow and brown. Birds everywhere and nowhere, rustling and singing their throats out. A steep alignment of a climb and tracks that branched off to be enticing for leisure and snuffling dogs. Of which, strangely, there were none, so early it was. Near the top there was an uneven meadow hedged in yellow gorse, and the other green-brown hills of the city filled the space between the neat boxes of Victorian and twentieth century homes. I sighed. And the sky above it all with racing clouds and patches over the sun. I say over the sun, like our local weather was something grand. We forget so easily our own smallness. The great blackness of void outwith this world in miles unfathomable, blah blah blah. I tried most of the time to get locked into the physical reality of the senses and the analytic mind. Put my attention where it best needed to be. At work, at my studies. I can think to myself, here, 'Trace with your own living fingertips this evidence of effort and diligence of numberless people. Those who made the books are more numerous than the stars we can see.' I don't know if that's true. But, to centre myself I could think acutely about the scratching of their quills. Dip, raise, curve along, point. The pigment of their inks, mixed by hand from local and distant flowers, well water and crushed beetles. And here's the moments anonymous peoples, children and adult, took just for themselves in doodles and flourishes. Centuries-old, still here is something that keeps going. I could take it and put it in a safe context.

But when you get up into a free view, ah sometimes all you can do is realise. Be forced to. Here's this frail cage of your body against meaningless winds. And here come the questions of cosmology and of God, hammering over the sky like doom. And you realise, with only one person inside of you, you are so easily cracked open and dispersed. Hands up if you feel the same. Hands up, swishing your arms through the thin layer of particles which surrounds us all times. Our living in this fragile element contributes to it a net loss, a tiny degradation. And the world's getting worse over time. And this so fucking predictable, like I'd been programmed to think just so, in these places – somebody's kind of a joke. When she gets up high it really gives her ... perspective. I took a deep breath in. I reached into the nearest gorse bush and pinched off a yellow bloom and smelled it and threw it away. I know I looked happy; Daniel smiled at me. Happy just to be breathing, I guess.

On a Bench Overlooking the Edge

We sat with our hands in our pockets. Shit, I thought. My hair whipped out and around my head. If I was going to be this fucking morose, I'd have liked it to have been because I was hungover from a good time. I felt Daniel shift in the seat a little; his knee fell against mine.

'Do you think Tom is still sitting at the kitchen table?' I said.

'It's bright today.' He raised a hand to his eyes. 'I think he probably is. That's my mum's house, down there. No, there.'

'Nice,' I said. The winds from the cosmos blew over us, hissing in the golden-red trees off to one side sending bits of them flying, and in the redoubtable gorse which made not much of a noise at all. The tilted axis of the earth made the seasons, and this was autumn. How can we believe in hauntings now? We are so little and always being obliterated, and as a species on the way to securing that completely. Belief in ghosts, in possession. However much I'd like not to believe, I can fully grasp why I do, or why I am able to fool myself: oh to be grand and full of diverse modes of being, to know extension of the self, to know God and demons and angels and the drawling, drifting spirits of enduring souls in such an epoch as this. It's the very end of everything, I thought. Though it was autumn, so, in that too, of course I thought so. But Tom was, anyway, he was haunted. Or bedevilled. I'd take for myself the strange, exciting fear in that, if I could haul myself out of this strange mood. Daniel leaned against me, or I leaned against him.

'What could it be in the book that's getting to him?' I said.

'You don't think we're overthinking it?'

'I want to look at the book again. I want to understand it.'

'Why?' said Daniel, 'You think it contains some mystery that has wrapped him in its claws? Don't be ridiculous.'

'I don't know,' I said. 'He doesn't seem himself, then last night, and this morning, and you said yourself a while ago, before I even noticed, that something was enchanting him.'

'I said you were enchanting him.'

'I never took you for a sceptic.'

'Sceptic. I believe in the beauty of this world and all that's gone before. But I think what's gone stays gone,' he said, 'this is all there is, Órla. It's enough. It's very beautiful, right now.'

'Aesthete. I just think he might be, you know. Something.'

'Fine. But seriously, you think he's – I thought you were so solid and – sharp. I didn't expect this,' Daniel said.

'Expect what?'

'You really believe he's got some kind of devil in him. Some kind of ghost. Or he has become a portal to the unseen world. On what evidence, there can be none—'

'All right, stop. You don't know me. You don't know—'

'The things I've seen?'

I said nothing. Daniel got up and walked a little way off to the edge, overlooking the city. We'd missed each other somewhere and spun off. I couldn't do this alone, I thought. I searched my head for what I knew of Daniel, in those weeks of our friendship. He was warm, twitchy, gentle, had a light comic touch, seemed to understand me on some innate level, seemed to understand everything by the map of his feelings and his mind, charmed by Tom – I'd seen it by then – keen fondness for me, responsive, clever. Yet now, when I needed his softness and feelishness, this coldness, judgement. Laughter came from behind us – a child, running with a brown Labrador. I watched them canter over the small field at the top of the hill. I wanted to be a little girl again. But I believed in ghost stories then too.

'Tell me a ghost story, then,' he said, 'one from your real life. Tell me what you've seen.'

The Cold Bitch

Once when I was a girl, about six or so, I said, my parents ran away. It was wintertime. We had just moved temporarily into this lonely house on the coast. My da was working there on a contract, restoring the house around us for some rich guy. We'd be back home by the spring, mam told me. The house was rangy, from the sixteenth century, hauled up from the cliffs it stood on – I looked it up years later to scratch the itch it had left me with but there was not much information to be had beyond the property value – it was worth much less in those days. I don't remember the sounds of sawing or workmen stomping through in their boots. I remember it being a heavy quiet place, even before my parents left.

My sister wasn't born yet so I had a bedroom to myself. The walls felt thick and cold all the time. The ceilings slanted at different angles. Everything, in my memory, was painted a heavy, glossy dark green. But I wasn't scared – I didn't have much reference for frightening things, I think. We'd always lived in old, ramshackle places, moving around a lot. So as children go, I was sturdy and not prone to letting my mind run on in that way at least. My parents, they don't talk about what they saw, or much of what they did. Only years later they mentioned it just the once, so I still don't have a frame of reference for what happened.

It was winter, anyway. I was woken up early in the dark by my mother clattering into my room with a suitcase. She was oddly silent, packing some things for me. I asked what she was doing;

she put a finger to her lips and pulled me out of bed. She did not ask me to get dressed, or even put shoes on. We went down the stairs and outside. I squirmed at the shock of the cold, and she slapped me on the arm, holding me up by it, and whispering. I don't remember what she said. Behave, probably. Da was behind the driving wheel of the car, cigarette in hand. Windows rolled up. I remember that because he normally kept them rolled down no matter what the weather, to let the smoke out.

We got in the car. Da started the engine and began backing out of the drive. Suddenly, mam jabbed at the windscreen. 'There she is,' she said. 'The cold bitch.' That's when I opened the door and let myself out of the car. Still don't know why I felt the need to do that. We weren't going fast, and I didn't hurt myself. I ran back to the house, slammed the door, stood up on my tiptoes and turned the lock. After a few minutes I heard Da knocking, lightly, then hard. Proper ramming on the door. Then he stopped knocking, and, after a little bit, I heard my parents drive off. They didn't come back that evening.

After they had gone, I put myself back to bed and, somehow, fell right asleep. I'd never been left alone before. I got up in what felt like the middle of the afternoon, made some bread and jam sandwiches, played house, put myself to bed. I wanted a bath, but I wasn't sure I would be able to stop the taps going once I started them – that was a big concern, that I'd flood the house and be carried out on a wave of water. That Mam and Da would be disappointed in me for not being able to look after myself. Otherwise, I was calm, collected; that's how I remember myself.

That night, the 'cold bitch' came to my door. I don't know how she had been with Mam and Da to frighten them so witless, but she wasn't in any way cruel or menacing to me. Her dress trailed on the ground below her feet. It was yellowish, hemmed with lace, like something kept folded in an old drawer. I remember wanting to touch it, and leaping out of bed to do that. The cold bitch just hovering there, in the doorway of my room, as I, chubby, little, ran at her. I tried to grab and pat at the cloth of her dress. I tried to put it in my mouth. I remember the texture of it, believe me when I say that. It was crumbling, stiff as dead leaves. She drew back. Whispering voices. A noise like cutlery being put away. I came forward. 'Please,' I said. Her face is hard to recall. She had a big mouth, if she had one at all.

I stayed out of bed, lying near her hanging there, for what felt like hours. I brought my plastic farm animals and played them with her until I got pins and needles and said, 'I'm going to bed again. Please don't let anyone come in the house.' And no one did come for another whole day. In the morning there was a piece of cooked chicken laid out on a plate, very pale looking and damp. But I didn't eat it. I made myself some bread and butter. And then I suppose my parents came home for me later – a day later? And later we moved out.

When I finally asked them, in a pique, why they left me, my da looked aghast. He said they hadn't left me: they'd been locked out of the house for two days. The locksmith couldn't let them in, the windows were lead paned and there was much debate about opening them by breaking, but it would have been very expensive, irreplaceable glass lost forever. Note they didn't say I locked them out. They were locked out. Mam said she would have panicked, but that I knew my stuff, even then. 'On the phone, you said you'd brushed your teeth all by yourself. No harm done.' That was all they had to say on the matter. I know I didn't speak to them on the phone, it had a loud ring and it didn't ring, the entire time when I was there alone.

Healthy Things

'And so, well, you're the only one that remembers it like this?' Daniel said.

'Maybe I've supplied extra details over the years. Maybe she was not anything but a curtain across the door, fluttering in a breeze. But I felt like she was more. And how do you explain the time spent locked in the house by myself? My parents were freaked out, still are.'

'Pretty strange, I'll admit, though I really think you could be remembering it wrongly. Surely they called the police? And you were six – it's just, this idea that you played with her, this ghost, with your toys, without getting scared – and you said you wanted to eat her dress and you put it in your mouth.'

'You find it hard to believe?'

'Very. Most children would have been sobbing and peeing themselves, I think. Most parents would have broken down the door.'

'Maybe it was my upbringing. Maybe my parents were different from most people's. I feel like I asked the cold bitch, "are you looking after me?" And I understood that she was, in her own way. Like, she was confused what I wanted, but that she knew I wanted something from her and tried to give it.'

'Were you that lonely? Did your parents care that little?'

'Her energy was positive towards me. Kindly, even. Or at least, not hostile.'

'You've lost me,' said Daniel, 'It's all a lot of granular detail for you to remember after all this time.'

'So. Well, I don't have to impress you or convince you. I know what happened to me.'

'You mostly know what happened to you. You've filled in, elaborated and expanded the incident, whatever it was, over the years. Your parents, for whatever reason, are reticent to talk about it. Perhaps an incident of neglect they feel guilty about.'

I crossed my arms and kept quiet.

'It's a huge amount to have happened,' said Daniel. 'Most hauntings are, like, an unexplained knocking. A cold spot. Some little imaginary face flitting past a window.'

'The rules of the world as you understand them are innocent until proven guilty,' I said, 'that's your game. The world is innocent of spirits until there's proof – but the proof you want is not the kind that spirits give. By nature they are ephemeral and leave marks only on the mind.'

'Of the young or eager to believe. Playful, imaginative minds.'

'Fine,' I said, 'let's get down off this hill. I'm cold.'

'Cold bitch . . . ' said Daniel, with laughter in his voice, 'it's colourful though.'

'Tease,' I said.

A Star Objects to Its Discovery

By the time we got back to the house, it was getting dark. Tom hadn't texted me all day long. I knew he would not be there, and sure enough, he wasn't. I should have gone back to my flat then, but I didn't know how to leave Daniel.

In the kitchen, the empty chair Tom had been sitting in when we left had a guilty look. Pulled out from under the table, a wooden statement. I believe furniture can be haunted – it is haunted and smeared – even sodden – with the residue of human feelings. Somewhere Tom was guiltily and a little madly walking out alone in the darkening October dusk with the diary in the pocket of his coat. I went and washed my face and Daniel made us tea, which I took with gritted teeth and tipped into a plant pot on the window sill.

'Well,' he said, 'very good.'

'It is very good!' I answered. 'Oh, what was the point of going out? We've lost him somewhere.'

'I don't think we needed to be minding him,' said Daniel.

'This morning you did.'

'Let's watch some TV. Badr will be home soon. You're welcome to stay for dinner.'

The offer was pleasant and full of brittleness underneath, and underneath the brittleness the strain of the day's events and underneath that, a kind of hope that I would stay and – I think, under all that patina – a little fear too, for our new friendship, and for Tom.

'What're you making?'

'Pasta and cheese,' said Daniel.

'So definitive.'

'Well, that's me,' he said.

While the water was boiling in the kettle I opened the back door and went out. I wanted quiet – Daniel followed me.

'You know, he'll be back soon. Last night was—'

'Like a dream. I know,' Strange intimacies, and now getting dark and all too much. I hugged myself. Even with my jacket on I couldn't keep back the creeping cold. In the bushes the dark was pooling, beginning to suck out the blue air. I turned and looked at the house. Briefly wondered if it was the house that was haunted, and not Tom. Consider: the age of this place suggests at least one person must have, at some point, died within its walls. Consider: its strange inhabitants and the kind of atmosphere that builds up over time like fat at the bottom of an oven. Old man Minto, the hermit of the downstairs room. Badr, who seemed to tend to the building like it was a kind of mistress, in his polish and adjustments a kind of devotional aspect. Daniel – for all that he swore for scepticism and against the spooky, just look at him. Clearly, a wispish, sensitive person of his type would be drawn to the ley-line feel of this place. Tom was the odd one out. He moved here because the rent was good, housemates seemed nice and they accepted his cat. Does anyone write a PhD thesis on a house? Not, just generally: specifically scale and map out a house like codicologists map the uniqueness of an old book. Does anyone truly have that kind of love in them for a house that is of neither historical or architectural significance? But a haunted house is the vessel and the text.

I wanted to ask Daniel what he thought of that, and what he felt about Tom, but I didn't have the energy. I took some gulps of the cold air and felt my own feelings clear with it, cold clouds out through chapped lips. Daniel laughed, covered his mouth. He also did not want to hurt me.

'Moon's up,' I said.

Daniel was beside me. He put his arms around me, suddenly.

We stood together in the hug. I hadn't thought him capable, but he was assured at it. With me in the moment of it as it opened up. I did not cry, but I thought about it.

'Forget it all,' he said. We pulled apart, and he laughed at something. We went in and ate what is always the right amount of pasta, too much, strung with tangy cheese and glistening with butter.

Tom remained out in the night.

Minto

Daniel and I fell asleep on the sofa, him on one side, me on the other, our feet touching under a thrown coat. I was woken by sounds in the house, a key turning in the door. But it wasn't Tom. I got up to investigate. In the hallway was a man, tall and hunched, with white hair he was sorting with one hand as with the other he rummaged in the post cubby and pulled out a stack of letters.

'Are you Minto?' I asked.

He turned around. A smile slowly materialised on his face. Though it was dark I noticed yellow teeth, and blue, protruding eyes.

'Hello! The very same,' he said in a shoogly, theatrical whisper, before turning back around and working on his post again. He made a discard pile and a keep pile. The discard pile went straight in the bin, and the keep went in the pocket of his oversized grey coat, possibly forever. He was humming. He went into the kitchen – I couldn't imagine him ever having been in that room somehow. I followed him in.

'Ah, are you one of the lodgers?' he said. He had a kind of refined, fluted voice that wavered between posh Scottish and terribly English. Sounded like a schoolmaster from a fifties film – Alistair Sim, that was it.

'No. I just. Go out with one.' I said.

'Lucky them, whichever one it is,' he said. He went to the fridge and took out a container of food and put it on the table. A sticker said 'Badr's turmeric chicken' on the front, with a date.

'Care to join me? The man's a very fine cook.'

I fetched cutlery.

'No plates,' he said, holding up a hand.

We sat and picked through the sticky, spicy chicken with our forks, saying nothing. Minto continued to hum as he chomped. Distracted or wishing to appear distracted. After a while he stopped, fork mid-air.

'Do you know what's happening with the blond one?'

'Tom?'

'Yes, the blond one. I have noticed he is a little odd. Now, if it's habitual oddness or sudden onset queerness, I cannot quite say. Just that to me he seems a little . . . lost in the fog.' Before I could answer, he forged on.

'Now, we're all a little foggy now and then. God knows I've forgotten to eat for days at a time, or I've not paid a bill – somehow it always gets done, very good they are here about that. But when someone is so off that it starts to unbalance the house, that's when I. Well. I go out on a walk and try to think of a solution.'

'That's what you were doing? You were on a walk.'

'Midnight stroll. I went to the Pentland hills.'

'That's quite far for a walk on one night.'

'Nonsense,' he said, 'it depends how time works for you. For some, like me in my old age, it is slower than for others. And you find you can get a lot more done when it is slow, though it can irk those who are fast fast fast.'

I went to the sink and washed my fork.

'Do sit, girl. Sit sit. Have more of that. There, good. Sometimes, my days last for weeks at a time. I only must remember to keep some supplies to hand, or risk getting fatigued as the day stretches on ahead of me.'

'I like that,' I said, 'though I don't quite believe you're entirely serious.'

'Oh? Well—' Minto paused. 'If I had to take an educated guess at what has happened to your gentleman friend,' he said, 'I'd say he is suffering from a kind of disruption.'

'Disruption of time?'

'Ah you're a quick one,' he said. He ambled to the sink and washed his own fork under the cold tap and poured himself a glass of water.

'Where do you think Tom is now, in his disrupted time?'

Minto stopped and stared in thought. His eyes were a paler blue than I'd thought, the colour of scintillations of light on water.

'Oh, I haven't shaved in too long,' he said, rubbing his grizzled jowls. 'Now, Tom, I'd say he's probably lost in another century entirely.'

'You've seen him with the book then?'

Minto looked at me. Man did not blink much. Owl head and a slight smile, 'Ah, what book?' he said.

'The diary. He's been reading the diary of an nineteenth-century man.'

'Well, that'll be it then,' Minto said. 'Look for him there.'

And with shuffling steps he left the room. And there came shortly after the sound of his door closing shut.

The Revenant

I lay dozing in Tom's bed, and it was Tom that woke me, flushing the toilet and coming in at seven in the morning. I checked my phone for the time.

'Where've you been?' I asked in a carefully groggy voice.

'Out,' he said with a sheen of sweat on his face. It was too little to go on.

'Okay. Oh, cold feet.' I said, and shifted to make room. He set down his jeans and tee-shirt, smelling of raw earth and of himself. It smelled like he had been lying on the ground. He had pieces of leaf in his hair. Many of them. I didn't dare to try and remove them.

At ten I woke up and got out of bed. The party was that night. Hallowe'en. I opened the curtains on the crisp-looking day, and looked back at the room. Mrs Boobs was awake and staring at me. We sat in vigil over Tom. His face soft with sleep. People can look so perfect while they sleep, I thought, so tender and wonderful. All that life held in safe hands. No worry or pain. Unless they are dreaming. But Tom's eyes were still. And was he the only occupant of that body, and had he been all the time he was away in this world of ours, or some other?

Around ten minutes later he got up swiftly and walked shirtless into the living room, and I followed behind like I was a wife, or a cat.

'Where is it?' he said.

Daniel was still on the sofa, with a mug in his hand and the

TV on. 'Hmm?' he said, 'Oh, Tom. Hi. The diary's in my room.' Tom stalked out. I looked at Daniel. He mouthed *humour him* at me. I picked up a pad of paper from the floor and scrawled in biro, <u>some kind of episode?</u> And underlined this.

We listened to Tom ascending the stairs, footsteps up to Daniel's room. His tread made it half-way back down the stairs, where he sat, and I looked at him, again dumbly like a wife, or a cat. I felt oddly like he had come down with another person. I couldn't see from where I stood if he had the book or not – I thought not since he would have had to have kept it down the front of his pyjamas. Nowhere else for it to go.

'Am I overthinking it?' I whispered to Daniel, who only shrugged. I wondered how Badr was doing. He was the only one of us at work today. Though Tom should have been. I got up and made more food. So it always goes. Breakfast, tea. In the midst of some kind of internal or external strife. Coffee, instant soup, checking your emails on your phone, chaos in the world, biscuits, the economy destroyed, a stadium.

The next thing I knew, Tom was in the kitchen with me, bustling about.

'Can I get some of that hot water,' he said. And he made himself a soup from one of my packets and sat drinking it while leaning on the counter as if nothing whatsoever had happened.

I let him drink for a while. Then, nearly bursting: 'Where were you yesterday?' I said, in as close to a correct, coolish, non-enraged, still meaningful tone as I could manage.

'Oh shit, I didn't tell you, did I? Company away day,' he said. Then he finished up and went off for a shower.

I took my soup to the doorway of the living room. I could have stood in the entrance to a shelled stadium. That would have done.

'He's cheating on me,' I said to Daniel, 'd'you think?'

'Hmm, maybe,' he said, bending his head to sip more from his mug, the sensualist. 'But it's the better option than what you were thinking before.'

'Fuck you,' I said, with affection.

I walked through the house, past Minto's door, into the kitchen, into Tom's room, back into the kitchen, and then to the back door, opening it but not stepping through as if I could be both standing in the warmth and out in the cold air standing in the garden. I snuffed that air. Mrs Boobs came and snuffed it too. I was upright on my place, I was disgustingly subservient to this man's actions, and needing, needing to know. The wife faces the sea her husband is sailing on, and does not know what is his fate, and it's the nineteenth century, and even now, some of us find ourselves so. What's he doing if he's not cheating on me, I thought. Daniel came up to me, with the coat on his shoulders. I wanted to laugh at him there. The world's least imposing gangster.

'Do you still think there's something supernatural, cold bitch?' he said.

'So I'm the cold bitch now? Me, the spooky one?'

'It's a beautiful day,' he answered, closing his eyes and raising his head up in the brightening light from the window. Dark eyebrows, darting eyes. Soft lips. Nobbly nose. Such surprisingly beautiful detail and I suddenly thought, with morning clarity, that we were forming a tiny cult between us.

'Something *is* happening with him,' I said.

'If he's cheating on you with somebody,' Daniel said, 'you don't have to overthink it. The strangeness is guilt, or something. Or perhaps he has secret business all of his own that relates to none of this.'

'I met Minto last night,' I said.

'Oh really? What – what did he say?'

I explained.

161

'Do you feel vindicated in some way, that old Minto senses something in the way you have?'

'Are you a therapist? Because that's how a therapist sounds, I think. At least, in shows.'

I opened the back door at last and went out. Bare feet on painfully cold concrete slabs. A snail there going about its business I stepped around him. Let myself enjoy the plumes of my breath. It was Hallowe'en, and the invisible was all around me, pressing on my legs like a cat. I didn't really feel that uncanny. Tom was a dilemma and a sliding desperation to which I felt sharply alert. And rightly so.

Plumping

Some days it takes four hours to get ready for an event because you have to pull your soul up from a deep well and shake it out, let it dry in the sun a little bit. You know what I mean? I walked home the forty minutes to my flat and climbed the three flights of stairs. Everyone was out somewhere. With slow movements I entered the shower, wet and conditioned my hair. Vee had some fine potions on her part of the shelf. I clapped and smeared cold white slime on my face. I think I was crying but the shock against my skin drew me out of it.

So, what I knew: Tom had vanished all day and into the night. He said a work thing. There had been the weirdness with the book. The book's sense of inauthenticity. Now a totem he could not live without to the point that even when he had it he thought he didn't. I hadn't slept. I was becoming entangled and with what, given he didn't give much away. I started shaving my legs. Slops of white dripped on my belly and went down the drain. Wine, I thought. I wrapped a towel around me and got the wine from the cupboard. I'd brush after. My teeth were foul anyway with the late night chicken even after a brush. In between the kitchen and the shower I decided I did not think in the marrow of me he was cheating. Stupid, I thought. What else? A bender wouldn't explain the oddness. A ghost then, or something inhabiting him, some obsession relating to the book, fuck anyone else's opinion.

But Daniel had been so reasonable that my lifelong belief in the – yes, I know, implausible – world of spirits visible and invisible was shaken. If I wasn't much for belief in anything else, why should I believe in them? I decided I had two options: 1. Call my parents and ask them again about the cold bitch incident, get something concrete on that or: 2. Mull it over some more before venturing to make any decisions. I decided on the latter. My parents would be unkeen to hear from me outside our allotted phone call day, and the worse for having the old bruise prodded. I rinsed off the conditioner and shampooed. I let the gunk that was left on my face stay on a bit longer. Cold steam about me. I leaned in to the narrow strip of heat. Ghosts though. The rattling window. The vacant stare and the yelling about stabbing. It wasn't much evidence. Tom's leaves on the pillow. Could be just a deep involvement with the text and its delusions, with the physical object which contained the text. His sweat-dirt smell. I liked this explanation. It played to my own obsessions. It allowed me some dignity. And hinted that whatever was off would be easily solved by waiting out til the book lessened its grip on him.

I got out and dried and put my loungewear on, black and loose. I had to pick up my party clothes from the tailor soon but too much thinking assailed me. Swirls of the nights past, the hill, the book and its weirdness and whatever it might be hiding. I padded into my room and lay myself down operatically on the bed, thinking of my haunted man, pushing back the idea of myself as a dull, everyday, cheated-on woman, then pulling that image to me again and hugging it tight with all its thorns. My little throw pillow said 'be well' on it, a relic from another relationship that had sickened and faded from this world. But I kept it because I wanted what it wished. He might be fucking someone else. That would be easier. Snap off ties. I looked up at the picture I had stuck to the ceiling: a forest in the mist from on high. What did it matter? We hadn't been going out long enough for it to matter. Get on with life then Órla. You've done it so many times, or someone else has done it to you – left, with little notice. Why this little game with yourself that it has to hurt? Revelling in being pained when really you are bringing that pain into being on yourself like it's a kind of obligation. I regret myself greatly, as an academically-minded woman, reduced to the cyclical obsessive.

Better minds than mine have worked this game out and kicked it. Stop then. Stop thinking. But better minds than mine have also burned in anguish for days. I yelled out an obscenity, at Tom, myself, the immortal fraughtness of relationships between people.

I determined as the only option that I would be in this haunted theory and keep Tom in my life for now, and allow myself to obsess in this one respect. It was so capacious an escapade; the diary entries had carried him out into the streets, all night, and had removed him some place I could not get to which I told myself I was interested in reaching for out of curiosity. He had seen some ghost of something, that much was convincing to me. Ghost of self-reproach, ghost of a conspiracy-hunter. I let myself dream myself then into all roles, turning them about to understand. I was Tom – his strangely vacant look and absent hours. I'd see him tonight, unless he wandered off again. I was James Lennoxlove, riding his foaming horse back from the ball, blood in his mind, then nothing, nothing, then dates of entry that seemed innocuous but were not. I wondered what the party would have in store for me, me as Tom, me as myself. And then, an inevitability, I could not fend off picturing him kissing some other girl, hand on her curves. It excited and appalled me. I thought of myself rushing in and catching him at it. Over and over on my little track, occasionally sighing to the naked room.

Walking Wounding

Tom called me in the afternoon when it was already beginning to get dark.

'We have to talk,' he said.

'Yes we do,' I said. I am fierce and he won't get me down, I thought. I was all dressed up, lipstick a shade darker than my own lips and applied patted down to a matte block. Eyeliner a sharp, strained flick.

I met him on the still-bright street, him coming languidly in his beautiful white suit like he had been born in it. I thought in fact I did not know much about his background, other than what he had thought to tell me – very little, and what I had seen and heard. That he was English and spoke with the chalky vowels that would make him perfect for audiobooks, and slightly alienating in conversation. He took my arm. We began walking in the direction of the party, two or so miles away.

'Well, look at you,' I said with an air of suave stupidity. Then, 'Are we talking?'

'I'm sorry about disappearing yesterday, Órla,' he said. 'I had to go and clear my head. I hadn't slept well. I'd had the weirdest dreams. And I – I decided not to just sit about and feel sorry for myself. I went out with some friends and lost track of time. I slept on a sofa. Felt like shit when I came back. I didn't think you'd spend the night at mine, and then when you had I felt guilty – and—'

It all sounded right, on the surface, though it was completely different from the work away day excuse. There are some people who are so charming that the red flags they give off are such a beautiful shade of crimson you can only gaze at them and smile a little ruefully.

We passed down a long road of fancy wine bars and pinch-points of milling pedestrians. We turned heads, us two, the way we were dressed and our frozen expressions. Other costumers would come in our wake, but none as fine. The city shifted around us, a few hydraulically huffing lorries and buses shunting ahead of us. The gangling queues at the bus stop spilling over the pavement and forcing us to edge through, break apart, blowing vapour in our faces the flavour of bad cocktails and sweet farts. I thought we should get on whatever bus would take us a bit closer to the house where the party was to take place but the kind of performance of honesty we needed to get into in that moment couldn't happen on a bus. Sometimes your agitation comes through at the level of your cells and must burn away. I knew even so early in it that this was an apex moment for us: folk can encounter such times in quite ordinary places, others in the city of their dreams, right before the turn to dusk, on the eeriest day of the year.

'What else, Tom?'

'What else what?'

We were pushing past a crowd and heading for a great stone bridge that crosses a waterway of cliffs and riverine trees. Posh flats overlooking it with the kind of view I'd imagine you'd get in a post-apocalyptic world that has grown verdant without us. My mind supplying the handful of survivors living by windows, surviving in the luxury of last days. Resting their elbows they look down on the crumbling vestiges of monumental architecture, striped trees, the slipping bodies of foxes through the ravaged underbrush.

'What else were you feeling when you saw me? At the flat. Cos I think you were going to say, and forgive me if I'm wrong – jealous,' I said.

'Jealous?'

'Conflicted then.'

'What were you up to with Daniel, if I should have been feeling jealous?' he said, stepping round an old woman holding an unnecessary golf umbrella as a walking stick. There was a hum in the air that was part crowd, part traffic, part swarm of inner bees.

'I didn't say you should be feeling jealous. I said what I thought you were feeling. Fuck me, I think you were jealous because you don't like the friendship I have with him,' I said.

'You know he's gay, right?' He said with ugly condescension.

I stopped. I worked out how best to present my face while my mind thought: no? But no. He isn't, I thought. Is he? Something spun out inside of me, revealing a great depth below. I thought of our feet resting against each other. I thought of talking with him for hours, just wanting to talk and listen and never stop. What closeness means. Tom was ahead now, white suit, dapper. And there, at my centre, the truer part: what did it matter, the definitions for what he – Daniel – and I might have? I ran my hand at the edge of the bridge wall. It was there for me.

'But you were feeling *lonely*, weren't you,' I said, 'when you were at breakfast? Outside yourself and us. What's been up with you, Tom? What's been going on?'

We walked in silence. Ahead of us everything stood rich and red-tinged with the sun getting low. I had used the wrong words, and I had no others. Something bubbled up from the void inside me.

'I miss you,' I said, startling myself. I cast around in my head for whether it was true at all, had been true all along, or I had made it true in saying it.

Tom stopped to lean over the bridge. Light played over his features as they moved through various guises of the thoughts underneath, settling on nothing, looking so arduous to me that all my frustration dissipated and I was concerned, more than I ever had been, that he really was in some kind of trouble. Spiritual or financial, something else, I had no idea. The water ran gold below us, on through the darkening trees, just crying out for a dipped arm to cling to.

'I can't tell you,' he said, suddenly hoarse. I had his arm. He didn't seem the type to swoon, but you never knew.

'What's the big secret drama, eh?' I said, with a bark of a laugh. 'You had a few nightmares and, uh, you've been really into some book? Tell me about it, maybe? I'm listening.'

'What?'

'Did you notice, with that diary you've been into lately, there's something wrong with it?'

He shook his head. I pulled him gently away from the side of the bridge and we walked unimpeded to the end. Sunshine was everything, before it began to leak out all at once. I had the feeling that Hallowe'en would properly start when it was dark, and I had to walk us quickly, his white coat tails and mine, black, flying. It seemed of the utmost importance to get Tom indoors before the light was gone. I spoke quickly, too, telling him what Daniel and I had potentially discovered. He said little, but I supposed he was listening. Everyone gets kicked out of their own contentment every once in a while. That could be all it was. The party, the party, I thought, rushing past old trees and the first headlights, walking ahead of Tom now, turning my head to check he was there, and stolid he always was. We were on time to be perfectly late. Daniel would be early, I guessed. He was probably carving pumpkins and throwing fake spiderweb around with – David, was it? We turned down a blueing suburban street of white and cream bungalows that at its middle point turned upwards at an angle that looked from our vantage point Escheresque. On the other side of the dip it was like a mirror image of the street's beginning, or, not exactly a mirror, a worse copy, off tilt. Even here, in this non-iconic part of the city, the streetscapes strung themselves uncanny. That was why I was here, I suddenly thought, taking a breath. That was why I remained all this time, because I could love a city so angular and ancient, full of stone secrets, folding them open. And so it was with my man Tom. Our point of commonality. I took his hand and down we walked.

Between

'This is it,' Tom said, fingering the map on his phone, scrubbing the highlight around our destination. We were both sweating. I made us wait in the cold a little longer – the sky still had a green tinge to it, and Tom was on the cusp of telling me something profound and delicious about his psyche. When nothing happened, I thought it might be a good idea to kiss him. He pulled back and touched his lips.

'Did you get any on me?' He looked at his fingers.

'No, it's kiss-proof.'

'I never believe that,' he said.

'You haven't tried it enough. It works.' And I leaned in to kiss him again, but again he pulled back.

'Don't.'

'Okay,' I said. I wanted to ask, now. About his violent dream. But it wasn't good timing – and it never would be. Suddenly he took me by the waist and spun me round. His hands remained on my waist. His gaze softened.

'Forgive me?' he asked.

I smiled, what else could I do?

It doesn't only work when you know what you might really be forgiving.

'Yes,' I said, 'me too, if I've ever let you feel like you are alone. I never meant it. I like you a lot, Tom. You're very likeable.'

'Yes, I am,' he said, ironic, smiling. He kissed me, then nothing was wrong, and we went in, and the party swelled for us and we danced.

And We Danced

Have you ever just waltzed into a place? I mean, really, in three-fourths time? Immediately we were in the door, Tom clasped my hand and away we went. Tom was an immense dancer; all sleek white movement, airy, as if he had practiced until his feet filled with blood, that old Hollywood glamour standard. Which he might have; I did not know him. We were white and black, fabric hanging over our bodies, we were our breaths timed with our skimming feet. I hardly knew what I was doing with my body and almost didn't have to. That's a lie – if I'd been clumsy that would have taken him down. But I am serviceable. We swung around the room, I held on tight. This state is unreal, I thought, the parquet floor moving beneath us and the room spinning golden and white and black from its static occupants in their costumes, clutching their cocktails and champagne. Some states of being are richer than others. The material of the moment, time itself and everything extant there and around you made proprietary, custom, of excellent quality, so that it drapes over you, satin, golden touched. We danced through the living room seamlessly into the kitchen and back again, the crowd surging around us and giving us air. We danced into the outside space, a stranger helpfully opening the French windows ahead of our sweep so we went on out onto the stone patio in the square of cast light. The music flooded the outdoors in which we turned a few times and then came back in. We must have danced unbroken for thirty minutes. But when I said I needed water, Tom dropped my hand

– we were like that at the sideboard, where the drinks were – he palmed me off to one of the hosts, and when I turned to ask what he wanted, he was gone.

Ballad of the Modernist House

I went and sat down with Daniel and Mark. I was talking to them, gulping water, but I was thinking of the ballad of Tam Lin. Tam Lin was the lover, the passive beloved, enchanted. The maiden Margaret, or Janet the maiden, who danced through Carterhaugh woods, plucked a double rose and gave it to him, to her Tam Lin – and we all know what that means. They held each other close pressed against the blossom. Tam himself was not a fairy but a possession of the Fairy Queen's. A human boytoy tethered to the otherworld. He tells Margaret he fears being given to Hell, that night, on Hallowe'en. It is Margaret, knocked up and vehement, who must prevent this, holding him tight, gripping the human out of the fey. Tam tells her he will be transformed into a newt, an adder, a lion, a bright bit of burning metal in her arms, and through it, she must hold him still. If she wishes to win her man, to stop the father of her baby being dragged to the devil. Which, in the ballad, she mostly does. I caught a glimpse of Tom's white suit as he slinked through a doorway, surrounded by six tall women in sheath gowns of ivory silk. I followed him with my eyes until he was dazzling against an underfilled bookcase (vase, white hardback magazine, fern) and blotted out the back of a large man with tall hair, black as a newborn colt.

I peered into my glass at the musky white liquid at the bottom of it. I drank it down and got another. The company bored me – Mark had a very unpleasant look to him, I thought – and I staggered off looking for something in the house, clutching my drink, climbing the stairs, bleering into rooms. Tom Mew, yes, Tam Lin, yes. I caught glimpses of him talking to other guests, to a man with a black mask over his eyes, a woman in grey satin with her hair impossibly high. Fuck you, I thought, with lighthearted venom. I should describe the house for you: from the ground floor, it was one of those millionaire's mid-century affairs that could have easily gone wrong. In other hands that style results in crumbling office blocks and blighted schools – great heavy slabs of concrete at an angle suggesting gargantuan collapse or upheaval, giving the central rooms a grand high ceiling. But with money, there's the design and materials to make a balanced and captivating space. Glass in long rectangular sheets, wood panelling, glowingly polished parquet, a strange, floating wooden staircase that peeled upwards to infinite height, it seemed, right before the doors. It worked beautifully. It was large and airy but still felt like someone's home. Some of that was the decoration, all the plants everywhere, including a giant dark-leafed swiss cheese plant that must have been growing there for decades. On inspection it was planted straight into a square of soil in the floor.

I took myself and my drink of the moment upstairs, the gap in the steps made me woozy. There was a cream-carpeted corridor that ran in a mezzanine overlooking the party's main stage, but I chose to go back further. I found a parallel corridor, interior. It seemed larger than it should have been given the footprint below. I found two bedrooms, one with a shock of red on the wall, the other all painfully white from furniture to floor. In another a study, lit by a single green standing lamp tall and gently curved like the light on the ferry of the dead, I thought. Dark green walls incongruously lined with dark wooden shelves of cloth-bound hardbacks and framed pictures of family. There was Mark, little, with his mother and another man, not the man I'd met earlier. Sad and slight, shorter than Maggie. Mark graduating from university. Black and white Mark in front of a nineteen-fifties car – I realised it was not Mark, but some relative. In the middle of the desk, in front of a closed laptop, stood a large pink cake with a lighted candle on it. I crossed the silent, deep pile carpet towards it, holding my breath. The feeling in the room was one of intense melancholy. I despise melancholy. It is a sentimental emotion. On reaching the cake I pushed a finger to it, up to the hilt– it was dry and woolly. A completely realistic cake made of felt. The candle was glowing and flickering, but it wasn't real either. It functioned like a candle, so I suppose it was as real as it needed to be. I blew on it; it went out, and after a moment of darkness it came back on again. I realised the small, shuttered window in this room must look out on the mezzanine. But when I touched the shutter to pull it back I had a horrible feeling that it wouldn't – that there would be a vista outside of a night world somewhere other than here. I recalibrated, steeled myself, and flung it open. There was nothing there. No window at all.

I left that room and found a large tiled bathroom, replete with huge, sunken bath that looked like something wholesale lifted from a Victorian boys' school. Then two more bedrooms that were more lived-in than the others, big soft headboards and a wrinkled pair of tights on the floor by a vanity. 'It's a house,' I thought. 'People live here, and I'm intruding.' I retreated, passing by the cupboard where Tom was briefly to lose his mind, though it had not happened yet. I heard a cheer from below. I heard a whole house seizing up around a population of strangers. I told myself I was having a damn good time, even so.

Interlude

Loneliness can come at you out of nothing, especially with the obscure sounds of a party and old music reeling below you. There are sound clips you can listen to, to recreate this intense effect – usually pop songs from another era altered to sound as if played through several closed doors. The feeling brought on by these snippets is a specific type of aloneness. Late in the cold hall of a dingy club, the place where the coats are or a red-lit back stair. Everyone else is in the dancing part, close and warm and sloshing beer around. You, though, you are wallowing in isolation. Run down, picking at your clothes, coming down off whatever, no one to love. It's fucking magic that someone can do all that with tweaks to a sound file.

On slowly and majestically descending the stair I saw out the window a glimpse of Tom's white back. I followed. He went into the space behind the foot of the stairs – there was another corridor there, with the cloakroom to one side, and doors and doors along it. Our feet clattered on the hard white floor.

'Tom!' I called. He was ahead of me, walking fast. Footfalls echoing, sounds of the party pressed hollow from all sides, muted chattering and laughing, glasses clinking. The corridor emptied us out into the back part of the house, an almost-mirror of the front. It was the place we had danced out through before. I could see clusters of guests to my right, and the merriment was set in and intractable. Tom hesitated a moment before plunging out

177

through the French windows and I hurried after.

We stood on the slightly raised balcony, garden sunken below and dark. Night sky with a frosty dampness in the air. I looked at him, he looked away. What was he looking for? I loathed this being the one running after; I wanted to be the one people chase. But perhaps that too would have been dreadful. He turned, eyes low. And I thought of Daniel, who never met your eye. And I thought, Tom's been drinking, he's been following something. He was a little out of breath. Shaky.

'Are you all right?' I asked.

He laughed.

'I've been listening to that music all night long,' he said, then, lower, 'it's getting to me.'

I had a strong need to touch him on the arm to prove he was there at all. I almost touched him. I didn't. Just then Maggie, the host, came out through the doors carrying a silver tray with tiny misshapen translucent bowls on it.

'Take one,' she said, 'you can eat the bowls. I printed them this morning, isn't it exciting, living in the future? Don't worry, gluten free. Please.'

I took one and put it in my mouth. It felt like putting a retainer in, but began to dissolve immediately. It tasted of passion fruit with an undertow of meat.

'Delicious!' I said, drool gathering at the back of my mouth. I swallowed.

'Tom, isn't it? Have one,' she said. But Tom for reasons unknown had turned pale and was pushing past us, back inside.

'Oh,' said Maggie. 'Oh well. His loss.'

'Yeah, well. Sorry about him. He's been a bit off today.'

Maggie smiled. She was an elegant lady, in all you'd imagined an elegant lady to be when you were a little girl: tall, smoothly moving, impeccable dark lipstick, hair that looked as if it had snaked itself into position that morning, a thirties-style diadem held impossibly in place.

'I've been watching the two of you since you came in,' she said, 'and I'm impressed, and a little unnerved.'

'By what?'

'By your beauty, yours and Tom's. By the way you keep gliding past each other in my house. You two lovers, my dear, seem to have different objectives tonight, and it intrigues me to see it.'

'What do you mean?' I asked, more for conversation's sake than anything else. I supposed I knew exactly what she meant.

'Oh, just that you're kind of, rambling about the place as if to claim it by touching everything – I've been watching. Oh, yes.'

I kept up eye contact, and smiled – politely I hoped.

'While Tom,' she continued, 'has been rambling about as if evading claims. He's a furtive type. But I'd say that's not typical for him? God, he's a sculpture though, a classic for the gallery,' she said. So it is with the rich, they can say whatever they like. But I couldn't be annoyed by her, angry at being found out, made insecure by implications, or even to laugh at them, coming from her, a woman in her late fifties at least. She won me over with the devil winking in her eye and her soft fluidity of speaking, 'You keep an eye on that one. Don't let him slip through your fingers.'

'I will,' I said. Murmured, like a good little swan.

'See you in another room,' she said, 'with your man by your side,' she said. With that, vamping off indoors, to another cluster of guests who all turned their heads to her, and raised each nearly-empty or white-slurred glass.

The Drinking

I rubbed my face and ladled myself more of the cocktail stuff and drank it down, seething it through my teeth. Then I fetched another, and had a conversation with an austere couple and their small, bashful teenage son, who peered down at me through his glasses like a wary creature caught under a magnifying glass. His skin was a mess, like mine was at his age, and I asked him something about school, and I asked all the adults about their jobs, and pretended to listen. I was seeking reassurance that there were people who were normal – and mostly they were and I loved them for it. I asked nobody if they'd ever seen a ghost, or if they felt slightly aroused at the idea of demonic possession, or the fairies stealing their beloveds. I went back to the punchbowl. I talked to Mark and Daniel on a sofa and in the kitchen. I went to the punchbowl. Hours passed. I went to the punchbowl, but I was strong. I chattered indomitably. I frightened an old lady by pointing fingerguns at her. That was when I went to the toilet and freshened up my make-up and had a long piss. Sitting on the toilet and looking at my overlit, not entirely Grecian, side profile in the mirrored wall I was hit with the clarity all toilets in such situations provide: a good gauge of my drunkenness. I decided it was necessary to stop drinking for a bit, now, and to reassess where my drinking had got me which was nowhere. Under the layers of conversation I had attempted to pull over it, my heart obscurely stung. I also decided I was ugly, and had a small cry.

Sometime around midnight I found myself on the stairs with Daniel, feeling empty, dizzy at the gaps in the stairs, a little anxious and drunk – party feelings. Tom was nowhere and everywhere, and a bottle of someone else's single cask malt whisky was firmly in my slippery hands. Daniel was telling me about the diary again.

'Shh,' I said. I looked him over. He looked so awkward, then, behind his glasses. He and the teenager overlapped. 'How old are you?' I asked.

'Tinder age, or real age?' he said.

'I can't imagine you on Tinder.'

'Lots of times. Every time was intimidating.'

'I'll bet,' I said. Poor Daniel.

'I'm thirty-six,' he said, 'same age as Mark.'

'No way! You don't look it,' I said, 'no grey at all, and you don't have the kind of – the kind of look people have. Old and tired like. You look young.'

'Well, thank you. I won't tell Mark what you said.'

'I'm twenty-eight. Sorry,' I said, then, 'I think I'm going to make some terrible mistake with Tom.'

'Oh, really?' Daniel was looking down the stairs and out the window at the front of the house. There was the man of the night, smoking a cigarette with a silver fox in a black tuxedo. The overhead light from the eaves lit him so that he looked like an angel in his whites. Like an angel who has sex, because if I've retained anything from Catholic school rumours it's that angels don't have genitals and so are excluded from that world of experience. In the dirty, manual way at least. I suppose they have a communions of souls or some shit. But anyway, there was Tom, like a seraph stepped out of heaven to sneak in a fag and get back before anyone saw.

'Do you think the fairies can have sex?' I said, sinking lower on the stair.

'Ha, yes. They have offspring, don't they?'

'I thought that was just changelings, ugly things that get swapped for pretty human babies,' I said.

'Presumably something gives birth to them,' Daniel said, looking at the contents of his glass; nothing. 'Or they're made from trees. Lumps of bog butter,' I said. I felt a realisation wanting to come on, like a migraine. 'What about ghosts?'

'What were we talking about again?' said Daniel, wiping his face with his hand. His eyes were soft and he was looking at Tom through the entranceway window and we were both looking at Tom through the window, and both holding empty glasses.

'I think Tom needs rescuing,' I found myself saying. 'He stands in the light and he dwells in the darkness. And neither are particularly bad or good, but they do need to be understood as states of being, that he is at the centre of. And I don't think he knows, Daniel, I don't think he does.'

'I don't know,' Daniel said, stubbornly. He rose and went away somewhere. I had decided. I got up and went to my man.

Rescuing Tom

Outside it was bitterly cold. The silver fox saw me come swinging – metaphorically. I wasn't moving my fists. He stepped aside and walked away to talk to the other group of white haired, balding smokers down by the driveway. Tom stood with his cigarette deft between his two fingers. It looked flimsy in my hands. I tapped off the ash. It landed on my shoe. Tom snatched it back, only to stub it against the wall and flick the stub away.

'Tom, what are you doing?'

He looked at me. Man was drunk as anything, or high, or drunk and high. Slack-mouthed he laughed, high pitched and too long, and wobbled his head.

'I'm waiting for them to come and get me,' he said, still laughing and shaking with it.

'Waiting for who?' I said. The shock of the cold air was getting to me. I was shaking too. We were both in suits, hopping from foot to foot on the doorstep like posh children who had wandered there out of the wastes.

'I feel like we're supplicants,' I said, because it sounded better. Tom looked around. He drew me in close and kissed my forehead.

'We are, Ore, we are. Someone good needs to come for us,' he gave a gasp, then in a lighthearted singsong, 'but I don't think they will. No, it's the villains for us. The villains in disguise of the most ordinary, run of the mill – ah, babe.' He started laughing again and lurched against the door. I was just surprised he knew what a supplicant was.

'Let's get inside,' I said, and dragged open the door. The warm air buffeted against us, and a few people in the party turned to take us in. Uninterested faces. I looked round for Daniel. Tom was leaning on my shoulder and he was heavy. Just like that, someone will switch from independent agent of their own good time to slumping rock of drunkenness and your problem now. I decided he needed his bed. But that was miles off. I cast about looking for the answer and there she was, Maggie, smiling slyly at us from across the room at the kitchen counter. I humped Tom's arm around my shoulder and monstrous we waddled and stumbled over to her.

'A bit worse for wear?' she said. 'Tsk.'

I nodded. 'What do you think we should do with him?'

'Oh, well, we have plenty of room here,' she said, 'I'll have Mark help you get him upstairs. The guest bedroom.'

'Brilliant,' I said.

'Yes,' Maggie said, 'brilliant.' I couldn't tell anything from her tone. I was drunk and eager to set down my burden some safe place.

Mark came over and took the other side of Tom and we got him upstairs and on to the bed. Tom sat up immediately, though he should have sprawled back. He sat up and I could only think of him in his bedroom in the midst of his nightmare.

Mark looked away.

'Oh, well, um. Should leave you to it.'

'Yes,' I said. 'No. I mean, could you fetch Daniel?'

'Sure,' Mark said. He had a very soft-focus face but when he smiled he looked more like his mother, part malice, part teenage glee at something salacious about to take place in his vicinity. I wondered if he and Daniel had ever been together.

'Don't smile like that,' I said, 'I just need to work out—' hesitating because I had no really good reason to want Daniel there. Not a reason that would sound sane to others. But what did I care of that, and I said quickly, 'He knows what to do.' And gave him with as much dignity as I could a cold shoulder until he hurried away.

Sitting With It

I did not want to touch Tom. He sat up on the bed listing mildly, eyes closed. I hate the silence of people waiting for something to happen. My own silence, in this case. He probably would have sung to himself or muttered if I hadn't been there. I tried to think of other times in my life when I had been in a situation like this and how I had overcome it. The job interview method for feeling like a successful person. It just served to make me realise how many other times I'd had to talk an inebriated man down off their short emotional ledges or make their way to a stomach pumping. And how many of those men were no longer in my life. The good ones pay you back in kind, I told myself, unlacing Tom's fancy shoes and throwing them gently across the room. I also wasn't sure what kind of role I had to play with Tom, now. Perhaps he would pass out of his own volition before any further drama started.

The door opened. Daniel. He shuffled into the room and looked helplessly. I felt immediately better. An assistant. A co-conspirator.

I slapped Tom's chest. 'The state of him,' I said.

'Yes, I see,' Daniel said in his low mild voice.

Tom was unbuttoning his shirt. Daniel looked at me, his hands gripping the doorframe. I answered with a smile. I remember clearly in my mind I had no idea what my smile signified but looking back I had decided that something was happening, the crux of Tom's moment of hauntedness, while we were all drunk and in a stranger's house. A crosscurrent of strangeness was blowing through the room, and I was weirdly elated. That must have made my smile come across badly.

'Mm, I need – I need to go,' Daniel said, and he slipped a little way into the hall.

'Just because you fancy him doesn't mean you can use that as an excuse to leave him in his hour of need,' I called out. 'Get us water, then, if you're going.'

I could have laughed. Daniel came back. He did a good line in excruciated looks.

'Oh come on,' I said.

'I'm not going anywhere,' Daniel said.

'Except for water.'

'Oh, okay. But I'll come back, I will.'

I sat back down on the bed near Tom though it worried me, though it made me fizzily excited. His body was tensed right up, his hands gripping the bed sheet like a woman in the midst of labour. It was to me an unnatural ability in one so utterly wasted, whose muscles should have been lax as old rubber bands. In a corner of my brain I was awaiting then some violent outburst, but another part of me, the part that saves or damns us all in the great moments of our lives, was saying it would be all right and that I must stay to be witness. If it was worse than rattling windows it would be actual apparitions, heads turning around three hundred and sixty degrees, deep growls, a body distorted further than human parameters allow, random Latin and Sumerian and the like. I knew, then, that I would stay through it all, if it did happen, mad bitch like.

I helped him get off his shirt and threw it by the shoes. He was dry and cool to the touch, his hair catching the light. I didn't like how red the room was. But then I did: what better place for what I was willing would happen soon. And the glow from the red paint set off Tom's blue eyes so that even drowsy they looked startling.

'Do you want to lie down?' I asked him.

'No. No!' he said, and he caught me in those swivelling eyes and I shifted back involuntarily.

'What's happening with you?' I asked.

'I'm waiting on him,' Tom said, and he looked to the doorway where Daniel had disappeared.

'You need to sober up,'

'So do you,' he said, and laughed again, more normally than before.

'Who are you waiting on?' I asked.

Tom looked at me and I couldn't understand the look. A shadow passed over his face. I thought about men, and the ways in which they look at me, and I couldn't find the right place to file this one away. I was sobering up, I thought. How long since the last drink? I wanted Daniel back. For water. But he did not come back for twenty minutes and, when he did, he was drunker than before and had no water. In the interim I went into the guest toilet and grabbed the tooth glasses and gulped down one glass full after another. Five I think. I had coaxed Tom into sipping some, when he became alarmed and got to his feet. He glared at his own reflection in the dark of the window pane.

'You!' he said.

I thought of what to do. In some stories the devil is a reflection. That of course is significant in an easy way to parse – you (as character) are playing your own devil – or the domestic space reversed. That's our room, our familiar body but just a bit weirder. Devil double that is yourself and not you and wouldn't that be the medium by which the devil could speak to us on his preferred direct yet unheimlich terms?

Then, as I looked between Tom and the reflection, I noticed it too. There was no metaphor, no academic lens through which to interpret. The reflection was not his.

Double

In the window pane was a sketch of the room we were in, and me at the end of the bed, and a man in the bed that was the shape of, almost but not quite, Tom Mew.

'Fuck,' I said, sotto voce. In case he heard? I don't know. I know. The face was looking up and I met its eyes.

'Who the fuck are you now?' I asked.

'What are you doing?' said Tom, loudly, and he had my arm. So, in the mirror, did not-Tom. It opened its mouth, and there was a hateful expression on its face that gave me the chills. Tom clamped his hands over his own, but the hands in the reflection did nothing. The pane of the glass began to rattle. I felt something in my back molars as if a low sound was building.

The not-Tom opened its mouth still further.

'Fuck you think you're doing,' I said, and I threw a pillow at the glass. It bounced off and fell to the floor. The figure got up and picked up the same pillow, in reflection. Behind and through it I could see the muddy suburban night sky and beside it myself. It held the pillow to hide its face. Tom was standing now in the same place as the figure. He held nothing.

'Stop, Tom,' I said, but he was raising his hands as the figure raised its hands, synced. And then I felt a pillow hit me and I momentarily stumbled and when I looked up I realised it had not hit me from the back – as if Tom had thrown it – but from the front. As if the figure in the glass had. And startled, I laughed loudly.

'What a funny kind of game,' I said. It smiled, sickly, back at me. But it was nothing. If you can hear me in my head, you're nothing, I thought.

The figure moved nearer the frame of the window and Tom was nearer, though not as close. The figure reached up and put its hand against the glass, fingernails first and dragged them down it making a slow scraping sound, though there were no fingers touching the glass, no real fingers.

I put my hands up to my head. I shouted, I think, holding nothing but wishing for a blunt object to use to smash that glass and disperse the thing, and Tom was at my shoulders and pulling me away from the window. And the noise—

A Violence

Jamming up my ears in screeching, din-like-a-fire-alarm-cheeping-til-it-bursts, high, make-it-stop noise, everyone-flood-upstairs-to-see-what-it-is noise, but when I left the room, it stopped. And I could not hear it at all until I stepped back across the threshold and immediately had to hold my ears. Tom stood bent in the centre of the red room, clamping his hands to his head. I ran to the window like some genius and pulled down the blinds.

And the noise.

Just.

Stopped.

'Are you all right,' I said, grabbing at him. He leaned into me, curling himself up like a child. Sobbing. I threw off my suit jacket, slid out of my shoes and drew him over until we were in the bed together.

'There, shh,' I said. What else could I do? I stroked his hair and his breaths slowly became even. Never had I seen a grown man like this. He kept his devastating eyes mostly closed and his mouth slack. I took a notion that the apparition had moved. How would I know? You know these things the way you can tell a scent shifting in a room. I closed my eyes too on this sudden feeling: there, behind my eyes and Tom behind his, we lay, listeners.

We could again hear the party thumping away down below. And a gathering outside in which someone laughed. A dry tread on the stairs. Daniel coming up. Here let it be said that I was not the frightened one, but riveted, as if deep unease was something you might seek out at a theme park. The tracks crank as the roller coaster edges higher. Time seemed to slow. I heard, really, another sound. The sound of someone in the room. Almost imperceptible sounds of someone standing still, breathing, watching over us. But Daniel wasn't here yet. I opened my eyes to catch it. Tom in sync sat up with me, holding my hand under the cover.

Against the far wall hung something shadowy, particulate, like the powder off a rose captured in old film stock. Gradually it fell. Gradually vanished. I could not turn my head away. I felt something sickly in the back of my throat. But as soon as it had gone I felt the weight of it lift. The wire of my blood, my shuddering breath too. There had been no better feeling in my life. I almost laughed from it. I almost raised my hands.

'Who was that, Tom?'

'James Lennoxlove, of Bitterhall,' he said. 'He's always with me, James, and I am James.'

Daniel Avant

'Here at last', Daniel said softly, carrying a bottle of something dark.

Tom looked up at him and I thought for a moment there would be a burst of strange yelling and screaming and I braced. But instead Tom smiled at Daniel and patted the bed. Daniel hesitated – and came over and kicked off his shoes.

'Light's too harsh,' I said and went about turning the sidelight on and the overhead off. The room glowed red. 'Womb,' I thought. I sat back down on the bed myself and bit my fingernails. Great spaces between us as we sat in our various parts. Tom propped near the wall, under blankets. Daniel in the middle, me at the very foot, legs dangling off. This tableau enacting the powerful rule of threes. A strange tale needs threes in it somewhere. Three strangers. Three choices – I scrunched up my face and tried to pin down only three, but my head just hurt. Three objects – we only had the one, I thought: the diary. Three ever-after haunted people. I was including Daniel in a haunting he might not admit to, having been offstage, momentarily as of course cynics always are. I wanted then something simple, three actions leading to a resolution and a happy ending but being not a simple person I knew this would not be my luck. Daniel wriggled and lay back, clutching the bottle to his chest like a baby. His head was in Tom's lap.

'I've been walking through this house,' Tom said, 'in a dream. A dream!'

'Órla, have I missed something?' Daniel asked.

Tom idly clapped his hand down on Daniel's head, 'Órla's seen him,' he said. He was running his fingers through Daniel's thick hair, while looking away. I see it now, that tender, important gesture, though at the time I could have hardly noticed it being so preoccupied.

'Who?' Daniel said, lifting the bottle to his lips, slopping some on his face. He laughed at his own clumsiness. Tom plucked the bottle from his loose grip and drank before he answered. I got up and went to the window and peered between the blinds.

'Don't – ah' said Tom. 'Ah. The man who I've been seeing.'

'You've been seeing a man,' said Daniel.

'Yes,' said Tom. He seemed quite lucid. 'You might have noticed I've been – not right. Lately.'

'Nah,' I said. I sat back down on the bed, on the end, and hugged one leg. It was getting late and the distant noise of the party downstairs was working again to make me the normal sort of gloomy. Home, I thought. My own bed. But something else. I looked over at the two men. My boyfriend and his flatmate, close on this bed, together.

'All right, yes,' said Tom, licking his lips, 'I've been trying to kind of keep a lid on . . . everything. Stupid. It didn't make much sense and I felt – embarrassed.'

'Embarrassed to be haunted?' I said, moving up. I needed to get in range of him, I thought. I attempted to push my hair back from my face but it was still up in fancy rolls. I touched my lip, and the lipstick on my finger was the red of the walls. Tom paused and looked back across to the blinded window and his glance caught me in the lip touch and just as I'd hoped – 'Órla,' he said. And then he was leaning over and kissing me. Deeply like a drowning man taking gulps of air, he pulled back, a face swimming, red colours, his terrible blue eyes. 'He's coming to take me away tonight,' he said. 'You, you two, are all I have left.'

And because I could not hope to make sense of it and because all I cared about in that moment was desire I just leaned over to sheepish Daniel and grabbed his bottle from his hand, swigged. Huge wet dribbling gulp. I closed my eyes. All the best things are done with your eyes closed. Eating something really good, kissing, pausing to take in the world through senses other than your exhausted eyes. I drank and thought about an old manuscript in a dimly-lit room, resting on a pillow. The unseen world spun about me in my drunkenness and darkness behind my eyes.

'You're one crazy fucker,' I said lightly. I got off the bed and shambled to the toilet to wash up. In general I had no idea how things would proceed but the situation felt potent and deliciously murky. In the toilet I flittered about for the light switch, then screwed up my eyes at myself in the mirror. Oh hello, another reckoning with my drunkenness. Had what had taken place really just happened? Or was I overtired and playing it up? The limit seemed just about breached, but not quite. I neither felt sick nor well and the tips of my fingers were numb but I was in my body all right. I tried to think what would happen next and could only manage an image of Tom on the bed, handsomely dishevelled. I peed and flushed the toilet. This room was pristine and every element had been selected for maximum knobby chicness. Marble ledges. Bronze taps. A shower with multiple heads that came from the sides. There were cute little packets and bottles for the convenience of guests. I fumbled through them knocking several to the floor. I dabbed at my eyes and unwrapped and bashed a toothbrush around my mouth and stared at myself foaming and snorted. I washed my hands and splashed my face with water, before realising my mistake. I attempted to fix my mascara while the room stood about me, judging. I'm coming for you later I told it. Maggie was fancy all right, I thought and I dimly visualised her piled up hair and bony, freckled neckline. I supposed I might get to know her beyond the bad first, and surface, impression and like her more. In short, I delayed. I delayed – I straightened up and walked out. There, in the bed, Tom and Daniel were kissing.

To Be Suddenly Unseen

Violent alienation from yourself is almost the worst for not meaning anything to anyone else. You know when you can tell a terrible inevitability? Picture yourself in a clearing in a forest. All the birds have stopped singing, not a single leaf moves, not even the clouds are moving; they have covered the sun. There's a sense that a spell has been laid down in the roots in the ground, in the black bark, long before you came, and is now hissing into the grove. Fate feels cool to the touch, settling down on you like that. Your own reaction to it is quiet. I stood against the wall and watched them go at it messily. Hands in hair and holding shoulders. Shaking. All of us, shaking, though they had forgotten me completely. In the few minutes I'd been in the bathroom, I had been scraped from the world like words on reused velum. Perhaps I was even invisible. I'd never been that before. People notice me, remember me. I'm brash and forceful, I know this. I know myself and the lines of me clearly enough. Here though were two men I'd thought of, I realised, as slightly opaque to themselves. Well, isn't that an icebath to your sense of stability. I no longer felt drunk. But I had a number of questions.

For the moment though I watched them not out of voyeurism but because I wanted to let them. I was the intruder. I had walked in from the party. Another guest, another woman entirely. Here were lovers going at it fresh and new and joyous and my mistake to have opened the door. They, in their innocence, continued not to notice me.

Tom and Daniel kissing, not stopping. They moved around each other: lines of gold and ink flowing sinuously together. Like they were describing a beautiful and awful thought in flesh before me and in me. Desire, being formed and being brought towards its obliteration in action. It was not a comfortable or exact feeling. That is not to say it wasn't also in some ways a pleasurable discomfort. But it took a while for me to know what to do next. Of its own volition a tear came down my face and ran into my mouth. I heard myself laugh and snivel.

They kissed; I watched. I watched myself; no one watched me. Then, coming up for air, Tom noticed me. Our eyes met over the great gap. *This is not Tom.* He beckoned with fingers over Daniel's shoulders. Handsome in his body. Shirtless. Kissing still, bending to kiss. I cringed, I shivered – feelings of a terrible depth and complexity overcame me and I smiled and I cried and reached out a hand. I wasn't wanted, how could I be wanted, to come between them now? Whoever it was with Daniel together there, ferocious with desire while I, while I. I went over to the bed anyway, stumbling a little, unsober and desiring more inclusion than anything. They drew me down. I kissed Tom or not-Tom. Daniel put his arms around us both. I kissed Daniel, and he, startled, kissed me sloppy back like someone on a dare. Then it wasn't the awfulness of the moment before but immediately transfigured into glorious bodiliness, dragging my burning self down into one delicious evolving second after another. Hands moved soft and rough over me and I moved over others, lost my white shirt and there was laughter and throbbing heat hearts, the blanket fell off the bed and then we seemed to reach the end of the moment, and all of us stopped, and looked around, as if puzzled. Tom shook himself like a dog shaking off water and laughed again, a little gaspy laugh at what he'd done – then turned to Daniel, still smiling and decked him. Daniel flopped down. Tom was up and gone out the door.

Silence. I looked at Daniel. He picked himself up, then the bottle of booze, took a swallow and shoved it, sticky into my hand.

'What the fuck was that?' I said.

'Fucking hell,' Daniel said quietly. We sat together in the bed and held one another.

There was a clatter from the ceiling and the walls shook.

'He's going upstairs,' said Daniel. 'Oh well.' He sighed, and clutched at the bottle, laying it on his stomach like a baby, looking at me with tender kindness. 'That was something, wasn't it?' he said.

'I don't know,' I said. 'I don't know.'

After There is a Touching Absence

Tom was missing for three days but in all that time Daniel and I decided – repeatedly decided – we couldn't go to the police because Tom kept texting me. Just using emojis of stars and stacks of books. Sometimes an exclamation mark. The drama consumed us both. I could put aside the PhD stuff for a while but I couldn't put off work.

At the end of my shift, I let myself look at my messages.

Tom had texted:

Aubergine

Upside down face

Waves

Hearteyes

Book stack

Book stack

Book stack

The latter three each about thirty minutes apart.

What a fog those days. I didn't quite miss him; I missed him like missing sugar when it seems like all the sugarcane in all the world has been pulled up and set on fire. Dipped mood, a sense that things were better this way, a sly, rotten hunger in the body.

Call

On the third day I wanted to do something that would make me happy, so I got out my Ouija board. I called Daniel up.

'Are you home yet from the basement of replication?'

'Yes – any news of Tom?'

'More emojis.'

'I'm beginning to think someone stole his phone,' said Daniel.

'I'm not. Anyway, we can talk about this in a bit? I'm coming round.'

At the door he greeted me with a stiff wave and an invitation to come in. 'I'm not a vampire,' I thought. 'Come on. My boyfriend lives here.' I sighed and grabbed his hand. He flinched. I held tight and led him into Tom's room. The curtains were still drawn. Mrs Boobs was on her bed, lying like a person would if they were sunbathing. She shifted and came and sat down on the floor with us, a little white loaf of bread. I took the board out of its box and arranged the planchette in the centre.

'Mrs Boobs must take part too,' Daniel said. I put out one hand and scratched her behind the chin. She made no noise, and did not seem to watch what we were doing with that deliberate inattention that cats have when they are most certainly watching.

'Put your fingers on this,' I said, nodding to the planchette. I put mine next to his. He took in a breath.

'You know, I read an article about the Ouija board. Did you know it named itself, using this thing? And that it was a device that was back in the table-knocking days originally seen as a

201

wholesome way for men and women to make contact. A flirtation device. And now, I don't think it's come up, but you have probably realised I'm gay,' he said. 'Just checking.'

'Are you telling the Ouija board? They might have a better idea than you do,'

He leaned over the board, 'Spirits . . . am I gay?' he said, then looked around, as if trying to spot a response in the room.

'If there are any spirits here who care if Daniel is or is not gay, please, make a signal through the planchette,' I said, then lifted my head. He was looking at me, right in the eyes, and I was startled by them, by something in them I still can't identify, a place we met.

'I wasn't certain what you were, at the housewarming.'

'It doesn't matter though, does it?'

I thought for a moment, 'No.'

'Are we going to try then?' he said.

'Thank you,' I said, hesitating, 'for doing this.'

'Ah spirits, where is our boy?' he said, still looking at me.

'Do you know, Daniel?'

He looked away and down, 'No.' A wave of paranoia flooded over me.

'Tell me, spirits, where Thomas Mew is,' I said softly.

The planchette began to move.

B   I   T   T   E   R   H   A   L   L

'Bitterhall?'

'The Lennoxlove estate,' Daniel said. 'Did you do this, Órla?' he said, very softly. I shook my head. 'Fuck,' he said. 'I don't believe you.'

'Believe me, don't believe me,' I said.

We both sat back, and let our fingers drop from the planchette. Then, after a quiet moment, laced them together across the board.

'I'm sorry,' we both said.

When I'm Gone

Daniel had a message from Tom at last – a potential location. I helped him load a bag into the back of Badr's car and then watched him drive the car off, holding my body with my arms, wishing I smoked. He was running off to get to the boy far in the North, where the land runs out. And me? Hours somehow drained away. I stood in the park, wandered there on my break from the tea shop. I stood looking between texts in my hand, barely visible in the smothering autumn sunlight and my mind barely audible over the rumble of a skateboard and a busker banging a drum with his palms and singing. In one text, Daniel was asking if I wanted to come with him. I had said no, it made more sense for me to wait. In the second, Tom's emoji list. I had read both parts of these messages countless times. I touched my face and felt the bags under my eyes. I felt about in my pockets for a tissue and blew my nose. A little gasp escaped from me, and I went up to a tree of some type and put it against my back and let the gasps come again.

When people go, sometimes they are really gone, and it's as if Tom had moved from one room of the party to another in an unreachable universe and I felt, grinding against my ribs, a sense that he would not come back. But would be everywhere. Everywhere was the dim reverberation of thirties music. In every place I was wearing my beautiful suit, and perpetually looking for Tom Mew, catching glimpses of his back as he split through the crowds.

How I imagine It Goes

I am standing in the road by Daniel's house, Mrs Boobs in my arms and Badr is by my side. Badr's silver car comes lumbering round the corner. Daniel is driving, but I cannot see into the car to see if Tom is with him. I have my phone on, but as in all dreams, the print is hard to read, shifting between states, first one answer, then another. I sob, the cat leaps from me. The car is approaching. And then, I decide: he lives. Tom is right there. And then I decide: he has gone north for reasons that many go north, a catastrophe. And there is no one in the car. And the police are standing, shadowy, dream-like police are taking my details. Whatever other faults he had, he was not that kind of coward, I tell myself. I tell myself at the counter of the shop. I tell myself in the library, staring at the nothing of the page in front of me. There are no texts while Tom is missing. I mean, every book is wiped, empty vessels, as much as he is plural. There is nothing to get from clever observations; everything has been taken. Except the hours to wait.

Tom Mew

Gully

I'm fine. Where are you – really – and with me there's a lot, two – I'll stand up and get orientated, just give me a minute, yeah – but there's a pounding on the rocks – here, listen, the wind's quiet – we can set this out – straight. Just – stay back. It's steep. No need for both of us to get hurt. You will. I think you will, or you are already dead.

So, now, right. Let me give you the whole outline, then we'll be on track: I was born – listen – on a corpse road under a spitting willow in a smashed up car in which my father had just signed out. Move on a few years, right, I was a little boy, I had a picnic in a field of bluebells that were the memory of my mother – I held them (mother and bluebells, not willows nor corpse roads). I was a happy child, I held them against my grey plastic or whatever that material is, feels like plastic doesn't it, the standard desks, and to hide my co-workers' faces with such things. Like a bunch of them so really blue that nothing beyond can exist. I was drinking coffee; bluebells – I was tweeting latest client acquisitions; rockpool with my grandmother shouting in her shock cold loving voice from the white part of the shore – I pressed some woman's head into a pillow yelling *get it*; bluebells and the shining light in the days before the days I had to be in. I was fine.

Now I get that this is all past tense. Because of you and other things. I'm going to stop calling you you now. There are so many yous. It's too confusing. It's like there's a box full of matches that are you and each one of them can go up and burn the rest. Woosh, that flare of heat. I was fine. I'm going to sort this out. I am here. And you are. And the sea, this day, overcast and the whole of the present and the past is crashing in you see and I can't – be anything. Cope. Forgive me, I'm talking bollocks again. I'm in some stupid pain, if I'm being honest. Let me just say it, explain it – before you decide if I'm worth pursuing. I'd totally get if you didn't want to go down that route. Well, now I've said this so far, I feel calmer, right, so let me just get my breath back. Listen to that sea. I'll get myself sorted, won't I? Don't worry. I don't think you do worry. About me. Why would you. I'm not sure if you're here at all.

The Structure

My life was circles I understood. The daily routine cycle is the same cycle for anybody. Wake up, get up, go to work, I won't go on, it would just be tedious. The start of the sex cycle is meeting the girl. This one I met in the club. Don't remember much about how we got together. The usual sex cycle is as you'd expect it: so, meet the girl, sex with the girl, maybe hang out with the girl or leave the girl or fuck a few more times then gone, then go looking and meet the girl. The calming circle was the bluebells, as I mentioned, just whenever I needed, think of bluebells for a nonspecific length of time until whatever is bothering you has been defeated. The fantasy life cycle interlocks with the others and is a new – no, a returning circle I didn't expect at my age. When I was little the fantasy life cycle was that my parents were not dead. It went: parents not dead, parents come for me, we go to a new big clean house full of toys, the reason they went away comes out. The reason was different every time. Sometimes it was a good reason like my father was on a special mission with the government and had to fake his own death and my mother's mission is to save me. One I returned to a lot was the bad one, where my parents had deliberately crashed because they knew I would be a bad son and had come back (from the dead) because my grandmother was that tired of me she made a kind of sacrifice, and so the big dream house becomes a kind of prison for us all full of terrible words gone over again and again until I had to murder them both usually with an axe or a heavy table or an antique blunderbuss I'd seen on TV. I was given anxiety medication after some outcry when I was little and that cycle slowly trundled to a stop. It couldn't really work that one anyway after my grandmother died when I was nineteen. I was free to think what I wanted.

The fantasy life cycle I only now – right now I mean, standing here saying it – get for what it was because it came to me in a different form, not the fantasy of reunion with my parents but union with another – now I get it. I know I should save myself. Fucking shameful. I've been kissing a fogged up mirror, right? I have drilled down in circles but now I know at least there's mud at the bottom, seawater, rocks around me and there are arms around to catch me up. Whether I deserve it or not.

Gym

In the middle of the typical daily cycle was how it began. I was standing smoothly lifting yellow dumbbells in front of the mirror wall with all the other people in the gym behind me and my body getting stronger, at that moment in the biceps. The tension of the muscle under the skin with no give at all, that was really satisfying. There's nothing like that feeling of hardness in your body, like nothing can hurt you, nothing can press in. I had on my favourite teeshirt which was blue and made me look even hotter. I like simple pleasures including the way I look. Simple. At the apex of my curl as I was prodding the bicep and smiling, Badr passed behind me, saw me and wandered over.

'How you been, Joe?'

He called me Joe because I looked like a Joe, a simple strong adult Joe. He knew my name was Tom – it was one of our things. Badr looked warm and expansive with a little smile himself. He had been going to the gym about as long as I had with no visible difference to his physique. We'd talked about that and him getting a trainer, but after some questions back and forth he decided against putting the work in to either building muscle mass or trimming down. Trimming down, that was what I liked; not getting musclebound but being my taut living maximum self-reliant self. Half-arsed gym was just a part of Badr's daily circle. Today in addition to his uniform of black sweatshirt and tracksuit he had a dark grey baseball cap on that said 'chill' on it.

'Alright, Badr. Nice cap.'

'Still the trouble, eh?'

'Yup.'

I had told him about the last girl and trying to be her flatmate and her putting the rent up on me when I started bringing other girls back.

'I have that room you know. Remember I said?'

'Oh yes. Still free?'

'Still free pal. Come on round and see it. Give it a shot.'

'I might just do that, Badr.'

I texted him in the changing rooms. I thought, what a muppet, what if he's still here all ready to go and he wants you to come over right away before you get showered. Something about the idea of him being close up beside me while I was texting him felt alarmingly intimate. Then I thought, I have no attachments and he probably likes the way I stink – he'll have to if we live in the same house. He was there in fact, but leaving when he got the text and replied right away, telling me to come round and giving me his address. I showered with simple pleasure and longer than usual.

Daniel

What shall I say about getting the tour of the house? It was a shabby crumbling kind of place. Boxes of cereal open on the fridge and the bathroom, that rough Lynx smell, but I didn't care – situation in my current abode was unbearable – it was time to step into a new place or die like a shark when it stops swimming. Badr was enthusiastic and welcoming – I guessed early on he must have been bullied as a child and did everything he could now – desperately – to make day-to-day life smooth for himself and everyone else. Seeing him at home clarified it all. He had a houseplant for every dropped friendship. He was one of the good guys that doesn't get anywhere. I slapped him on the back, I listened to him talking. I could be around him a bit and move on at the next opportunity.

I could see the mysterious door where the hermit owner of the house stayed. Badr introduced me to Daniel. I saw Daniel out of the corner of my eyes that first time. So I can't tell you anything. Not yet.

I went through the downstairs and saw the room I was going to take. I crawled all around that place testing it out with my sensory organs. It was a done deal. I would move in, into the new sex cycle that had just begun – if I'm honest – with an overlapping of the last one. I got myself set up to be a better man in a little while and Badr would hold me to it meanwhile and my cat would hold me to it, both kind soft beings.

And Daniel?

I don't remember the days without Daniel. This is important: the time between meeting him and knowing him has compressed under the weight of everything after. I can just about remember the early days of knowing him, making myself talk louder and more confident than I felt. I told myself it was the beginning of a new cycle so I was going to feel rocky. If I believed in astrology, I'd say something was in retrograde – that messes you up, right? I don't really know anything but I'm sure astrology has to do with cycles too. I respect that, I just don't believe it. Funny now there's no moon or sky and only the end of the land and the sea has all the answers I'd ever been asking for. I remember the night of the party – let me keep this. I remember the night of moving in. I got it into my head to think Daniel was a soft thing too, shook his hand – pleased with its dry firm grip – and went on my way, trying so hard to carelessly slot him as a detail only for the new rotation. But even that early I felt the first shocks of coming disruption as he sat with Órla and I saw them together and myself pretending to be outside of it all. I took to the room where Daniel was not to try and find my footing there. I slumped into swearwords and laughing like roaring, trying to hold up my picnic bluebells – you'll have already worked out that I had other distractions which were all variants on the bluebells – like he was just some ungracious scrolling on the singular surface moment of a day and not. Already. Fuck. I sat myself solid as a side of beef in the living room with my friends and the desperate warmth of Badr and we talked about somebody's girlfriend and my job in advertising and media. Which I'd explain was a lot of meetings and strategising war for things that don't matter. Yeah, right in front of my colleagues, I didn't care then. As if they didn't know. And I drank a beer and another beer and each sip made me think it was my lips that were foaming not the drink, I was wrenched inside because I was moving into the place and I knew, as much as I resisted: he is something. Daniel. This is not a circle this is an end, a gap, a plummeting point.

Daniel, when I let myself see him clearly at last in the basement of the university, looked like this: a quiet man, watchful eyes, a tripped step look. I mean the kind of person you look at and think nothing, then look again and get startled – what am I trying to say? Some horror that is not horror, the rollercoaster loop-de-loop of someone who sees you but who is also a lot of other things at once. Emblematic embedded eyes. Step it back: they were brown eyes, I think. I mostly saw him in low light always.

He was four inches shorter than my six one and looked like he didn't care about food or sunshine but would be rosier and darker if he did eat and go out and didn't work so much but might not know how. He looked like the wind from a mountain was blowing on him and he was barely standing against it but in a fierce determined way, even when he was at rest he was holding himself against that wind. He liked to wear lots of layers. He loved jumpers and touching things with his fingers as if checking their quality. I've never thought about anyone more than I've thought about him and it shows, like I've exhausted all my thoughts on him and then pumped myself round the track again twelve more times.

Let me tell you, sexuality didn't come into it. It was just a door creaking open to let the fucking ghosts in. Daniel was a harbinger. Everyone is drenched in ghosts – there are so many more dead people than alive – so it takes a cut to let them get in. My cut was Daniel. My means of infection was the diary. This I am just now setting out from myself, from my fallen position. Now, inside, I'm glad of the windbreak, this stove, aren't you? I can taste smoke in the back of my mouth and it reminds me

I'm still alive. I had to stand on the edge where the breakers come in before I even would admit it: I wanted Daniel to be near me always because I wasn't cycling, I was falling and the darkness was already rushing past me.

Daniel, Daniel

Fear was a new feeling in my adult life; I thought I'd put that fucking brick down on my road from childhood and walked away from it forever. What could I fear when everyone I'd ever loved had died already? Before the day I moved into that house, I breezed through life, I was healthy. I was blowing by fast and sleek and no impediments; work was shit – Cloudberry Corporation, ad campaign planning for fuck's sake – but life in Scotland was an improvement on life in London, where I had been before, in that at my new work no one cared after five o'clock, and drinking was mandatory but not skewed with upmanship. I was too young to complain about the cost of pints and rent – necessities had been a gouge for longer than I could remember, and my grandmother's money softened that a little anyway. Life was all right, before. I had Órla on board, a girl who seemed like she wasn't easily hurt and would be a good friend once it was all inevitably over between us – I saw she was smarter than me, but did not worry, since I guessed she was smart enough to be kind to an, let's face it, idiot, like me once the fucking was done.

I saw Daniel on the side of the room and put him away for the moment but as soon as I was leaving the flat, that first time after I agreed to move in I was afraid of an unknown pressure of wanting. This unknown shape. This Daniel whoever it was. Wanting things is the worst possible thing. You should never want. You should just fucking *be*, right? That's what better men than me had told me. And especially not to want to the degree

I did. So when I moved in I threw myself into work, so when I was living there I was out a good amount of the time, out with Órla, in with Órla, who seemed to like Daniel a decent amount, and gave me an excuse not to talk to him and an excuse to look between them and get coffee and sip it and go off to work and hear her talk about her funny odd little new friend.

Thread

Fear though, it had sneaked into my life and I couldn't shake it. Things change, all right, but I'd always been in charge of that change, or could see the shape of it. I was good like that, adaptable. So. Like I said, this wasn't about sex. I wouldn't care, would I? I could fuck a man. No worries there, though I haven't. Hadn't. This was like metal filings finding out about magnets. Only the magnet is so unassuming they think, why this magnet. Why now. I am being honest now – as honest as I can be, and sharp with myself, because I am so lost and truth is a small iron thread coming out of my arteries through my chest wall and you'll tell me I have to follow it up hand over fist somehow out, somehow into light again, out from under the shadow I'm in. It might lead to you, it might not. It might kill me. I am repetitive, you'll think. Shallow, a whole load of other judgements. Fuck you, I know, don't look at me. So are all people who are in a crisis or in love or full of ghosts. So are all people. It's a lot. It's a lot.

A Partial List of Objects I Unboxed at Cloudberry

The ones I remember:
- On my first day, a box of a thousand shoelaces with the name of a celebrity stamped along each in Arial Black font, to be handed out at a national football match.
- A box of fake maps to 'stars' homes' in a small Scottish town where none of the actors actually live; I don't remember what this was for.
- A box of white tee-shirts, torn up and with fake blood on them, advertising a new crime drama for an online network we represent.
- A box of samples of gin-flavoured dick-shaped gummies for some club.
- A box of holographic jumpers to be given to local 'influencers' who were fans of gymnastics.
- A box of seventy obsidian black shell-shaped objects with screens (that were not phones) whose use and associated company no one in the office could work out.
- A box of anatomically correct dolls without hair (an ill-advised campaign to do with alopecia awareness).
- A box with nothing in it but packing peanuts.
- A box of plush polar bears with their eyes crossed out, to signal their extinction; a promotion for a computer game.
- A box with leaflets of infographics that detailed not just our

company but individual people working there (all women) including their estimated clothing size; a promotion for a new clothing app.

– A box of American flags and guns in the colours of human skin, complete with nails and some with freckles and warts; a promotion for a Chinese gambling firm.

– A box with 3D printed food snacks that had gone mouldy; a promotion for a new 3D snack company which went immediately bust before we could give them feedback.

– A box with mocked-up old scrapbooks and photo albums; a promotion for a genealogy service.

– A box with toddler clothes advertising a breast milk enhanced beer (we told them no).

– A box with several mer-unicorns stuffed with recording devices.

An Introduction to Him

To understand myself I'd realised early on in life I had to understand one or two people at least very well and mould my thoughts to their shape to keep myself tough and on course. I'd done it in the past with friends and work colleagues though suffering from the move north and the small cultural barriers there were between me and people at the new workplace. There are always bits that get lost in translation, jokes that won't work, etcetera. But I had the form down. A couple of my early friends and girlfriends were the biggest role models, but none of the later ones had more than a bit to add to my repertoire. Usually, after I was into my twenties – whether partner or person of interest – their influence faded when I left their company. And I became different again, with only a little of the residue in the ways I dressed or a motion of my hands retained. Different again: another circle of being, but with these little bits of continuity, new wheel but still a wheel. So I keep – kept – myself together.

After I moved into the Minto house I read and understood the story of James Lennoxlove and sucked it wholesale into me sort of accidentally. Nobody else knew it really, not even Daniel, who had the diary – who had stolen it, and like most any thief had missed its real value. Mark MacAshfall, whose diary it was, also never knew the whole story. He knew the facts but not the story. I was the only one who got that. It gave me a wilder wonkier shape because of that. You should never get an original insight, they are the road to madness, because they might be wrong, and that reflects on you, or they might be right, and then people might be disturbed. That's what I'd thought all my life, based on empirical evidence. Yet here I fucking am. At the end of everything.

James Lennoxlove's diary came to Daniel from Mark who I knew previously by chance – his stepfather was a client of Cloudberry and once I had to go to Mr MacAshfall senior's house to explain a device his company was using to collect and monitor the notes of the most profitable songs in real time. He hadn't invented it; he played the piano to me in a room upstairs and made me taste a wine he had laid down from the year of my birth – sweet charred cork and purple musk with an entrancing death lily edge, he said. Mark came up and extracted me. We sat in the kitchen and the sun cast long golden rays between the stairs. I told him about my grandmother's villa on the edge of a town in the Cotswolds. The electrical substation where I'd hang out with friends and drink cider and smoke roll ups had barrels of pink and white flowers planted around it to make it look prettier. It was the kind of place, I said, that looks like either everyone is about to be scenically murdered and or endlessly and in booming self-satisfaction votes Tory which amounts to the same thing – I was pretty drunk at that point. Mark laughed; a pug sneezing. Less scenic to be murdered by Tories, he said.

He told me about his family – convoluted to the point of interlooping – after a while working his way to telling me about a relative who was potentially of interest, whose diary he had just rediscovered and who he thought he might write a biography on, if anyone still read at all, he said.

'He called himself James Lennoxlove,' he said, 'but nobody knows what his real surname was.'

'Did he call himself Lennoxlove?' I asked.

'Yes,'

'Then that was his real name,' I said. Pretty smugly, if I'm honest.

'Well, maybe. If you think of it like that. It's just – there were no Lennoxloves recorded before him, and I mean anywhere, though he claimed he had an older illegitimate brother. He claimed also to live in Bitterhall, which is a place that does not exist. It's possible he meant "Bitterhaugh" or "Bitterhill", both of which might. The only thing I've found that's real with Lennoxlove attached to it is Lennoxlove Hall, but the Maitland family lived there. Lennoxlove Hall is in East Lothian – not far from here. The mysterious James Lennoxlove wrote in his diary with no firm locations or even dates.'

'Pretty weird for a diary.'

'Mmm. It covers a small section of his life in, best guess, the early part of the nineteenth century when he was, apparently, a young man. I've had the book analysed by a codicologist and handwriting expert who told me that the writing marks it out as from that time, and done by someone educated, though most Scots were literate, so that narrows nothing down. The only thing she could find odd about it was the ligature of the binding, which is made of an unusual material – black silk threads of Turkish origin.'

'Pretty interesting stuff,' I said.

'Ah, you don't have to be polite – I know it's probably not, but,' he said, 'that's not the fascinating part, really. Lots of things have details lost to time. In the book, you see, he describes witnessing a murder that I have reason to believe, though no evidence as yet, that he might have in fact been involved in.'

'A murder,' I said.

'I know, right?' Mark said. He stopped briefly to bring me over a coffee. The wine with its grating heft and wordy descriptions had left me tired. I had nowhere to be while I was able to pretend to be in a meeting/liaison with a client. The house had this unbearable gentle luxuriousness to it and Mark though hideous to look at was a clever, funny bloke, and he pushed a plateful of small cakes covered in thin icing in my direction.

'Thanks very much,' I said, stuffing one in my mouth. The icing was lemony. From the study on the floor above I could hear Mr MacAshfall singing and bashing down operatically on the keys. 'How do you know he was involved?'

'Family secret,' he said.

'Are there skeletons in the cupboard?'

'Something like that,' he said. 'Either way the diary is fairly well written, full of strange tensions. But anyway I'm stuck right now with either proving that my relative committed some horrible deed – I don't even know for sure who it was that was murdered, I'd have to delve into local records, if I can figure out where is "local" – or writing my book on him even if he didn't do it whatever he might have done wherever. But also, I'm stuck for a very stupid reason.'

'Oh?'

'Diary's gone missing.' He made a vanishing shape with his hands.

I came away from the house of the MacAshfalls with a short-burning curiosity and a promise to help Mark publicise his book somehow if it came about – he assumed I must know the right kind of contacts. I forgot about all this until a few months later when the book materialised before me in the Minto house, in the grasp of the man who my heart was at that time choking on. And I stole it myself, and read, and didn't tell Mark I'd found it, obviously. Though my own reason for getting stuck was. Well. You know.

Diary

James Lennoxlove told me his story. I saw right away why Mark was suspicious, even without the sudden and unlikely name. The entries seemed intent on stuffing in the details of a life as much as possible but without any sense that they were something a person would write. Best comparison I could make was that they were like the fluffy mini-series my grandmother used to love: well-made and sumptuous but not like the way people would have actually lived. Aristocratic lifestyle porn.

According to Lennoxlove, he was a friendless young man, living in a manorhouse of honey brick in the East of Scotland, with most of his forty rooms overlooking wide butter-coloured oat fields and an ancient wood where his father had taken him hunting. He saw fairies, he said, once by a bridge near a ruined churchyard, but provided a way to shrug this off by saying it was while he was on some tonic for a migraine. Lennoxlove wrote for his readership (whoever that might be was unclear) unreal thickets of smoke-like mists trailing over coursing grounds, and drew attention to the curling steam off a horse's back and the thick spongy quality of the paper his lover used to write to him, that kind of thing. The sheer volume of detail made the eyes water. The foxes' tails hanging dripping blood from the servants' windows. A huge book of accounts that had landed on a child's foot, leaving them lame. Memorable was the duel he fought with his brother over 'some jest', naked except for their swords, on a moorland, both giving up immediately due to the cold. Nothing dull happened to him, even as nothing happened. BBC costume drama, like I said.

From twelve to eighteen, I used to keep a diary. Days don't happen the way James' days did. Lots of 'nothing important happened today' and football scores and how I'd got fucked off with my best friend at the time and we'd fallen out because he had said something dismissive about my favourite band. James Lennoxlove had no friends at all to bitch about, no attachments barring his brother, and, later, the lover who he only seemed to be with hunting in the woods – and in the inn, which got honestly wrenching in the superfluous detail, not just the encounter that happened there, but the beds and aspect of the room and the sound of feet creaking over the boards outside. If it had been today he would have featured threadcounts and the wifi quality in amongst the descriptions of humping (which were weirdly vague, but I suppose about right for the time).

But I couldn't stop reading and chuck it as a wholesale lie. There was some point to it. And like Mark said, something that drew you in: his lies were beautifully crafted and winking, I thought. I don't have time to read many books these days but I know the difference between ornate fakery for a laugh and trying to muddy things for a secret reason of some kind, a hidden narrative that leads somewhere. A hidden motive. I pride myself on picking up on these things. And the façade holds, I think, up until the point where Lennoxlove reports how he went to the Hogmanay ball and saw the murder in the stable, then it sort of – crumbles. And I imagined everyone would have got that. Now I wonder.

Lennoxlove talked about seeing the glint on the knife and feeling the heat rising from the wound – he couldn't have felt that from across the room. He could perhaps see the light on the knife but it was as if that was all he could see – the point of focus

227

of his eyes trained down to just that as if to avoid – as if not to see – the man murdering or the victim, I still don't know. And at one point he wrote 'I must keep going, I thought, as I rushed and then I turned and I made strides for my horse.' I must keep going at what? Leaving the stable? There's a problem there, right, with the order of the words. I would tell Mark, I thought, reading it the first few times. I would go to him and give it to him. James Lennoxlove was his relative – he implied direct ancestor – and he would want to know and to have the time to choose what to do with the information.

I held onto the book though, fidgeted with my ideas of it. Not doubting myself exactly but looking for enough proof to show – before I went accusing a stranger's great-whatever-grandad. Daniel was always above me in our house, wandering, looking for it. He would be embarrassed – the thought ran through me like battery acid in the chest, that idea, that Mark knew Daniel had taken it – I did not know they were good friends; I imagined a scene and my part in it as instigator. Who likes to be exposed like that? Who likes to be the exposer? So while I held off deciding what to do I read it again, up to that part, to see if there were clues of a growing madness that made the incident unlikely, or signs the whole thing had been written as if to lead up to this part for some other, special reason I could crack.

Timing and Presentation

I stayed up. I procrastinated. I listened to the walls creak. I must have read that first part of the book six times. It isn't long. A possibly-pretended year of a life. I stayed with it. I grew to love the richness and the textures. How the youngest servants would run out and pick up windfall apples, scampering, he said, like rabbits in caps. I was sold on its vision even as I knew it was fake. It was like a film I watched over and over. No, like an ad. I was being sold an image of warmth and complexity, and behind that I thought I could see what the company was, what its mission statement was, the inept marketing manager and the brilliant young art designer. That kind of thing. I kept on my path. I put off having to show Daniel up. I'd plumb the mystery, and Mark would just be in awe at what I'd found, and in the end everything would be smoothed over. By my last read-through I'd almost decided it was too like modern life, wasn't it? That pretence of perfection. I had deleted all my social media accounts a while back. Bad relationship moment, too many reminders of my own failings and that didn't allow for a clean shift into the future. I was good at clearing out old Cloudberry tweets and online docs too, kind of famous for it because at work that's the kind of sad thing you get famous for and get told you're famous for in meetings as you let the pen fall slack in your hand and you time and pitch your laugh precisely. I fucking love the internet. I hate it for my own self, as I said. I hate conflict and exposure and drama, but I love the kind of cultivated reveal that's possible. For people who like to make a display of their minutia and make it stilled and beautiful in a way you can't manage in real life, all heavy breathing and stumbled words and tangle. James Lennoxlove didn't have the luxury of writing allowing his work to be read and then deleting afterwards. It had to be all out there forever or not at all. But he managed its presentation so well, it became a kind of curation that wasn't possible, I thought, for things made long before the idea of the internet. I wondered if this might lead me to the secret. I don't think it did. The book was still old. The life in it was still fake but beautiful. The purpose wasn't embedded; there was nowhere to click through to another site, the one that expanded on the original idea. It was just lines one in front of another. I read it again to make sure.

I got to the point where I gave up re-reading it, satisfied I'd inferred everything, but still couldn't find the answers. And so I sat, the whole book in my head, running the images back and forth, with a funny tick to my heart and too much of it. It was the same night, a long one that held me like fingers in a fist, I slipped out – did he hear me go? Órla didn't shift – and got a night bus to the gym – one of the few things in this city that never closed and worked out for two and a half hours hard, nodding at the other insomniacs with shadows under their brows and furrows of overlit teeth showing – got up a steam on me like any number of James' real or imaginary horses, then went for a run in the darkness. I had the book in my kit bag with the dirty clothes. I wore a warm coat though it wasn't that cold yet. I don't know now what date it was, what day of the week, but I was gone all night. Like a dream I ran without effort, bag on my shoulders, striding easy under streetlights and by a canal at one point and past countless empty shopfronts and a handful still with goods inside, lights on but doors locked to all comers – I don't know, I try to recreate it like James would have done, but the order's muddled and my life is chaos now and catastrophe even then, when I didn't know it. Running through this insolvable problem made it feel at least like it could be something easy, even though I was no nearer to getting it. I stepped on another night bus and got off at the part of the city that's on the beach and not really the city at all and then I ran along the shore, heading south – I think – blood full of bright horses and servants' aprons and crystalising lights in front of my eyes and I was dropping tired when I climbed on another bus and sailed homewards. At the end of the run I presented my findings to the air just outside the Minto house.

There was no way to know, there was no evidence only toneless text and I might understand it okay – I understood most things, if I had the full facts – but I'd never have proof that it was a story told out the side of its mouth let alone work out *why*. I wanted to believe that James Lennoxlove was lying to perk himself up. He might have been a poor man with a bad life trying to build himself a nice fantasy mansion. Perhaps he had given himself a newly discovered brother for just the same reason I gave myself back my parents.

That wasn't a deep dig for the amount of effort spent. I went inside and stood in the hall. Mrs Boobs sat on the stairs glowing white as the space inside a circle and looked at me with narrowed eyes.

'Darling,' I whispered to her, putting my hand out to meet her bending ear, 'you don't know, do you?'

I was cold in my sweat and my lungs still burned and though I was strong I was dizzy and all this might explain the sudden shift of the hairs on my neck and the sound – close, Christ I jumped – in my ear, of a voice right up near it as if from someone standing behind me.

'I can tell you,' it said, 'if you'll let me.'

James, James

I never loved a boy, and that's a fact. I never fancied a man. I had
no space in me for it. I never saw a ghost either, or believed
in them, or believed anyone who said they had seen a ghost
wasn't doing it for the attention or because they had dodgy eyes
and wanted to see one. I never heard voices. I was a picture of
gleaming mental health. I was so in my body I had to give it to
other people hard just to make it through the weekend. I had
no twinges and no weak parts and nothing deviant and nothing
branching and nothing but that straight path that goes all the
easiest ways, paved with primo paving stones. I didn't even
have to wear glasses. I still don't need them but other than that
I am not what I was. Past me would say I've diminished: it's true
I can't be looking good, here, now. I can smell myself. The last
time I saw my reflection it laughed at me and was another man.
There are waves in my hair and I mean water waves, and my
lymph glands are swollen with nineteenth-century dirt. I'd also
say that I'm not diminished *enough*. Don't look at me like that.
I fucking know.

I didn't see James that night in the hallway of the Minto house.
I saw Minto. He had just unlocked the door in mime-like silence;
that's the way he moved. I didn't know it was him at first – in
the mostly dark hall, and never having seen him – and thumped
the space above my heart, that gesture you do for shock, and
muttered, 'Oh, hallo.'

'Hallo and halo to you, fair youth,' this white-haired blur said. Like that.

I made my way towards the kitchen as if I had been going there before the interruption. Minto followed behind. He held his hands in a funny way, like a tired praying monk, limp. Praying to the pale flowerbeds, I think now, that line the sides of the corridors wherever he walks, (he told me this another time – it was a method he used to make himself go anywhere, to think of a way prepared beautifully). I made myself cheese on toast and he hung about the whole time in silence behind me, or sometimes shifting to the side of me, not in a creepy way, but watching what my hands were doing. His face was padded weirdly, most of it going under his eyes and some on his cheeks, making them disconcertingly full.

'You haven't asked what I know,' he said.

'Mm,' I answered. I was at that point stuffing my mouth with hot food and my body was loving it. Liquid cheese oozed on the diagonal and between my buttery fingers.

'I know that you're the new boy,' he said. I nodded without looking up, 'I know that you have a follower.'

Minto: this large and crumpled man, bristly, pale husky eyes, pyjamas under a shabby but expensive-looking striped suit blazer, primrose woollen scarf, hot pink slipper-booties. He was swaying lightly on his feet. I thought through my own shit; posh old drunk, what a shame. Insomniac too, or up ridiculously early. They say old people stop sleeping so much. My grandmother stopped sleeping the night through a month before she died. She had a lot of photos to organise she said, but after death the albums were not around. I remember a fire in the back garden, odd yellow smoke falling flatly over the edges of the pit. Obliteration is organisation of a kind, a controlled permanent filing into particles of carbon. Me and her were a lot alike, really.

'Ah-huh?' I said, thinking food food food, and waiting for the total exhaustion to take me down though still I felt all awake. Minto raised a thin, red hand and extended his pointing finger towards the empty space to my left.

'There,' he said, 'he's quite clearly there. Hello, friend of my houseguest.'

I turned – yes I did – to see – yes – nothing. But not *completely* nothing. The universe had been opened to the idea that there was something, and through that fissure something hissed completely silently and completely unreal, but only for now. At the time I'd snorted. I'd had enough and bustled my plate to the sink and went through to my room and Órla sleeping there, my landing spot, and the cat came up and arranged herself on my feet and in the dark I fell towards safety, for perhaps the last time.

Occupation

The ocean is full of plastic. I've touched plastic things dozens of times today. Small nubs of it, smooth flanks of it, crinkling skins of it. Touched it with my hands, my lips. I feel the gyre multi-coloured flop and spin. Plastic is in the gullets of guillemots and stamped into valleys of landfills. It's a weird, upsetting occupation of the earth, if you think about it – our production, natural since it comes from us. I think at some point in the distant future what's left of humanity will look on plastic with appalled nostalgia – like it's amber from another era where our secretions could not be stopped – but that day I sat under a dodgy light on a plastic and petroleum-product chair attempting to open an acreage of boxes set on the floor to meet some new-birthed plastic and petroleum products and pretend I was happy doing so. I struggled with layers of tape, finally snapped them with my teeth. The latest plastic simulation of a thing, thingness being adspace, in my work. I plunged in up to my forearms and packing peanuts swelled around me like smooth blood cells and my eyes closed over and the sounds of the office receded. I wanted to just sit with my hand in there, rustling. I wanted to sink into the slurry of dry tiny pieces. I had not slept. Out by the neck I slowly raised from the box one of fifty toy mer-unicorns. Mallory in her tall heels primped over and eyed it, and me.

'The vodka people, right?'

'Yeah,' I said, turning the thing. It had a switch that set it on and it began to sing an unpleasant upbeat tune. We listened in silence. I liked Mallory for that.

'Well,' she said with a sigh, 'it started off weak and it struggled in the middle there, but by the end, it really managed to finish and be done.'

'How much did they pay for this?'

'Too much. It's got to be in violation of some of rule about flogging booze to kids. They should have just stuck with the cartoons. But there was muttering about them too.'

'Who would want this?' I said. We looked at each other.

'No one. It's going in a hole in the ground, to sit there for a thousand years.'

'Such great triumphs mark out our days from the lineage of humanity,' I said.

'Funny. Who said that?' Mallory asked in a tone without any sense of enjoyment. That was also part of the game, and I liked her all right for saying it, and I desperately wanted to walk out of the building and start running and run to the sea again, or up the cliff. Instead of answering I imagined a corner of a dark woollen picnic blanket, and the way cheese and butter sandwiches gleam and bulge when tightly bound in cling film, melting slightly from the heat of a summer's day, and how they feel as they come loose and my childish fingers poke flute holes in the soft white bread.

We would make a copy, Daniel and I, spending some hours in that long oppressive basement room – I can still feel the air conditioning blowing my lips blue. Do you know what precious means? I thought it was a slimy word used in jewellery copy and by Gollum. But though it has an ugly sound in the mouth it means more than important; tiny and rare and not self-replicating, and so mortal though longer-lived than either of us will be. I thought *precious* afterwards as I lay hard in my bed, almost crying.

I thought of Daniel's hands on the neck of the new thing he had made. It was worth a thousand years of occupation of the dirt for that, I think.

Recycle

I touched the smoothed edges of the rock where I came to the end and thought of plastic inhabiting everything. Microbe-sized multiplying and seething in its shiny ever-new pill bodies. I'd been able to avoid thinking of all this, when I was fine, before. So now I thought of the ionic surfactants that wash down the drain. I thought of the rare metals in phones dragged out of the rocks in unknown poor regions of the world, names I don't even know – the county or the metals. I thought of the phones I'd tossed away when they began to run slowly or just look a little tired. I thought of factories making plastic goods and realised I didn't know what they'd be like, though I have watched videos before of production lines. There's a lot I can't see clearly – all I have is the conveyor belt and no other details of the warehouses or people working there. What the work does to their eyes or their fingernails, I don't know and can't bear to know. I thought of the volume of plastic shit being made at these unknowable factories spewing out, like the doors of factories were mouths or anuses, factories like bodies. I thought about the sticky backing glue on labels I had peeled off at work. Boxes of new textures and shapes immediately discarded. I thought about guilt, which I didn't really feel for any of it. It's my fault and it's not, since I am going to die, I thought. I thought of myself, standing here, how easy it would be to take a step forward and stand nowhere ever again. I thought of seabirds' guts. I thought, isn't it stupid. Some children when they learn about dying are horrified by the idea.

Then there are others who think, well, that's one way out, and that stays with them all their life, that sense of horrific possibility. There are others who don't think either of these things but I'm too tired to think of them.

I tried to think of every good thing I had done and all I could manage was standing under a tree in somebody else's garden, with a man I – I wanted. I'd fucked everything else up, even just by existing I was just a walking carbon footprint. I had never loved anything as I should have, I had lacked capacity to see between wanting what I was told to want, and my real desires. And even when I finally dimly got the hint there had been a kiss that almost but didn't happen, and the name for that's a ghost kiss. A kiss that does happen can be a mistake but a ghost kiss never is, aching just beyond the borders of myself. A kind of human texture. I hear hail falling in the grass and on my clothes and his. I shuddered. Later we'd go a lot further but it won't count. I'm lost again – timing. Here, at the end. Small stones fall when I move. The grass is damp and the winter sky is nothing worth recording so I do, staring at it with my phone until my eyes hurt. But I'm inside, I forget. You're here and I'm down on the ground and I fell? But I did not die. There's a fire going. I'm in the grate sending up sparks, and my skin is blurring. I need someone to lean against me so I can be in one place. Stay with me.

Doubling

We walked into the building of the university late at night with
the infernal bright shit that so characterised the work that
I was spending my life on. Down past some security doors and
into the padded room, and I felt the fear immediately – that the
door would close shut behind us forever and we would die and
desiccate in there. It was not my only fear.

Stopped dead. Daniel looked back at me and smiled. He hadn't
said anything other than, 'Here's the machine,' with a wave of his
hand like introducing a work colleague.

'It doesn't make the copies out of plastic?' I asked. My voice
cracked under the strain and I winced at myself. My heart so
fucking loud, like a much younger less used heart. Go back to
being the way you were before, I was thinking. Órla never did this
to me. This was dire. I have never loved airless rooms. Too many
memories. Rooms press in and crush you like grinding stone gears
and no one overly cares where you are, ever really, you could be
missing for hours and no one would think to go looking.

'No, the machine uses different resins,' he was saying. 'It's not
in its mandate to copy post-twentieth century objects.' He was
placing the thing in the copy tray with finicky care. I saw the
veins on his hands, the raised bones. He had a small red scuff on
his left hand, near the middle knuckle. I followed its progression
as he moved the toy about, splaying its legs, straightening out
its shiny green fishtail as much as it would go, brushing out the
cheap shitty silver mane with his fingers. Will you listen and not

tell – I was worried with a rising alarm in my heart that I would – at a slipped moment – be somehow tricked into kissing him; that was how I thought of it, like we'd stand too close and I'd lose my sense of decorum, bend down, my lips on your lips. I didn't have thoughts, my thoughts wanted to yell, it's the room itself! Don't get confused! And yelled drowning me out white cold as I watched him pull back and go about his business. I wanted, with a kind of shocked heat, to reach out and hold his hand up to my lips. I could imagine the skin cold against my own cold hand. It would smell of citrus; before we left the flat he had been peeling a mandarin. 'I am getting confused,' I thought, and tried to puzzle out all the reasons why I might be mistakenly feeling like this – I hadn't been sleeping. I was not gay, nobody had said that about me: nobody at school had yelled it at me or shoved me into a wall for it. Nobody had implied or inferred it. Not that it mattered if I was, I told myself afterwards, if I was. Just, right, no man looked to me for anything other than work – and sometimes to double check their form at the gym – that was all I had to give, the rules were set. There below everything in that horrible cold dry room, the tops of my ears burned. Nothing about this made sense, so perhaps it was my body telling me in its twisted way I had a virus brewing, a shivering, high temperature boiling up and my subconscious made a mistake with the input. You could blame reading over and over the sensual sinuous diary entries of James Lennoxlove, colouring my understanding of the world so much I could get fearful pleasure out of this. Because that's what it was, I see it now. But then I was thinking, wanting isn't like this, doesn't have the feel flavour shape certification or panic of this, so this isn't wanting. I was overtired. I hadn't been sleeping. Nothing had to happen, I wouldn't make any kind of mistake like that.

Passage

I went to get coffee and I held that instead. It's this century's substitute for rest or closeness, unity that requires no other hand but your own to utilise. One of the many, and more reliable and available in public now that vaping has left cigarettes as historical. Fucking vaping, the flavoured condom method of substance dependency. Coffee is customisable comfort that doesn't need other people except for workers in the chain of supply, I suppose. Can't ignore the world economy, especially if it's how we get interpersonal only with ourselves. I had made a career on the fringes of this sort of self-securing by the object, the image, the smell or the burn of a drink. I was like the high priest of it. No – ha – really another worker too, just one of many soldering meaning onto the endlessly passing things with a series of little taps and clicks.

Anyway, I went out through the doors. The hall smelled of fresh paint and nineties carpeting. There's lots to register in an empty building when you are trying to buy coffee so you can avoid the man whose presence is causing you actual mania. You walk carefully to avoid making noise, then get self-conscious about what that means about you and switch to good strides. The hall extends away from you as you walk down it. Something crackles, shifts. Wall surfaces; ghosts. I went into the nook for coffee, stood for a moment staring into space, then pressed the options I wanted. A hearty old stream shot out of the machine, invigorating the air with fragrance. Behind me a long way back down the corridor I could hear a slow, steady creaking. Sometimes your mood is a Dutch angle through which you can see the world and it's only going to look bad, that tilted. I kept my head down, didn't I? I didn't invite it in. At no stage could anyone say I had let myself go completely. No, I got taken by the crazy. Or the weird reality, I don't know. I don't know! The creaking came nearer, I kept busy. Hand around the cup, so warm, the colours on the cup a solid choice, the logo resembling a major chain but not actionably close. I selected the options for Daniel, thinking he probably liked a standard cappuccino with a twist. For some reason, 'smoky woods' was a syrup flavour. My finger hovered over the button. A sound came from a few metres away, shuffling. Snuffling, like a horse tickering, the sounds of a bridle in a horse's mouth. It kept coming closer. The machine beeped up closer still and the second coffee was ready. I sipped, I swallowed a hot mouthful. I turned around two cups in hand, face calm. Daniel had followed me – or, some other person with a job to do crawling in this empty hive.

Nothing. No one.

And then, walking in from my left side, a figure. There was a sick feeling all through me like death, like the system going into shutdown, greyish beats, no air.

The figure turned his head to me as he passed, then kept walking down the hall. My own head was facing forwards – I held myself upright, on duty, believe me, against any of this – so I saw little of it, only registering a horror and dirty coils of snail-brown hair, and only when he had gone by me, about twenty seconds afterwards I turned in the direction he'd left in. Nothing, no one. I stared. Still nothing re-materialised. I started breathing again in a gasp. A sick feeling – fuck me. I knew he had not gone into any of the other doors. The keypad noises would have alerted me to that. No. What had I seen, then?

I stood for a while composing a self against a world that had rotated its agreed-on boundaries. Come on I told myself, it's just tiredness – here, breathe in the coffee – it's just a moment you will find yourself thinking back on in pubs – disassociating with a group of mates talking about spooky things, but you – you won't say, give them your moment – so weird you have to unhinge a part of your worldview like a snake unhinges its jaws just to accommodate the animal it's eating. But I was used to getting through; I had good core strength, I could run a mile in four minutes. I could live through the childhood I had. Later I'd be able to – digest. And so I shook my head and pretended to scoff and became an approximation of fine and went back into the copy room to face other kinds of dangers, now seemingly less obscure and wreaking.

Still

Still the night had plans for me. Daniel wasn't at the end of the room by his device. I found him in a kind of cupboard off to one side – the air here smelled like blackcurrant cordial, less sweet, more sawdust, the wine I'd drunk at the MacAshfalls'. It was from the inks. Daniel pulled out a container of liquid leather to show me – the stink of it – mammalian, dangerous. I took a deep breath in to show him I was not afraid. I pulled back spluttering.

'Smells like an uncooked hamburger dropped down the back of a radiator.'

'Yes, sordid isn't it? There's a bottle of gilding liquid up there. And dirt.'

'A bottle of dirt?' Daniel wanted to make the objects as close to real as possible, and real things stink, and are coated in their filth from being here – from existence. I admired it and I hated it, just how deep he was trying to go with authenticising things, but that was good – to be operating in a higher layer, above my weird, base confusion. 'You'll be able to convince everyone it's real when it's not.'

'That's not it at all' Daniel said. 'Well, now you've said it. Maybe. But it's more – verisimilitude. And excessive pushing at the limit of what we can do, how far we can go.'

'Dirt would really lend it credence. Get the right patina on it, and it's like, why even have the real thing?'

'You're testing me, Tom.'

I picked up a bottle of ink from a nearby shelf, 'Kells blue 0004. That Kells?'

'That Kells,' Daniel said. 'You don't really think this is all some kind of master forgery—'

'No no. I think it's pretty cool. Just, has to be in the right hands. Otherwise the world would be overrun with fakes, instead of your choice few.'

'It's still a pricey and difficult thing to do, and there's a lot of paperwork around to prevent forging.'

'Unlicensed forging.' I looked at him, tilting my head. This was good. Pick at him, I thought, until he bleeds. But on thinking that – repulsed myself. It implied, if I thought about it, a skin stretched between us – skin stretched out on the air – or the skin of our bodies, interacting, pressing up against us, hairs raising in the scented squalid warmth –

'I just want to keep the old things safe, Tom,' he was saying, 'that's all I want to do. To keep the originals in perfect condition. And I get to do that here.'

'I don't think it can possibly do what you want it to do, Daniel,' I said. I really thought it all was a miracle; a disgusting and dangerous miracle, if you looked at its constitutional parts.

He looked away, turned back smiling, cheerful, 'I'm here to change your mind. And I think you want it changing.'

Patter

I remember, I pulled the collar up on my coat and ploughed into the frigid air. Daniel going fast at my side to keep up, a bit of the look of a narrow-faced dog. The late stub-end of the night – first there were the city's elegant stone tenements, their staircase railings glowing black with condensation under the orange lights, then shopfronts and desolate empty buildings, then the hedges of the gardens of bigger houses set back on lawns a distance from the street and from the network of back lanes we were going along, like servants rushing so as not to be seen. A stray growth – tendril or bulge – in one of those hedges or a binbag, guts got at by a seagull is as needed and helpless as a small scream of passion or despair I thought, 'We are lashed down, we cannot spare ourselves.' Bloody tired I was from so many emotions – really, an excess of them – or the fever of them – which had in the long hours worked itself through, I thought, with that little scene or hallucination over the coffee marking the worst of it. I did not on the whole journey need to think myself into old, happier times to get by. I was beyond that. My trusty body was just intent on getting me home.

Some time along one of the back lanes, Daniel stopped.

'It's starting to sleet,' he said. Stupidly I looked up, and a gritty piece of hail booted into my eye. Daniel grabbed my sleeve as I covered the eye and swore. We looked around for somewhere to shelter, 'Here,' he said, and shouldered open a door in a wall.

In the garden we stood under a tree as the sleet turned to hard pips of ice. The tree was wide enough that we could both stand comfortably beside each other against the trunk – we stood beside the tree anyway.

'It's really coming down,' I said. Daniel leaned his head back and I blinked, and could just about make out his eyes under a diamond of shadow. Between him and me were all our heavy clothes. His neck looked good. I didn't know why I thought of that, just then. There came the kind of sound they make recordings of to help you send yourself to sleep – a sound that becomes music with drumming tickering rhythms of its own, belonging to no one.

'It's beautiful,' I said, and stiffened in embarrassment. I think – now, when I must be fucking honest – stiffening in self-containment and stiffening in another way are not so far removed. I could see him clearer, his head and neck the only things exposed, the long lines of his throat, his hair overlong on his ears. I don't think he thinks of himself, I thought. I think he forgets himself in his work. I felt close to tears, but with one eye shut it must have looked like I was winking all the time.

'Do you think it'll break the windscreens of the cars?' I asked.

'I think it could,' said Daniel. 'Wouldn't that be amazing?'

And I smiled, just a little.

'You know, I think that I get you a bit more,' I said.

'In the light of this; I've a violent, subversive edge?' said Daniel.

'That's right,'

'It shouldn't be cold enough for this,' he said, barely in a whisper, and the din of the falling hail nearly muffled it.

'Yes,' I said.

It had happened; I had let myself look at him. The hail pattered, lost its rhythm and stopped. I stood a little removed and very upright, wiping my hurt eye. With nothing else to do I scooped up some of the hail and shoved the pellets in my mouth.

Say, 'How does it taste?' I thought. 'Say something like that to me.' But Daniel said nothing, and we went on our way.

Corpse Road

I said that I was born on a corpse road. That's not an exaggeration, I really was. Remember I told you part of the fantasy cycle was bringing my parents back from the dead – I'd start with the half-hour before I was born. I'd start with calm images gathered from the photos – there were many photos, once. My father in his Ford Cortina, griping the wheel smiling not at the camera but at his young wife, humped with foetal me. Both of them fair haired – that type always die tragically, don't they, either that or they're Nazis. Anyway some neighbour on the street had taken it at their request when they were bringing the car home from purchase. He looks like me if I had an (also blond) beard and serial killer glasses. The side-on image makes the whole – the windscreen unshattered, his body fresh, lolling arm on the driver door. It was a summer's day, when I was born. I was meant for summer days, all of us alive – my mother in the back seat, I decided, chosen for ease of entry with her giant belly, and her need to shout full-throated curses and groans as I tried to fire out of her from a thornier exit. My mother, she had looked happy and shy; she had been nineteen, my father twenty-two.

The road that was not exactly the straightest to the hospital but the prettiest – goes through a long ride of trees, over the hill from the dappled wood – of picnic fame – and through pastureland with a river and its oxbow lakes. The road has been widened since its first use, but on one side you can still – if you pay attention – see the things that look like stiles that are for resting the coffins on. A small high Anglican church is up ahead – a large willow planted right on the tight bend opposite it with a curved mirror hammered into it to warn of traffic bearing down – and this is all I have to change – I have to make it so my father looks in that mirror, instead of being distracted by some operatic birthing scream or general mindlessness. I've always hated willow trees. I've always hated that little church, though I only ever saw it once, the day after I passed my driving test.

I stand in front of it (I'd parked my hired car in the tiny church's car park). A mirror breaks at the moment of my crowning. I come from the place that mirrors show. And I wondered if the willow retained the memory, and in what way it knew, by the texture and weight of a car slamming – crumpling – a horn sounding – and my mother, sobbing and falling out, grappling and gubbing on the road with glass and light trembling in her hands. And I have already almost made it out of the mirror, sopping wet. Some shard of its glass must have still been in the gouges in the bark – I was too fearful to investigate or stand at the dusty bend and feel about for it. I rubbed my Adam's apple and kept my shoulders hunched. My mother dies when I am three and my grandmother considers it not right to talk about it. No, she didn't die that day – no, she did – I wanted to be Victorian for a while because if death was in vogue I could be fully allowed it and the forms for it would be clear and there'd be plenty of people like me, plenty of death for the Victorians. It was normal to have a tragedy, one was not complete without it. But this was the early two thousands, I'd missed the Neo-Victorian by a couple of decades. And I was too well-built for life and had too many friends.

So part of the fantasy was that bit, rewinding, adjusting. The rest was: in our beautiful house my young parents and I lived together none of us knowing how to cook, eating toast for every meal and playing computer games together. I didn't have to extract myself from this dream when I turned eighteen. When my grandmother said I should leave home and then croaked in the back garden in the middle of throwing a box of my things into a fire – don't get sentimental, she had said, as I slammed my door. When I was eighteen my mother was only a year older than me, and I could have kept on imagining myself as small, and theirs, and loved, but I did stop, because that's what I did. If you are trapped in a crashed car you pull yourself out. There is no other thing that occurs to you.

Contained

Reviving hot drinks in the kitchen. I felt light; I watched the night sit in the garden and heard Daniel's voice. Mrs Boobs came to me, tail a question mark. I was tired – good. I didn't want anything. We played about with the copy and the original. Daniel laughed at them both like they were the same thing.

'You know what's worse than this?' I said, raising up the copy. 'This,' I said, raising up the original. 'The wifi spying on us, listening to everything. It's a lumpen device of late capitalism.' Daniel looked puzzled, I think because it probably seemed like I was angry, all of a sudden. I wasn't, I wasn't. I think he got it when I got up, rushed for what I needed, took him outside and set the thing down and poured vodka on it and then lit that piece of shit up.

'Yeah, life is weird,' I said, standing over it, breathing in the acrid justified smoke. 'I think I'll be thinking about your copier, you know, for a while – trying to get my head around it, before I can have an opinion. I normally know right away, if something's right or wrong.'

The device fizzled, made sounds, I leaned in, heard, just then, I swear, a piece of Daniel speaking, or was it Órla – *Tell me how he was* – it said. I knew it was us, I knew it hadn't been said yet. I leaned in.

'Do you hear that?' I asked.

'You have a strong moral compass?' Daniel asked.

I looked at him. Silence. The air in the little garden jolted me awake. Looked at him. He didn't look my way. The good smoke of our breaths met in the air.

'Let's get back inside,' I said.

We had to peel off our clothes – such a stink on them. We threw them into the washer. And then I stood there and then something in us realised, right then. All of a sudden, I thought – Daniel wants me too. See, all this time I hadn't known. Not true, liar, said a voice in the back of my mind – you want him, you want to hold onto him – my heart started drumming. And all that we did was stand there a little while in the cold of the kitchen like we had each forgotten our lines. It's all right, I thought – but I wanted, as well as to feel his skin against mine, to put my head on his shoulder and cry, just sob. I hesitated. Then said I was off to the shower.

Thought Silencer

I turned the water on full blast and the heat up to almost unbearable levels and punched my face against the stream and muttered, fuck fuck fuck, under my breath. Everything that had happened and not came back to me that night in waves. I doubled over. Desire – longing – hail – the long muffled room – the uncanny passing figure. I dunked my head and said haaahh and put it back into the water and waited for the pressure and the heat to unknot my thoughts, but even after coming out and drying myself I was still full of a miserable energy. Another run, I needed out – I put on a lightweight fleece over my running gear and headed for the door.

Out on the flat foot down thudding over tarmac road and the black frigid night for hours. I didn't listen to music – I listened to the rubbish of my brain shift about until my muscles below burned so much I outran thought, and I kept running. And I ran to keep from— I ran into cold and hedges and nothingness. The lone buses with the anti-junkie lighting beaming blue and cold. I puffed and ran, dodging bins – cars – some early-arriving tourists wheeling their bags. Drunks clustered on one of the bridges – I always forget street names here, they don't seem to matter against the age of them – raising their cans at me as I fled past. I turned hard right and let my legs go long and unkinked on the downward stretch of the centre. I passed a woman out late walking her dog – startled her with my heavy panting, but was gone too quickly to apologise, if I even could have spoken.

I got so thirsty I could think of nothing else but dropping down – falling and staying there. I licked salt off my arm, I listened to my pounding exhalation – I stopped and bought water, drank it messily, ran on. I ran towards the dull shape of a hill – heading for the path up it – but got confused in the dark and wound up running along towards the cliffs. Didn't care. Couldn't care. Kept running. At a turn in the path I heaved and threw up. I couldn't remember what I had for dinner – If I'd had dinner. I shouted once and ran on. At the top of the path I saw the plateau of the cliff going out in front of me and the lights of the city below like a city below a transparent sea. Not like the cliff. Not like here, where the sea is uninhabited, I think, but softer if I had dived in. If I do. If I stayed for dawn there, then, I'd have been late for work – I just lay down for a while feeling my chest exploding and the wires of my muscles burn and overhead I could see the woollen sky come down closer and closer like it wanted to get a look at this flea – this ant – in the wet grass. I felt like my heart was going to crush itself. I closed my eyes and gasped in and out. Time went black and I didn't know anything.

When I came to myself I felt both better and worse – worn out but rejuvenated – real and unreal. I crawled to the edge of the cliff and looked out, squinting. Where was I in all the world? I had no thoughts, I wasn't myself. As earlier with Daniel, when I'd worried I would accidentally forget myself – forget all my established sexuality and my desires up until this point in life and try to kiss him, I was struck by worry – that I didn't know myself – that I had no reason to be here and then some close and dangerous reason would present itself to me. The most obvious being that I'd run up here in the night to try to throw myself off the crags. I crawled over a little further, feeling the folded edges of the bare rocks jutting out. If I kept wriggling forward, this desire would shake hands with gravity and fulfil itself swiftly on the same path far below on which I'd run earlier. I gasped – a noise like shock and a laugh – I didn't want to die, I hadn't thought to do it. I hadn't thought I wanted anything, just to run. I wanted to be held.

My eye still felt sore and I rubbed it – rubbing more dirt into both of them in the process. I winced and said, 'For fuck's sake Tommy,' and pulled back from the edge and rubbed and rubbed away. Eventually I sat back and thought at last.

'I didn't come here to do anything but run,' I said. 'Anything else is just coincidence.'

I don't know if I'd thought how easy it is to make mistakes just because you stop thinking and let your body go where it wants. That was astounding to me. I'd always thought my body was a pretty reliable self-attainment machine. And it did do then what it was meant to – my eyes cleared themselves, my heart wasn't about to pop. I sat on the cliff, weak but strong, got up slowly and walked down again. In the grass at the foot of the hill there was a huge puddle spread out, with the orange glow of the sky reflected in it. I came to it. I stood over it and saw my body in the dimness. The rest of the city pulled back – there was only grass and sky and myself.

'Come closer, here,' it said.

I was standing right over it. No thoughts. Slowly I lowered myself and tied my shoelaces. No thinking. I couldn't. I was mostly blankness, dehydrated, a dip in blood sugar, a couple of nights of no sleep – this is how close we are to becoming animal ghosts of ourselves. I leaned over the puddle and looked at the face in it. It was not my face, not my body. I got up quickly, making no noise and walked on. Hands on the back of my head. Home to bed. It must have taken me forty minutes to get back, but turn me upside down and shake me out, you won't find where those forty minutes have gone.

The End of Being Tired

There's a room. It's where everyone loves you, all your mates are there. You're gathered round in some low-lit, cosy place. There's no sound at all except a high wind of a storm. You can see people laughing and smiling, you can feel them very close to you. It's warm and it's never ending. You don't have to worry about how little sleep you've had. Money isn't even a thing. No one is going to turf you out. You're not going to fail to do something right. You're perfect, you've always been perfect. You touch your forearm against another guy's when you raise your pint and it's fine. No one flinches at the touch of you. Your grandmother is resting in a room upstairs. She doesn't see what you do but she's alive and she's well. She just doesn't feel like getting out of the bed. Two strangers, younger than you, beautiful, work behind the bar. One is heavily pregnant. They smile fondly over at you. There's a vase of bluebells on every table, by each twinkling tealight. The room is totally silent. Everyone is speaking but there's no need for sound. You catch your own eye in the reflection in the mirror above the fire. You're loved. You're safe. You will never feel bad about how little you are again.

Habitual

I entered this new cycle reluctantly, but soon gave in to its plans for me: a few snatched hours of sleep – then work in the day time; Órla's during the evening – or out with her, or at the gym; then as little time as possible at home until it was late enough that I wanted to run. I did want to, I think. It was a need. Just like the changes to my diet. Where I normally ate three regular meals and drank as many coffees as work sociability required, now I ate something sugary for breakfast – some gross chocolate bar. At lunch I tugged the sliced meat out of sandwiches. I had to eat this in private, so no one saw – in the stalls at work, cramming rolled up ham into my gob and flushing the bread. You can manage any pattern your body needs to fall into, even if it seems a little weird – you can make it work for you. It can be done, it just takes a bit of fixing. That's what I told myself. Do it carefully, know it'll probably right itself in a few weeks. I was losing weight, I was feeling like my internal organs were slowly and without pain dissolving into a gel inside my skin, while my bones were like rubberised pipes. At the same time I was in better shape than ever. I could run and run. Badr stopped me one afterwork-sesh in the gym. 'Haven't seen you in a while, Joe. Seen you less than before you moved in, what's going on?'

I just laughed and told him 'It's the work, man.'

He looked serious, 'Ah, it's that. Well, keep it up. Don't let them find your weak spot!' he said, and I knew that he thought it was want I wanted to hear, and I almost started crying.

'No chance of that,' I said and laughed, and he slapped me on the shoulder, gently, so as not to knock the dumbbells to the floor.

Right as Badr was going I saw that man again – the one from the puddle, the one who had passed me in the hall. In old cartoons, you could always tell what object a character was going to lift up, a book or an apple or whatever it was – these were distinctive because of the layering of transparencies, which gave them a colour scheme that was a little brighter, that you came to recognise as though it was more ready and willing to be lifted. I saw him with that kind of feeling, though by then I was used to him. Almost. He was part of my days and slightly above it all. His face below the dirty hair had a foxy look, what I could see of it, as he kept it turned away when I – made cocky by its constantly appearing – looked up and around for it. I began to think 'that coy lad', when I saw him. Which made it easier – made me smirk. At the end of long runs, towards the dawn, I would see him. He peered at me, or passed by in a flicker – I was sure it was him – through absurd apertures like puddles, cracks in fences, reflections in the black screen of my mobile or work computer. He was there and it was like he wanted to be seen even as he obscured himself – he wanted to speak, but he was reluctant.

Plans Moving Forward

At that point, within my new cycle, I felt less and less of a need to speak – at work or any other place. I wasn't sulky or grim, just quiet. When you don't need to speak you shouldn't. When you don't need to eat or sleep, same – like I said, you can deal, your body finds out a way. You should always wash though, out of consideration for others.

I took the diary around with me more often, as a kind of guide. I had noticed that entries after the murder were longer; Lennoxlove wrote about a woman who was a rider in a local hunt. He didn't describe what she looked like, only that she was 'spirited, clever, compassionate, well-educated, the best of all in all disciplines they put a hand to' and 'unwed by the terms of local conditions, but nevertheless unable to be mine.' He referred to this woman as F. I got stuck on this section, puzzling. It was, after a third look, written a little differently, less thick with waving corn and the sound of feet on gravel than earlier parts, more on abstract feelings, but with urgency. More like the writer was running out of time, or running off on an obsession that did not allow them to look elsewhere. I didn't like to stay at the Minto house to read it, because Daniel, still obsessed himself with finding it, might drop in at any moment and ask if I had seen the book, which would be embarrassing so I took it out to a coffee shop with me at lunchtime or after work. I found a place that stayed open later than anywhere, a real greasy-spoon place near a theatre, that could do me a mug of tea for cheap and a plate of just a bit of sandwich meat chicken or ham if I wanted it served up without any judgement but a tired friendly smile. I drank tea, ate meat and read the diary through, one entry at a time, sometimes coming before work too, gnawing on the diary like it was my main meal.

Through it all, Órla was cool. She didn't ask me where I'd been, except once when she was staying over and I'd gone out for the night and gone off to work without answering any of her texts. We sorted that out. Even though I was a bit screwed up over the Daniel situation, I knew that I shouldn't rush through anything – I needed to sort my head out, the time would come when it came, that sort of thing. Most of all I didn't want her to feel any discomfort or discover my thoughts, so I was better after that. I got her flowers and chocolates. I asked her about her day and listened to the answer as much as I could. I began blinking and seeing black spots, which made it difficult to keep a straight face. I feigned a lot of extra work – stress from that could really cause all that had happened to me – so she accepted it like anyone would. She started asking if I was looking for another career. I told her I was built for media PR, that even if I didn't like this job, I was going to start my own company one day soon and really learn to thrive. I just had to push myself a bit here. All nonsense. Don't get down the road of lies next time, I told myself. It only makes it harder. Because of my lies I had to agree to go to the party at Mark's place – Daniel knew Mark from childhood and it would be a 'great networking opportunity', Órla said. She would have been right, too. And I liked Mark – guiltily liked, knowing what I did, I was almost his employee, his gumshoe – and I liked old Mr MacAshfall, weird as he was.

Gifted

I finished reading the diary for the fourth time – there's no point not savouring things, especially if you're trying to understand them – in the greasy spoon café. I closed the back cover and it gave a satisfying creak. I finished strong, with the last sip of my tea, which wasn't too cold either. But as soon as I'd done that, put the book down firmly on the table, I felt something slap me on the side of my head. I looked around – I looked down. There was a narrow, wrinkled leather thing at my feet. I picked it up – it was a shoe, but not like any kind of shoe I'd ever seen. It looked almost like a ballet shoe, but black and with a thicker sole. I thought it must be handmade for a man from the brogue-like design. For a man with smaller than average feet. Someone had thrown an antique shoe at me. I ran my hands over it – it was clean, and the leather wasn't old. I looked around again, no likely culprits. Just the shoe. I wish I could hand it to you, that shoe, so that you could hold it in your hand, feel that it existed. I sighed, put it in my pocket, paid up and left.

In the course of the next six days I received, from the anonymous thrower: a second shoe; a pair of balled woollen socks; a long pair of patched brown breeches; a worn but clean white shirt and a malt-coloured tweedish jacket with a sagging collar. All came to me in various public places – all with no evident person behind their delivery – unwitnessed by anyone else. On the seventh day, a small knife with a bone hilt slid itself across the table of the café at me. I had returned to this particular spot in the hope of gaining more things. I felt wired, jolted awake. At the same time I didn't feel like I should show the clothing to anyone I knew or mention them at all in any kind of context, even hypothetical. Did I think they didn't exist? Did I know I was waiting for the whole set before I would act? Well, here it all was, with the final piece being the knife – I rubbed the grain of the bone handle with my finger and thumb while across the room, the same woman I always paid the bill to plunged a metal basket of battered fish into hot oil. I knew instinctively this was the last thing I would get. The knife blade was silver – I could tell from the fact it had tarnished. And I wondered about the significance of a silver knife, and I wondered if I was supposed to fend something off with it – or if none of this was real, if I could fend off madness with it. An imaginary knife is not nothing, I thought, putting it on the skin of my finger, poking it in and giving it a flick – gave me a small pain I sucked on – a real enough taste of my own blood against my tongue. Then I panicked a bit, thinking it was probably a filthy knife, come from I didn't know where. I went and washed my hands. When I came back to my seat, the bill was in a little dish with three hard white mints, sitting right beside the blade of the knife. Nothing was settled, though, I thought, looking at my finger, a divot out of the flesh.

Alight Here

It was dark when I drove by the station and dark as I doubled back to it, several hours later. I had been driving around for hours this time and in some ways there was nothing else to do with these hours – dark was a larger than ever part of my day and my senses were too – not in a bad way, necessarily. Just life – changing. The question of what to do with the clothing, real or unreal, remained with me. My runs in response, or simply due to a new cycle, were being replaced with driving around at night, hours spent pushing up into the countryside, northwards each time. The clothes sat in my kit-bag on the passenger seat. If I had wanted to dress up, I couldn't have done. Whoever had owned them, they were about half my build, with tiny feet. They stayed with me. I took them where I felt I had to go. Prowling up the A9, crossing deep into inky mountainous places that must look good in the daytime – I recognised some of the names and looked others up after – but for me in those hours were only a curve of the road lit up, the occasional skirting of tiny roadkill or, once, a deer.

The station had a kind of bunkhouse near it, but I couldn't bear the thought of going inside and being turned away from a room – there was bound to be none for me, in such a small place. So I parked and I went walking into the nothing that is the damp autumnal Scottish countryside – hearing my shoes skiff on the rough surface of the road where the lights of cars circled the hill roads but never seemed to reach me. I am being dramatic; I wasn't there for long. Just long enough to look at the sky where the stars

265

were out and the high wind was under the stars and I could hear a river, rushing, down on the other side of the station line. Or perhaps I am conflating two moments, one where I stopped at a train station with a bunkhouse, another where I stopped in a passing place and went to a river. The darkness made both seem to happen in the same place at the same time. Dreamily I stepped off the road into the slippery, sheep-eaten grass and went downwards. Did I cross tracks? I might have had to scale a fence, I don't remember. I had my bag slipped over my shoulders.

Seen

I meant to go to the river and look at it, but when I got there – whichever dark river it was driving itself loudly through this empty country – I thought perhaps I was coming there for some kind of assignation. And pretty swiftly I saw a path on the other side of the river that seemed likely for me. It was a hiking trail. I crossed the river – it was not deep for all that noise. It bit icily into my shoes and made my life miserable, but was no risk. There on the path – ahead – was the figure. I'd never seen him looking like this. He was almost naked, his body glowed in the little light from the moon. I walked up to him – he didn't disappear. He looked at me shivering. He was small.

'Here, you must be freezing,' I said, and I unzipped my coat and threw it around him. He looked up. I still couldn't see his face clearly. The cloud came over the moon and it was hard to make him out. But I knew it was not a lie; I knew he was really there, and that we had been meant to meet. It was an inevitability that felt like a hand in a hand.

'Come with me, back to my car,' I said.

He said nothing. He might not have been there I thought, in a moment of panic. But I could see his outline, I could hear him breathing. His hair unmoving in the wind, though it was pretty long and wild.

'You've came,' he said. 'I'm glad.' He sounded faint. I got one arm over my own and dragged him back to my car, where he stood faint and stupid after I opened the door awkwardly guiding him into the back seat, one hand gripping his arm – wiry thin – the other pushing his head down, crushing his messy hair. Oily residue – I wiped that hand on the back of my jeans hoping it wouldn't leave a mark. I turned on the engine and fired up the heat. In the overhead light, small as a candle, I saw him clearly, though he kept turning away, all skittish. I sat silently waiting. I coughed. He finally faced me, in the mirror anyway. His resemblance to Daniel was uncanny. I almost cried out his name. But I only stared. Slowly his face became distinctive – his own – as his mannerisms shifted it. A certain lowering of the chin. His eyes softer and more intent at once, like someone after a day of destructive bad news who hasn't slept since, who has understood his situation is changed forever and accepted it, but never let his body recover. It's not so hard to recognise, when you see it. He, under my questioning stare, looked around himself with a smile on his face – bemused, polite, pleased, I thought, but not wanting to seem so.

'You've some things of mine,' he said, almost so quietly I had to process the words before I understood them.

I unzipped the bag and pulled out handfuls of the clothes, 'This?'

He nodded and took them. He removed my coat, covering himself a little for privacy.

'Why did you throw your stuff at me? That was you, wasn't it?'

'I've been getting nearer you,' he said, 'sir. It took a long time to get so close as to be – in my own flesh again, or something like my own, I don't know whether it is or not.'

I stopped, and thought.

'How did you get nearer?' I asked.

He nodded his head at the bag. I pulled out the book.

'You're James?' I asked

'One James of many, yes I am,' he answered. 'And so are you in your way. The better side of any James.'

'I'm not sure I'm really getting you.' I said. Now I was warm – I had kicked off my shoes and torn off my socks and stuck my feet on the dashboard, nearest the heat – I thought I was getting sleepy. This was more and more a dream. My eyes were flickering over. I had seen his face in a painting, or I had seen it through an open window while passing. I didn't remember who it belonged to.

'Do you dream of his deeds? Your hand on the knife holding his neck and all?' he was saying. Soothing voice, sweet voice. I woke up at a knock on my window.

'Are you all right?' said a woman standing there, in weak white daylight. She had a parka on; a torch in her hand. She looked alarmed. My bare feet were still up on the dashboard. I wound down the window. She was a policewoman.

'You can die of hypothermia you know. With wet hair too, goodness me.'

'Yes, fine, I'll be off,' I said, wiping my face. 'Sorry to have scared you, just pulled over for some rest and fell asleep.'

Fed

I came home – evening again, like I had been just out at work, hadn't been gone the whole day. Órla was there waiting with Daniel. I waved at them. All I wanted was to crash into my bed, to not have to think any longer. But they were there, wanted to talk. I sat down at the kitchen table – the book was on it. Had I taken it in with me or had it always been there?

'Hi guys,' I said. Then, 'I'm off to bed I think. Wow, long day. Lots going on at the office. We've got this big – big client – project in. Breathing down our necks. All the time.'

'Tom, do you remember what happened last night?' Órla said.

'Yeah, of course I do!' I said, 'I had some trouble sleeping, and you woke up and got out of bed. And you got Daniel.'

As soon as the words were out, I knew they were true. But I also knew that my drive into the mountains was true – that I had met someone who had Daniel's face, who I'd given the clothes I'd found – back – because they were his clothes. My head started to itch. The skull behind the forehead. I couldn't dig down to it – I had to work hard to keep a calm look on my face. Some things are true and not true at once and it's just sorting out what point in time they are true and actually happened, what day of the week you had what for dinner, for example. Or if something is yet to happen, or will happen in a different form. We can calculate trends, you know. We can foresee any number of possible outcomes.

'Do you want some coffee?' said Daniel, 'I'm just putting the kettle on. Having a fry-up, too.'

There's a feeling children get when they know their carers are hiding something or lying, but also know that they are lying out of kindness, and so decide not to press or uncover the lie – helpless white grubs on the underside of rocks, squirming – but can't quite work out why they don't – why they go along with it, like a game – like a game is better than not having a game, I suppose. It happens loads in adult relationships because we want to be both carer and child to each other. Or I should say: we want to move our pieces around and have them accepted by the people we are playing for.

'Yes, please,' I said. I pulled back from the table – loud scraping chair legs, just horrid – to look at the soles of my shoes. I was wearing shoes, but they were clean. It was damp, though, I remembered. Any muck might have washed off in the river. I wondered where my bag was – not here – but Órla was talking to me, so I didn't get up.

'Yes, I'm fine, did you get back to sleep?' I was saying. There was hot food in front of me and I ate it like a beast. Like a man. Bacon and eggs and fried toast and mushrooms – even though I hate mushrooms, I always eat them when they are put in front of me, flinching but firm with myself – and beans, soupy cheap tinned beans. This was Daniel's food. He couldn't afford to get the good stuff on his salary. I think it also did not occur to him to buy himself nice food.

'I'll pay you back for this,' I said.

'Oh, don't worry about it. You can make dinner some time,' he said.

Then he and Órla were gone, and I was sitting in an empty room. The dishes looked like they had been washed.

Bedding

I showered and staggered into bed; into the bed where I had – had
I slept there? – I couldn't remember. I was ruined with tiredness.
I pulled covers over me – a small cry, a small, shifting weight:
the cat.

'Are you looking out for me?' I asked her. 'Do you know if
I went? Did you know I'd gone?' I had my eyes closed. She settled
and began kneading on my chest. 'Who was here, while I was
away?' I said, or I thought. I imagined Daniel and Órla, lying
together all pale, like a long-married couple waiting for death –
I thought that was the best thing, a miracle, to hold together that
long – I saw them doing it – I saw their whole lives up until they
were old, spent there in bed, still as glass. And at that I dropped
into the pit that's in all of us, and I waited for some other part of
me to wake me up.

In Bitterhall

I began to have all these dreams. I don't remember if they were one after another or over the course of a few days. Or before the clothes, for that matter. They seemed long, like films. Like BBC mini-series of existence. I remember it only now. I can see out the window the sea is disappearing. No, you're right. The ocean. The ocean is disappearing, and I'm still, somehow, alive.

James Lennoxlove is writing at his desk. A servant comes in; not a servant for the house; he has dirty boots and an uncompromising look. He says, 'Come out, master, the light's dancing in the sky, strangely. Will you not come?' And Lennoxlove, startled, says yes he will. And they stand together in the field between the stables and the ghillie's house. 'Dear James,' says James, 'thank you for telling me about this.' And the second man is so glad he sighs. And James is both me, and you. There's a look of the green and red northern lights running over our clothes. It's like if you set fire to wire wool – ever done that? It burns in a rolling way, in an epic way, though small. James must go back inside; James must go to the stables. I don't know these men. I am both of them, in their sweat-stiffened clothes.

Flatmates

When I woke it was dark again and I began crying; not that I meant to, not that my heart was broken or my mind or anything – just some switch got flipped between unconscious and conscious and the tears bubbled up wet and quick and without any reason. Night tears going down my fingers, going into the corners of my mouth. Had I dreamed of anything – had I gone anywhere again? But I was wearing only the boxers I had gone to sleep in. I pulled on my pyjamas and shoes and walked out of my room, expecting – chaos. Expecting overturned chairs. I had the realisation, slowly, that someone was at home where I was at home as nowhere else – in my own body. This new person; do you get me? Am I making sense? You could say I was pushed aside from myself in that home, and that anything might happen. You could say anything. You, you, a plurality of others. I stood between the table and the doorway of the kitchen and I touched my face and a sob came out. The shock of that led me to start crying again. Great abandoned sobs and tears going through my fingers. But I wasn't sad – I wasn't hurt. I've never really cried, not at anything. My grandmother would get upset with me for not crying. But I never could, until I cried like something was crying through me and I followed the instruction then, of my body, or whatever else it was, as I would with any kind of arduous process – knowing it would be over soonish, and by the sounds of it no one was in the house.

Except Minto.

Minto was sitting on the black sofa in the living room. I eyed him, he clocked me.

'Hallo again my dears,' he said, and ran his fingers through his white hair. I almost turned around to see the person he was also addressing – but again, no one, but not and entirely no one. I thought about laughing and wiped my eyes – sat on another chair. The television was on with no sound, set to a documentary about the deep sea. Small frilled things frisked across blackness. Minto, for his part, was dressed in a summery-looking suit with a huge camel-coloured coat over the top of it, and at least three scarves, all of different red shades. He had fingerless gloves on – I marvelled at those. The last time I'd seen fingerless gloves was in a Dickens adaptation. He had painted his nails matte white, perhaps with correction fluid. I realised it was pretty obvious that I had been crying. My face felt red and raw from my outburst earlier and worse, Minto may have heard it, the sobs I mean. Even someone as strangely removed as he is had noticed. But Minto was only looking at the television – perhaps he had seen but perhaps also he had never paid much attention to anything.

'They're getting worried about you, you know,' he said.

An Interesting Discussion

At first neither of us said anything else. A large van rumbled, beeping down the street and in its wake, seagulls crying. A beautiful smell filled the air – some kind of cologne he was wearing. It smelled like the woods in summertime, green and fresh. I'd assumed he would smell musty, like the old shut-in he was. The cologne made me more curious. If he was able to put on cologne maybe he was able to make other kinds of choices about his life. Maybe he was not the old kook I thought.

'You mentioned last time that you saw someone else with me,' I said.

He looked up and smiled kindly. 'Yes, this young man here,' he said in a reedy voice, gesturing at the space beside me where a small table held a lamp.

'Well, the thing is,' I said, 'I'm struggling to picture him. Bad eyes, you know. Could you tell me what he looks like?'

'Come, don't condescend. But I'd be glad to, be glad to. If there is honesty in your heart! He's quite short, yes, with dark hair that's very thick. He looks awfully familiar – and he's dressed for a party. I mean, a costume party.'

'A costume party?'

'Nineteenth century servant clothing, with breeks and shirt. Some kind of pastoral theme. I'd say he's just about to put on a mask, and mingle with his betters.'

He paused as the television showed a coral reef, darting yellow fish.

'Oh, you know who he looks like? Our other houseguest.'

'Daniel?'

'Is that his name? I can't keep track you know. They come and go, ebb and flow. Like tidal creatures. I love them all, even the naughty ones who don't pay their bills and do a flit into the night. There's always some reason for that,' he said, looking at the space to my left. 'We should never judge someone's actions too severely, if it does no real harm to anybody.'

'Minto,' I asked, 'I hope you don't mind if I call you Minto?'

He folded his hands and nodded, smiling again. 'Nobody calls me anything else these days.'

'How,' I asked, 'how can I make this other guest more comfortable? It's just – he's always with me, I think. But I don't really know what he wants.'

'Och, I think he should tell you himself what he wants,' Minto said.

'I'm so tired,' I said to myself.

'Then that's a sign you should be resting more than you are,' he replied. 'You're wasting your good looks, and it's a national tragedy.'

Presentation

When I didn't say anything, he went on. 'Now, the thing about your guest is, he's the sort who got me into trouble back in my younger days. Just after my wife – you know, at the university, in the hall when I took tours, I was a fair public speaker then and the stories amused until, well – admin changes, a brisk new air comes in and the faculty start to talk – I made too many of the others alarmed, and they needn't have been. I told them who and what, the old desks and the furled beasts sitting on them, the room with the cold always in it was from the ladies, you see – but nobody wanted to be told that. I had to get the train up every day for the commute, and the bus. And trains are full of that sort. Buses less so – but you see them, sometimes, from the windows – standing mournfully in the fields, resting on old ploughs, pipe smoke, staring at me as I rushed past, since they always seem to sense it – too long without the human kindnesses, I think . . .' He trailed off. 'I used to scream and shout and get all red in the face. I used to write to people, 'What's this all about, please help me, I will kill myself if I can't find the solution.' Well, that all falls away, eventually. Madness, they said. Lots of small pills and time on the West Sands walking Bonxie. By the time I'd settled in for the hard weather and grown to like it, you know, I would even wish I could have made a decent career out of it, become an expert, but there's no legitimacy in that area of study. I've read an inordinate number of books and I can tell you, there are too many cranks. Their own worst enemies, some folk. Too little rigour of testing and analysis. I was always for hard science where it needed to be, with a coat of softness for palatability, not the other way around . . .'

He trailed off again. In the silence I got up and made us tea. He held the mug in his red hands, wincing a little.

'It's not for me to go and change an entire discipline, or create some kind of hybrid new one. I see that now. And early retirement, and tea on the train up there for the last time, I spilled all over my nice white shirt. Piteous looks at my final address to students – ah well, all behind me now. You see I have no bitterness, not at all. I just need to be quieter, more than I am, cautious towards anyone who might not understand. That's why there are always ones like you in the house, sort of a reassurance. Very kind of Badr to go and get you for me. Ah, but I'm off on a tangent now. I go on a bit. Sorry. Not so used to talking and it all comes out in a dramatic monologue. What did you ask me again?

'About the other one.'

'Mm,' he said. 'He wants to tell you something terribly important. But he looks like the kind of man who struggled to speak all his days. I had lots of students like that. If only there was such a thing as patience in this day and age. But while we have made many advances, that has become quite old fashioned.'

He sipped his tea. 'It doesn't tell you a thing about his character, mind you, the shyness. Did I ever tell you about the time I threw a desk out the window? Only a small one. It killed a man walking below in the street.'

Finding

I went to my room and got ready to go out. I was going to take the diary to Mark, I fully intended it. But first I needed to go somewhere where no one else was and clear my brain and work out – the right thing to say. The thing that would not make Mark believe I was insane – it could get back to Cloudberry, easily. It could do any number of things to harm my career. I would not like to find myself turning into a Minto before the age of thirty.

I would ask him about his cologne another time. It was really very nice.

Tears in my eyes again as I put fresh gym gear in the bag. Why? I yelled out a little noise of frustration as I packed. Mrs Boobs looked up from me from the bed with eyes so wide I apologised.

I walked out the house and headed for my car. I needed rolling fields, oak trees and little rush-lined ponds. I needed acreages of black and white cows and honey-coloured stone. I needed peace and truth and order. All of this was a little hard to get in this far part of the north and in this season of dying. I drove out anyway, heading in the direction of Ayrshire, though I'd never been – I dimly knew there were milk cows there, close enough – sixty on the country roads, nothing coming in the opposite lane, a roundabout by a woodside development, and blinking, there were fields, laid out stripped to stubble as they were. Somewhere about an hour south of Edinburgh I spotted a small river with trees along it and feeling tired decided it would be fine. I parked up at the side of the road.

He would come, I was sure. Any part where there were fewer people, in a landscape he felt comfortable in. I called him only 'him' in my mind. So far he had been James, but he was also Daniel, or Daniel-like, or ghost, or a singular hallucination from sleep deprivation, somehow shared with Minto, or indulged in by him – he had known the figure was there before I had, hadn't he? I thought – he made me think of him, the bastard. And now I was stuck with him. But I didn't have to be. You just have to face these things. I had the diary in my hand and I was walking in a field down to the river, just as I had the day before – or was it longer – walked down to the river. Where that first river had been shallow and broad, dark under a deep infinite dark, and biting cold, this river was grey-green, deep and narrow, fringed with leaves and grasses, those tall plants that have an umbrella of white flowers in summer had left their skeletons to wave in the damp breeze. I saw a brown shelf of mushroom on the skinny stump of a tree. I saw crows walking in the fields beyond the river. Out of a patchy blue sky sparks of snow were falling.

I got to the riverbank and I stood close to the edge. It was too wet for sitting. I waited and thought I should look at my phone, but then, that looking at my phone might make me seem distracted and uninterested. I wondered what rituals were needed to summon a person perhaps caused by – causing – a breakdown in the normal order of my life. I thought about how to punch him; I had the feeling if I tried he would stop being incorporeal. I pictured giving a black eye to a ghost. I'm not ashamed to say it now. I'm hungry – wait.

Okay.

I opened the book. Some flap on the edge of it was loose and I worried it with my fingernails. Stopped because it was an old book, and didn't need my help getting more worn. Then – I heard it—

James, came the whisper, so quiet – I had dreamed it. I had mistaken the wind for it. I did not move; the wind in channels ran around me.

There was a bang, a metallic dunt, and I dropped the book.

Someone had hit my car. I could see them out of theirs, looking around. I ducked. The book – the diary – it was in the water, sinking. I grabbed it, nearly falling. My arm covered in slimy water, my fingers feeling of nothing, my heart contracting to a blip. But I had it – I pulled it out.

The book was not totally soaked. I looked around one last time, and there was nothing, no second car, not even crows near me. Nothing wanted me except to torment me.

Nothing made sense. I was feeling faint with the cold and the shock. I was sweating and swearing – I clambered back to the car, slipping on the wet grass, and my car had a smack in the rear bumper, but no terrible damage – lights all present – I shuddered and got back in, and drove home, slowly, with the sense that the world was full of figures watching me from the countryside, disinterested, leaning on farming equipment or staring out from the windows of the old cottage rows. I don't know if I saw them or if Minto saw them through me or if I had fallen asleep at the wheel and dreamed my way through them, the overlap of dreams and actual progress home. I was fierce though, and my body digested the shock. By the time I came home and washed my hands and dried the book in the oven and sat with it again at the kitchen table, no one could have told whether I'd moved all day or not, or even guessed that I'd almost lost it – the diary – not so many hours ago.

Katabasis

I could hear the city around me as Órla dragged me through it, though what I or she said to one another I couldn't say. The sky was this grimy pale gold, while, I kept thinking, the night is like two hands about to snap – closed to crush us between them – any minute now. I had trouble swallowing, I had a pressure behind my eyes and it felt like I had a sinus infection. Now, thinking, I suppose I was panicking, a little. I had the diary in the pocket closest to my heart, like a Romantic. I kept raising my hand to touch my pocket unthinkingly until I made myself stop. Just because I had almost lost the book didn't mean I would again.

'It's sunset,' I was saying, but Órla wasn't listening. We were on the long downward slope heading towards the MacAshfall place. I forget who decided we should walk there, however long it took, but it was good exercise – I couldn't remember the last time I'd gone to the gym perhaps Monday? What day was that? Or this? It's not like an inner ear thing, to know the schedule, it's okay to lose track sometimes. I had already decided it didn't matter to know my place in the world as much as to convince others I did, while I busied myself with this other more important work. What was the important work? I was so determined then – going so fast. Towards some goal. Man in the river. Pages with the gleam of a knife. My whole life up until that point – but if I kept going, I didn't have to be afraid.

I almost whacked an old woman in the face with my shoulder, my suit tails whipping behind me. We were late by then, Órla said.

But the night would be good, I thought. The finality of a phase approaching. Very soon I would be handing the diary over to Mark and telling him what I had found, which was that – what? Ghostly figures. The silhouette of someone against the sun. I knew almost nothing, at that point. I felt buoyed too, seeing Órla energised like this to take me to the house where I could unburden myself of this thing, share, with the one person who might understand, the story of all that I'd found and got carried away into. To make it stop, if it could be. It meant perhaps our cycles – I mean Órla's and mine – were aligned and would continue longer. I felt like I could do with her, like a stabilising wheel.

'Where on earth did you disappear off to?' she said, walking ahead of me, backwards. 'Are we talking about this?' Sharp like a bird crying. I would try to listen, I thought, indulgently.

'I'm sorry about this, Órla,' I said. 'I had to go and clear my head. I hadn't slept well.'

'I mean, I get that – it's just, you seem a little – '

'Yeah, I've not been sleeping – I've been having the weirdest dreams. And you went off somewhere and I – I decided not to just sit and feel sorry for myself. I went out with some friends and lost track of time. I slept on a sofa. A leather sofa,' I smiled, I rubbed my lips, which were dry. 'I felt rubbish when I came back. I got rained on. Got myself soaked. I didn't think you'd spend the night at mine, and then when you had I felt guilty – and – '

'What else, Tom?'

'What else what?'

She would either know the truth somehow, or she wouldn't. That's what I thought. She would see I was concealing this great story behind the lies. It hadn't rained for some time. The river. The ghostly people in the fields sending up smoke lines that no one saw. The lies were all there to make a web of constructions indicating what had actually happened. If she could read in between, then I'd know. A tram gave its strange echoing ding; the greyish department store on the corner was leaking people like blood. A lowering grimy light, my beautiful clothing glowed and hers was crisp and black. We had slowed, we briefly held hands. We were young and light, we understood. We sped past a patisserie and a jeweller's. This part of town was smart and we were heading towards the future. I tapped my jacket again for the book, to feel it comforting and waiting there.

Through

As we walked the crowd thinned, and then we were on a bridge across a gap in the city where the river flowed far below. I stopped part way, unable to go any further, struck with the knowledge of an action repeated before: crossing the river. Though at this time at a great height – the bridge fell away on either side for thirty feet at least. But I was flying over it. I had to look down and see if he was there. If I was there next to him. I had stopped to look. I asked to borrow Órla's lip balm. My lips were fine but I needed to plant my feet down, there above the great hollow in the air. It struck me I didn't have a plan for what to say to Mark when I saw him again.

'What else were you feeling when you saw me?' Órla said. She must have said other things that I'd missed. 'Cos I think you were going to say, and forgive me if I'm wrong – jealous.'

'Jealous?' I tried to work out what she was referring to. I leaned over the wall, locating some trees, yellow and red as a fire, and used them to ground my vision. I rubbed my face, and the leaves on the trees seemed to crackle and disperse into the air. I gave a hard sniff.

'Conflicted then,' She must mean the morning. That morning? A morning? All the mornings stretched back along the riverbank behind us, every morning that had existed since the city was built alongside it and overhead. The setting sun glinted on three hundred years of mornings. And I had a flash of the man, who had Daniel's face and Daniel's slight, compact body – working away at the banks of a river – I thought fishing. I almost called down to him. I hoped he was warmer now. Tying some wire around his hands, threading a needle – Órla meant the morning when she and Daniel and I had breakfast together. I must have seemed cold to her.

'What were you up to with Daniel, if I should have been feeling jealous?' I said.

I was speaking mechanically. Staring out across time, across the chasm of time. Alongside a field of green corn, James Lennoxlove was rushing on his horse, with their long shadow cast over it. A haze of morning mist swirling with autumn leaves broken up to particles. The accounts to be read. He pulled sharp on the reins. Down to the river he rode instead, where we would meet. I saw from a distance the white of his eye, looking for mine.

Somehow I was still in this other present.

'I didn't say you should be feeling jealous,' Órla said, 'I'm trying to work out what you *were* feeling. Fuck me, I think you were jealous because you don't like the friendship I have with him.'

'You know he's gay, right?' I said. My head was in a dark barn with lamplights, burnished metal. I was going to be free of this, somehow, telling Mark. I didn't want to. It was soft there, softly lit. Órla opened and closed her mouth. I saw silver time in the water, running in crisscrossing lines like the fishes for Daniel's net.

'But you were feeling *lonely*, weren't you?' she was saying. 'You aren't – you seem – a bit out of it. What's been up with you, Tom? What's been going on?'

I didn't speak. The fish in the river multiplied, branched out into channels, black and silver streams of fish, and the man was waiting for them to reach him, and everything was glinting. Faster than the current. A temporary overload. I blinked, seeing fish trails in cutting water. Feeling wet pages under it, held in my hand. And then behind me, just out of my line of sight, was the man. He wasn't in the river now, he was walking with us, towards the house, and we had stopped – making him late. He had an appointment there.

'I'm worried about you,' Órla said, in a brittle voice.

'I can't tell you,' I said, pushing myself back from the wall. My light mood was gone altogether. My rushing thoughts gone cold for the time. I heard a faint buzzing – so many days and what had I really done with them? Sucked back thoughts. He wanted. I heard him want like a faint breath in my breath. Órla gently took my arm.

'What's the big secret drama, eh? You had a few nightmares? You've been really into some book?'

'What?' I rubbed my face again, my nose stung, my eyes. I couldn't focus. Tempting to say to you, I saw the sea and it was so welcoming. I saw a circle in the sea, going round and round, saying, fall into me and don't have worries any more.

'Did you notice, with that diary you've been into lately, there's something wrong with it?'

I shook my head. It was better to feign ignorance, to keep the threads separate.

MacAshfalls'

Do I decay, right now? Have I fallen already? Do you see the stars are out, there, through the gap, there's one. No, probably space junk. I want a coffee. Do you want one? The stove doesn't burn like it should. Wait. I'll keep feeding it though. Sparks come over me. Sparks enter me. I won't. I'm still here, for now.

Órla had sensed I was tired – I was tired, wasn't I? She'd stopped speaking at me – like birds singing in the end what she had told me, making no more sense – and dragged me off towards the party. I saw the long women in silver white dancing and the men their slaves dancing too. Never mind we'll talk about it later. For tonight we'll just have a good time. Words in that vein. From me, from her. We walked up and down some suburban hill streets towards what was going to happen talking little, consulting the map on my phone – I couldn't quite understand how to get there on foot without it, not knowing I'd already been set on this way a long time before I'd even realised. Maps in my mind were overlapping – empty countryside sprung up for a moment and faded like a camera light going off – then dimness. Are you still with me? I can't see you. Blinded myself from staring. At flames. At the night dark up here. We had arrived at the MacAshfalls' house. I patted the book in my pocket. I pat the book in my pocket.

The house seemed even more like a magazine spread: giant beautiful green leaves, the wooden panelling and the slant of the roof – I think even feeling so bad I made a note – at the next meeting, talk about the narrative this house would add to their business. People love this sort of space. A couple of online pieces accompanied by pictures of this would work like a charm. A warm light suffused it at that time of day. Beyond the tiredness. The people were the only corruption – out of time themselves, the interwar look, short chinned, rosy, white satin, only the cigarettes in long holders were missing, because it would be inauthentic to us, now, to be that authentic. I eyeballed a couple of Cloudberry clients as we passed by, but they didn't recognise me in my white suit and purposefulness. I was suddenly struck with the thought that we had passed from the outside into a place where a mock-up of the nineteen-thirties was ongoing in a strange kind of experimental set-up, itself taking place in the time before I was born, the nineteen-seventies – overseers in heavy-framed glasses gripping clipboards just out of sight, some head-ups in their carpeted conference room were the ones smoking constantly as they watched us through black and white monitors. I was in step with my own mission, but the overall aim was something higher than I could grasp. A question of how we behave in circumstances where our mortality hovers above us – can we feel its white wings gently brush the top of our heads? Can we feel our circuitous pointlessness?

Almost with a cry as the music of this strange set washed us further in I grabbed Órla by the hand and took her in to the dance. Blindly ongoing the dance. And white and black, and a kind of emptiness around us – we were in fact the only couple dancing. I steadied myself in dancing, and holding her warm hands. The music swirled us two specks tossed us about. But the song ended and all at once I all but dropped. I'm not good at this, I thought. I can't do this. Órla guided me to the side, and Mark – Mark was there, holding up glasses for each of us. I slopped the liquid across my lips as I drank. Fear in the depths dragged me, a weight. But I was smiling. I should have found it fine to hold that fear. I am strong.

I – with wiser options available – split myself in two. In one version, I took Mark by the shoulder and led him to a quiet spot to discuss the book, and what I might know. In another I walked off on my own and found myself drinking meeting nobody's gaze bent under the sense that all my life I had been a mistake and that I would always slam into a crossroads, knowing I was lost, because where other people have strong internal compasses I had none at all. I might have navigated by the stars but I had no stars. Daniel you could have printed stars for me, I think, out of nowhere. Then I'd know. I'd be steady. But I'm not allowed. I tried so hard not to put my head into my hands and cry.

Circling

Then he came, flickering, the notion of him, and places began not just to overlap but, like, stitch together. Someone dropped their hand to their chest and their necklace sparkled. A candelabra overhead almost guttered in a breeze I couldn't feel. Someone passed me a tray of hors d'oeuvres and I pretended not to know what to pick. The waiter said, 'Oh this one, definitely the best,' and I saw him briefly and he smiled, and he was not the waiter but he was himself the man who had insinuated his way into my life.

'Get away,' I said quietly. I don't know if he heard. I stood upright, I furtively knocked back drinks – tasting only the salt part of them or else the fumy, fragrant part, like drinking hothouse flowers and clammy stagnant air. At one point I was talking to a Cloudberry client about 3D technology turning us all into objects to be scanned and read and our originalities must be discarded in the after effect or we would perform clunkily or worse, become redundant. I must have done well, because the small crowd pressed around me was laughing. I had Órla's hand again; I led her outside – how many hours had passed. We spoke and I was nearly crying though holding back. He's here, I nearly said. Red crackle in my voice as I talked so I flitted from group to group so no one would find me out. Nothing else was under control, not even my sight was to be trusted. I saw Órla dancing with my tormenter. I saw her sit down beside him on the steps. I drank, there were always glasses rising to hand and salty, humid booze slipping past my lips.

Wander

It grew so late and no hours passed. All the while music came winding from the vinyl records, sounds so relentlessly ambiguous, upbeat and sad at once. I danced and I ate something hard with a slippery savoury paste in it. Another source of dissonance led me upstairs. I saw Mr MacAshfall bashing on a piano in a high room of the house that was not visible from any place in the street. His guests were immortal his pose seemed to say, or they'd died in their finery in garden bunkers in the first fall of the Blitz. I wondered if there was an experiment going on. I knew there wasn't, but if I pretended it made it easier than the fact that none of it seemed stable or to make sense. Still he played away, waving at me. I raised a glass back and hesitated. Then with no more greeting forthcoming I left. Why had I tolerated him or even looked for him? The real thing I was looking for was – some help, some notice – not even a guide to all this but someone to hold my hand and stop my sobs coming up like stopping a sneeze. To be understood is all I ever want. I know I don't seem the most —but if you see me and I'm there. I see you and you're real. If we don't notice each other we are both at risk of dissolving. Blipping out. It terrorises me, being seen, and existing when there are so many other better things people could be looking at.

I was in the kitchen and my palms had nail marks pressed in them from me making fists all night. I saw a window and blackness beyond. Then wooziness. My nose stung. Wasn't this an— Perfume filled the air: of woodsmoke, cut across with sex heat semen – I walked quickly dispersing it – with the smell of party sweat Chanel and spilled white wine and cold tiny pastries cluttering back to fill the void. The sound of a river flowed around me, a hand grabbed my arm, I could not feel my feet. I shook off the hand and walked away, trying not to stumble. I went upstairs two at a time, gripping the rail. Had to get away. A river in my lungs and in the woods black at night. An owl cried. Straw and horse shit stamped by hoofs into the white carpet. I passed by everything and into another century, up and down the floors. I see it, it was there, these blasting pictures that did not belong to me. You understand. I could have managed if not for them insisting on me because I wanted them to.

Sliver

I wiped my face at a sink, someone was using the bathroom and they yelped but I was out. White stumbling steps. I wiped my nose which had blood on it – my fingers had blood on them. And shocked laughter burst behind me like a flower in a hedge. I scrambled through the nearest door – white, close fitted to the wall – and closed it behind me. It was a kind of walk-in wardrobe, close and delicately fragrant with a Jo Malone type scent – my grandmother and her friends' houses – a sensor light turning on as I came in. Coats made shadows in fingers on the floor. The book – that would help – I pulled it out and in my fingers it fell open to an entry after the midway point:

> J and the hunters returned to Bitterhall about two, and went into the house for refreshments, leaving the horses to the grooms. I stayed a little while. I have always loved J's horse almost as much as my own. It is a great black stallion with a white star a white saddle. No one might normally ride him unless they were very much the master of themselves. I decided I would brush him myself and led him into the stables. They were full with hay; the hayloft overhead was flowing over, sending golden arrows of straw down upon my shoulders. I brushed them off with the horse-brush, laughing. The men removed the leather saddle, reins and snaffle, and joked about the hunger of hunters who have only caught a fox. I said we had not caught any beastie at all. All that had happened was a dog had caught a thorn in its muzzle.

I blinked and looked up at the room and there – I could see Bitterhall clearly before me. I couldn't have dreamed something in such high resolution. It stood grey-stone austere in the frail wintery Scottish fields with double wings and stables and a long winding drive through a ride of naked winter trees. There was the smoke: something burning in the courtyard where the stable hands were huddled. The room's walls were still faintly there. The room itself was both tiny and massively vast. I felt my breathing speed up, and I pressed my back to the door. But out there was only more chaos, and in here, at least, was what needed to be seen: One of the stable-hands hailed me. He was walking towards me and I was walking towards him. He had Daniel's face. And the clothes I had recovered. And he was standing right in front of me.

'James,' he said.

'I'm – I'm not James,' I said, voice high and stupid. I wasn't James. I had a small, pinched feeling I was not James to *him*.

'No. But I call you that if I want to,' said the man, 'Here and now. And why not, if it's James' diary you carry about with you. Who else could you be?'

I was in the stable. The man was standing beside me, holding a horse's saddle in his arms. He hauled it up and hung it across a half-door. Inside the stall a sturdy black horse stood, large as a house itself almost, facing the wall, tail flicking. Stink of hot horses and cold sweat. Further back from the horses a table stood with a lantern on it. Bedding in one corner, where there was a lantern, a rolled pack. I did not belong here. He belonged here. In fact, he had invited me in to his particular home – the size of a sleeping roll, the warm bodies of horses. I went over and touched the top post of the stall. It felt real: I got a splinter. All the while he watched me, even as he rubbed his hand on the leather of the saddle, smoothing it down like it was the horse itself.

'I've a splinter,' I said, holding up my hand. It throbbed –

suddenly deep in and unexpectedly raw pain. I thought, what if it gets infected, what if I fall ill, here, in this stable, and I have to go to my bed and lose a week or more, or die from it.

'Let me look at it,' he said, moving with terrible deliberation to me. He wasn't – I thought for the name – Daniel. Not Daniel. He was his own man, and not mine either. But he was, in a way. Mine. Like an extension of myself. I shook my head. He had my hand in his. It was rough and had dirt in the cracks and it was held roughly and made my hand dirty.

'Aye,' he said, 'well . . .' he bent his head over my finger. I felt him gently nibble at the place the splinter had gone in. He pulled his head back; a little piece of the wood stuck out from the teeth. He spat it out cleanly.

'You could have used your nails,' I said.

'Suppose I could've, sir,' he said, looking away. We were both ashamed. I knew his nails were trimmed too short to have been any use and that my own would have worked. He'd done it the best way he could. He held my hand still. My ears were hot. The horse stamped. I could hear muffled music, silken, playing through the wooden walls.

'Well,' I said, 'then – don't do it again,' he gently let my hand go. He turned to his work. I walked over to another stable where a mottled white and grey horse was facing outwards. I put my hand carefully on the top of its head.

'Wait,' I said, 'one moment. You were talking about the diary? This one?'

I held it out to him. He reached out but drew his hand back.

'No, you're to keep it,' he said.

'Why?' I asked. 'Why is it mine?'

'James,' he said.

'I'm not James.'

And then I was only in a wardrobe, lost in a rack of old coats.

Finally

The book was on the floor – I had panicked, caught in a confined space, drunk and too tired, and I'd dropped it. Again. At least not into water this time. I rushed and picked it up, cradling it in my hands. Some part of the back had come loose – stupid, I thought, stupid, stupid. I licked my thumb and tried to smooth it down. The corner came unstuck completely and I began peeling it from the leather, swearing at myself.

In the gap between the back sheet and the binding was a folded piece of paper. I gingerly tugged it part of the way out and saw handwriting. I knew I must look at it, knowing there was a clue in there – there must be, or I wouldn't have found it. But I couldn't – I couldn't, my heart was beating like something was going to burst. I put the book back in my pocket and burst out of the wardrobe instead, expecting to walk into the dazzling white length of the corridor. But I was in another place – a room. And in the room Órla, looking up at me with concern. There was a window ahead of me and I had a horrible sensation – raised hairs on my neck – that the window had just been vibrating as if struck. As if I'd banged it with my fist.

I folded myself up and backed onto the bed. After a while I said, 'Órla, something's happening to me.'

'I know,' she said, 'I know it is. I'm sorry.'

'I went into the place in the diary and he was there,' I said, putting head in hands not knowing if I wanted to tell her – just letting the story come out. My throat was burning like I had shouted. My words rasped; I hadn't taken a breath in too long. If I had done anything to harm her, it would be unforgiveable.

'Did I hurt you?' I asked.

'You've been hurting yourself,' Órla said. She came over to the bed and sat at the opposite end from me. I wanted her arms around me; anything. I wanted not to feel myself like a pulled tooth, flimsy and rotten. Someone came to the door, and Órla barked an order for water. I pushed my head down into the pillow.

'I want to know,' I said, 'but I'm so tired.'

I think I must have seemed drunker than I was. Órla had taken off my shoes, jacket, tie, shirt, at some point. I was warmer without them, under the covers, but looked around for the book until I had it near me, held to my chest. Órla spoke calmly.

'Yes, I think we all have questions about what's going on, with you. I hesitate to say with "us" since that's not—That's not—'

I am alone, I thought. I've never been scared of that; who isn't alone? But then, just then, I was. It hit me in my guts, it tore at me. I am alone.

Then a small voice inside me whispered; you are not and will not be alone, not with me here.

'Daniel's getting water I think,' Órla said, 'though he seems just as fucked as you. What a party, eh? And you know these people. These fucking folk. I don't think they've noticed anything,' she was talking on and on in a reasonable voice. I was grateful for it, amazed to be honest that she could be so free of drama. I shifted position; the book was in my hands under me, and I pulled it out and put it against my forehead. Cracked soft cloth. It smelled – faintly – of the stables.

'Here,' she said, and took it from me, 'I'm just putting it down so you can stretch out. Get some sleep.'

I tried not to get worked up. If I said anything more to her I don't remember. I did something with my eyes closed – something like I slept, but a busy sleep.

Red Room

In the red room there for a bit I must have slept and under that I was remembering the urgency of the diary page hidden – beneath the folds – and the strange eroticism of the man in old fashioned clothing biting the sliver of wood out of my finger. As I came and went from myself I felt a body lying beside me, at first stiff, then soft with sleep. And then there was a second standing over me, watching, breathing. I kept my eyes closed for safety. I felt better, less unhinged. I wondered if the drinks had been spiked – that would account for the disorientation. I did feel faintly sick. I kept my eyes smartly closed and I thought about what I might have missed in the times between going into the wardrobe and waking up standing in this room with Órla there and the look on her face. It felt like being stolen from myself. I thought, 'Okay, something terrible has happened to you – what now do you need to get over it and feel all right?'

Órla sat up beside me.

'Just off for some water since Daniel's not come back with any,' she said. 'Dying of thirst. Don't go anywhere.' The bed released and she was gone.

Someone was coming up the stairs.

I pretended to be asleep. The worst thing now was if Mark came – I could just about cry at the idea of explaining I needed more time. But no, it was Daniel there in the doorway. He stood – the light fell around him, making him a silhouette. Like here, you standing by the window, a silhouette with the stars at your back, candle flame illuminating your hand. Like that yes, a dream almost. Exactly. Then Daniel was fully there and the door closed behind him with a boardroom click. Light from the low lamp bathed his face, extending shadows on him. Then or now. I felt like this was the first of many future times I was really seeing him clearly, letting myself see him. He was awkward in his formal clothes. His overgrown dark hair on his ears, and his eyes were long and glowed in the light – not amber, I'd want to say, something livelier, like silty water in the sun – and his lashes dark. He was drunk too. He fussed with his jacket, taking it off. He had a soft-looking, stumbling-looking mouth that my fingers somehow remembered being inside.

'Daniel,' I said.

'Here.'

He handed me a glass of water as he sat down on the bed. We were alone, then.

Kiss

A wind blew from a distant inland place and I found myself shaking. Between us, the air crackled like a pelting of ice about to hit us both, already too late and smacking into us. So suddenly this comes on I thought, because I didn't have the perspective yet. All I felt was: make the storm break, make it stop. I felt a pain in my fingers – a kind of shock – a kind of shock that is the moment before touching. No, it was never like this. Believe me? I reached over for him and pulled him near. His hot breath and my hot breath. I kissed him. Just like that as if our mouths and tongues together had been a form the universe was waiting to shape all this time. If you unsettle yourself anything is possible. That's what the night had proved. There was no accidental slip of the lips that led us somewhere I didn't want to go. I wanted – to go – I did.

As I kissed him I saw that other place, only briefly; I smelled bread cooking in an oven and heard a creaking of wood and leather, the sound of a brush on a wet floor – smell of fresh hay falling loosely, horses, sawdust, pipe smoke, mud being washed away. Two selves crashing together overlapping two selves imaginary or from long past histories, I didn't care, I pushed my tongue in. Daniel filled the world in then with himself and it was cologne and sweet-salty booze and a hit of chocolate. His face gritty – not gritty. Stubbled. I opened my eyes and pulled back a little; it was Daniel, wasn't it. Yes. I chose this, I thought.

Even as I thought that I felt myself as two people: one making the choice, the other judging it, loathing it. A small part of me was pointing at something moving under – I moved back from that part. It stretched its shadow out along towards me across the floor of my being, touched me with shame – Órla it said. I moved back to Daniel. But perhaps it was not shame but tact. Because Órla was in the room again, watching, silent. There was nothing I could say that would make things any easier, right then – no excuse or comfort – and my lips felt stung and good – that would invalidate what I had just done. So I just looked at her. My mouth tired and red. Daniel's too. We had chosen to. Our handmarks were all over each other. A redness on his arm from my hand. My God, I thought, is this what it's like?

Daniel put his hands up and held my face.

'Tom. You're fucking gorgeous,' he whispered. I took his hands and held them against my face.

'I'm sorry,' I said, 'I'm sorry,' apologising for my whole life – and to the shadow, and to Órla, and to my own self for not letting this happen sooner – but this was the only time it could have.

'Shh,' Daniel said. 'God, I have you,' he said. Or did he say it later? Órla was beside us, and warmed us and we made a figure together of our arms and legs. And we didn't stop kissing any more after that, exhausted, fired, drunk, fell back down together, holding on dearly tight. I think I spoke, I think I whispered, 'Don't leave me yet.' Daniel's back against my stomach. Órla's neck against my mouth.

Waking

It was still dark. Sounds of the party breaking up came from outside: cars leaving the drive, goodbye, drive safe. Little car honks. I fumbled around but couldn't find my phone to check the time. I wasn't hungover though my mouth was clothy and I desperately needed a drink. Daniel was lying beside me, a thin slice of his neck lit up red in the white light from the toilet. And arm with no owner poked out from the lower sheets. I swallowed A white cold line moved down me, sank into me. I got up and put on the rest of my clothes. I went to the toilet to fill the glass, but I saw the diary on the floor in the light – falling across it, an arrow – pointing to Daniel, then moving to point to the door.

I wanted to say goodbye to him. I was pulling him up to do it. 'Get up, Daniel,' I thought, 'get up.' He was awake and a horrible smile came on his face, and I realised he was not dead and I might be. A scream came up the back of me. My hands were hot with blood. There was music playing again, wasn't there? In a moment I was free.

The hall was dark and full of ways to go. I passed each one on careful steps not wanting to meet Mr MacAshfall and his forced cheeriness that would force me to be cheery right as I had come to a piece of my real self. Not wanting to meet Mark's mother – had I briefly seen her? Impressions of hair and a pinched neck, some judgements, my sloppiness. Not wanting to encounter anyone at that tilted hour but Mark himself. There was a chance he had gone to bed, but I thought it was a small one. I went downstairs into occasional light and a kind of dry comfortable atmosphere. The MacAshfalls ran the public parts of their home warm. The last of the catering staff were carrying biodegradable sacks out to their van through the open front door; if they noticed me they didn't want me to know they had. Kind, I thought. I was barefoot, unshowered and almost round to sobriety, a depressing prospect for anyone to see. I dumped myself on the staircase and waited for them to finish. As they were exiting, one of them looked up at me and gave a louche army salute. I raised two casual fingers, immediately thinking it was like something an emotionally hogtied man might do watching his only brother set out to sea on an unworthy vessel. He closed the door behind him and was gone forever.

'You're up,' said Mark. He was coming from the living room area. He had changed into some less smart clothes, but by anyone's standards his pyjamas might count as formal wear. Navy silk, matching slippers.

'Mark,' I said – I strolled down to meet him business mode on, and in the kitchen we sat on high stools at the marble bar with our faces rearranged in those shadows. The red of the counters only made Mark look even more doughy than usual. He took out something white and thickly creamy from the fridge and began eating it slowly with a tiny spoon.

'Enjoy yourself?' Mark said. He was still a little drunk.

'It's been a strange night.'

'I'd imagine,' he said – smirked.

I sat silent.

'Do you want anything, Thomas?' he said, gesturing broadly to the kitchen, 'we have lots of leftovers. Or I can make you a drink?'

I asked for water. He got up and made me a glass with ice and a cucumber slice from a tub in the fridge. When I had drunk it all down in silence, I was ready.

'Listen, Mark – I have that book you were talking about. The diary.'

'Oh really! Yes, I thought you might.'

I stared at him.

'Daniel took it,' he said. 'The idiot stuffed it down his trousers and ran off. I knew you'd moved in with him. And that you might remember our conversation. So . . . ?'

I tried to straighten the timeline in my head – hadn't he told me before I'd decided to move in? I took a brief tilt towards paranoia. This is a set-up, all that. But I gave up and took out the book. I put it on a clean space on the marble bar and opened it to the back, where I had left the folded piece of paper.

'Mystery deepens,' I said.

Mark scoffed in amusement.

'Look at that.' He leaned forward and unfolded it. And this is what it said.

An account of himself by James O'Riorden,
written 16 May 1820

You will have read this diary now and perhaps there is no one who will ever see this letter as I will conceal it well but still I have to write it. I am compelled by my moral sense and the awareness of the precarity of my soul for what I have done and what I have not done in the matter I related as if I was James Lennoxlove, the master of the house of Bitterhall. I am not that man. That man is a figment, based on a man of a different name in a similar social position. I am James O'Riorden, no one of importance, a servant only in the house of the other 'James'. I wrote in his words, unable to tell it myself, and to ease only myself. God forgive me!

I was born in Ireland and taken to [illegible] very young by my mother, three or four years old. My father she left behind and

306

all to the good, she said, that he stayed, and kept his surname with him, while we took another. For this reason I am not afraid to mention O'Riorden here, as there are no records by which to find me. I was raised in a part of that city that is considered a very low place indeed. But still I went to school, because as you can see I write not badly. I learned more refinement in my letters while in the service of the 'Lennoxlove' family, the father of 'James' requiring even his grooms to be able to read well and keep reliable accounts. This was not out of charity or some noble goal but to enable no man to feign ignorance if some goods of the house or money etcetera went missing. When I was first employed I had additional practice as I was required to keep a legible diary of the horses' eating habits, stool, teeth, and overall look, so that the master could keep track of their flourishing and make adjustments. Very often he would comment on my dismal handwriting and I would attempt to improve it before he next checked it. This first master 'Lennoxlove' was always looking to the improvement of the breed.

But it is about his son I write, the man I wrote as in guise. I was in the barn on the last night of the year (I will take care not to write which year, so that neither I nor he am incriminated). It happened differently to how I said, but I think dear reader you will have guessed so, otherwise why should I write this?

I was nine when I came to the house. James was fourteen and had his schooling by a tutor. The master was in his full health then and very strict; I saw him beat James – nearly a grown man – for riding out late on a fine summer evening. He did beat him in full view of anyone passing, hitting him with a strap until James fell on the courtyard stones. The master made him stand and hit at him again and again, until at last he fell and could not get up. It was as if he were beating me, the pain I felt for James, who I carried home. He cried but afterwards was a colder, more defiant sort to me and to all. I had such extreme affection for him, which I kept almost silently and unseen. I took care not to be servile in my manner but always restrained and quickwitted – I knew he would find nothing but disgust for me any other way.

James would ride all the time he was not kept by other tasks. He grew fair haired and tall, strong and well, with a charming smile that I saw him give only while on horses, and later, to women with whom he wanted to get his leg over. Still I do not think he liked horses overly but for the feeling they gave him of freedom on the quiet lanes and the leaping of hedges while chasing down some poor fox or other for the dogs to tear at. When the old master died and James inherited, he put some of his money in to further increasing the stock and to expanding the stables.

I turned the page.

To mark his first year of manhood and the new though ongoing improvements he was making, James held a ball at 'Bitterhall' and invited gentry from the nearby estates and from [illegible], where he had lively society friends – poets and advocates and the like. The ball ran late, but James slipped away before midnight. I was minding the guests' horses and trying to compose some poems. Another man who was to help me was away with his sweetheart, which pleased me so I could work on my compositions in peace. James came in loudly, kicking at the door, and with a very fierce look to him and asked me to prepare his horse, which I did quickly and saying little. He rode out and I closed the doors behind him. Later I heard sounds of the horse cantering near, and went out to receive it, but she dashed past me into the stable. Two riders were now on the horse, beside James, a man in common clothing who looked pale.

'Sir,' I said.

'Oh, it's you,' he answered, and lifted the man down. 'Go to the house now please, I'm about my business,' he said. He had the man by the shoulder. Barely a man, it seemed, by the look of him, with a thin young face, wary and frightened. All I did was nod and stepped outside. But after came a sound of disorder – I rushed in. The man was resisting, feebly I thought, and James stood to him angrily holding a knife at his throat.

'Sir,' I said again, cried his name and begged him not to hurt the man. But he, seeing that the man would not stop shouting, killed him there with the knife and after it was done had me bury the dirty straw.

I have no idea to what end James brought the man to the stable. The body we laid in a ditch by the road and I said to the other servants I'd heard it was a vagrant from the city had committed the murder in the early morning, and so this rumour duly spread. After we had returned from the road, the master cut his palm and mine and squeezed a little of our blood together into a brandy cup. We both drank and he declared us blood brothers, loyal unto death. I do not know if he believes it, or believes that I could be so easily taken in by the power of an oath surmounting a horrible act. Just because I am loyal to him – this he clearly knows, how deep my affection has been for him since our childhood.

I have never said anything and never will, not in fact for loyalty but in shame, except that I found I had to say it in some way however cowardly, because my heart couldn't bear to keep quiet, and so wrote it like a kind of story. And now you have found it – never mind, it is likely that when the backing has come unstuck I will be dead, I am only waiting until the stables are furnished adequately and the horses are not so disrupted by the works before I force my departure from this world. I expect to go to the devil in due course. But I will see James there in Hell, I think, many more years after my own going. The man he killed, I learned later, was the son of a blacksmith in the nearby village. I want to write his name, but it isn't possible without drawing the crime too clearly. As it is, it will stand better if there is an element of untruth about the thing, even with this confession.

Invisible

'Oh my God,' I said.

'Very mysterious,' said Mark in a flat tone.

'Yes—' I answered.

'Oh well,' he said, slapping the paper down on the counter. 'I suppose it was too much to hope for neat answers and that.'

'What do you mean?' I asked. 'It's right there.'

Mark drew back, and played with the paper – turning it over and around, craning his head. 'No – am I missing something?'

I sat shaking, looking down at the confession. A cold wind swirled in my head, though I couldn't think why.

'It's right there. James, his life, what he saw.' Mark touched the paper, and I knew, 'Mark – you don't see anything. You don't see anything.'

Mark eyed me over his mug, then flashed a clever look. 'Did you know, Arthur Conan Doyle's father saw fairies dancing over St Gyle's Church and drew pictures of them ascending into a descending blue night sky. Not unlike,' he said, gestured vaguely at the sky – a woolly orange – 'this one. They locked him up because he was a drunk, too, if I'm remembering right. I'd say that reason, rather than the seeing of things. It's not unforeseeable. An inability to fit into this world, to be stuck between this that and the other. It's the chemical straitjacket, these days, for that kind of offense.'

Put on prim, businesslike tone. Wry smile. 'Oh, yes,' I said – mumbled – got up. 'I'm messing with you,' I said. 'Anyway – I have to be going.' I was walking away, 'Thanks for the party—'

I left the paper. I must have been shocked then to leave it, to leave the only proof behind. Blank or full of writing – I don't know. Do you know? What was written and what wasn't? But I had to leave. I saw a meeting with Mark and my bosses, all sucking on their teeth. I saw my humiliation, everything falling to pieces. I was already at the front door.

'But. I mean—hold up, come back.' Mark said, 'Or you just need—'

The path through seemed to shrink. There were more people than I thought, and their voices rose up around me. Until I got to the door and slammed it tight.

Company

A stick falls in a room made of plywood on the edge of a precipice, a gorge over the sea. I heard the seals slab themselves up on the beach rocks. Can you hear them? They make strange calls. I sigh. I have been drinking in a party in a city that doesn't exist and I don't know how far out I am in the fields. The car is a way back on the main road, probably. It smells like the sea but also I smell, of cigarettes. Sweat, a bit. Not too bad. This bothy is the place to die in, very chic and echoing – and lonely – fucking beautiful. Even the stove is the perfect accessory, polished but someone before me used it, I can see old ashes in it, which makes me feel. Reassured. It's real. How better could you get? James is with me, that's true too. Oh, I know, sorry. Sometimes he crouches on his haunches. Sometimes he looks at me so sternly I want to laugh. James is the groom. James is the master. His book is far off – I left his confession, can you believe that, how could I? Quite a state. No choice or else shown up – but the miles contract accordion-style and I hear a music that I will not hear for real again until a few years from now, at a party, at another party, when I am well. After the party, when I creep downstairs and see everyone sleeping curled up on pillows on the floor and against the sofa. Whose house will it be? The two Jameses asleep in each other's arms. Me alone against a damp wooden wall trying not to be a part. I slide my foot forward and look at nothing and you. This is another life, the right one. But even there we make poor sticks, we curl up and go soft.

Deep North

I drove up all night when I was still way over the limit. I am fucking ashamed, of course I am, don't even ask. Until I got to this place – following nothing, following a line crawling on a blank screen – our end of the world which in this small country seems to be every edge, even the inside parts are precipitous. You can turn around twice and find yourself about to fall off this country.

I sit here by the fire. I'm trying to concentrate, get the edges of myself – to know – holding them somehow. My phone was in my pocket. It wasn't the source of the music. Nothing was but I was. I stare into the flames and let the focus of my eyes go; there's the stables – approaching – night this time. As if I could just lean forward into it. I replay my entrance. Night this time – I approach the stables – there is a horse under me, a man sagged over in front of me, like he's drunk. I hold him in place with one arm – into the stable and there is the other James and I send him away. And I turn to my man. Some nothing scooped up off the dark country lane. He begs me. I say, you don't want something true at last? He looks away. And then the pit of my stomach. You can find yourself doing something strange and awful so easily. And then the knife, and into his neck. I see it again. I breathe too hard. I see it again; the glint of blood by lantern light. Horses stamping and beginning to make noise at the fright. Everything slips. Clattering horses. A low wailing. All such sounds, a din rising over me. My hands on the wheel slippery from fear, sweat. I've never been held so strongly as I was by you. And other things that run dark over my hands.

At some point there was a harsh sound and I shook my head. I had the phone in my hand and it was calling – Badr.

'Hi Badr,' I said when he answered.

'Tom! Oh, man. We've been looking for you, ay? Whereabouts are you?'

'Oh I'm up north a bit. Far north coast.' I looked up through a rainspattered windshield and saw a stove with the warm eye of a fire winking in it.

'That is a way away, man, phew,' Badr said, sounding impressed. 'So what you doing there, you all right? Daniel's been going nuts. Órla too. Bit of a stress.'

'Sorry about all the fuss. I went for a drive, and then the road was so nice, I just – kept going. You know how it is. Just one of those times when you just need a holiday from your life.' I looked at the grime under my nails and felt my nasty breath. I shivered in my clothes. They were fine but they weren't clean. Nothing was, except the space around my phone: clean, small, safe.

'When I need a holiday from my life I just go to the cinema, see an action film,' Badr said. 'But naw. I get you big man. When you coming back?'

'Dunno.' By the window a gull hovered on the currents. It was day; the bothy was steady against a hard wind, my breath in clouds. I closed my eyes. I wanted to tell him how beautiful it was here, dawn especially, which was happening now. And then there was no one who saw it at all and it was more of itself that way.

'So you're way up there. I think – you have an address for where you're staying?'

'Let me check,' I said. I walked out to the car. The sky was high gold over the plain of the heath with scratches of clouds against the upper atmosphere. I thought, 'I could take a picture and post it. But I'm not doing that.' I opened the car and the GPS turned on – Badr went on talking in my ear – I peered down. For some reason I was shaking – tears streaming stupidly down my face – but everything was fine. 'It's just beautiful here,' I think I said.

'Okay, cool,' said Badr. 'Okay, so, mate, someone's going to drive up. Join you for a bit maybe. Would you prefer, eh, me or Órla or would Daniel be the best for this. Or someone else . . . ?'

I muttered your name into the phone. The Atlantic air should not look this good. Maybe it's late, I thought. It's winter now, already. I had slept, hadn't I – ball in front of the stove. Like a soot sprite, from a cartoon. A stand of thin trees marked a property a hundred yards away. I blinked it away. Besides that and the road there was so little under the sky. I could hear the ocean breathing in and out over the hill and down the cliff to the beach, rope ladder or careless slip. My hand dropped to my side. Badr's tiny voice going nothing against all of this. My master looked at me. I followed him away.

Conflare

James and Tom were frozen. They went outside anyway. Whoever made the bothy constructed it so that the door didn't have to open into the wind. James and Tom couldn't stand to be far from the heat of the fire – funny how little it takes to get down to a wire thinness and vague with it – they missed nothing of their life, they were a dot on the surface of a rock, a lichen, a hole to whisper in. James and Tom held some heart of rock they had pried out of the ground many hours before up to their mouth and said what they wanted, for five minutes straight. They had never been so honest. And it didn't matter at all.

Tap water from the outside pole they sucked through chapped lips. James whistled; Tom turned. Horses ran across the fields; one horse – each frame of it – four hooves off the ground and a steaming back. Like an intro to a lavish television show – like an advert for summer here where the land had given up as well as out and was the low browns of nameless dead plants and windflattened grass, stones scarred under the light. They walked to the gulley where the little crooked stairs led to the beach at low tide though it was high now it was narrow and James and Tom thought they could have jumped it. Or could have fallen in trying to and been rushed away into the grey churn and fallen into the kelp forest and the mouth of a basking shark, the nets of a fishing boat trawling for silver fish. On the rocks that made the gully were jellyfish of lichens, big rusts swimming against the soft brown of the cliffs below the brown of the empty land, always above the reach of the sea. There was a cave at one end of the beach, visibly drinking the water in. Tom and James listened; the waves wrote about themselves above the wind, the sound of pen, scratching. They walked into the cave, then, or another time.

A group of players are scratching on fiddles in a big warm house and there are men and women dancing. James and Tom can hear them, almost as if they are in among them, among their flicking sweat and swirling dresses. Their sweat runs down as Tom and James touch the hard rough wall. They can smell the alcohol on their breath and a feeling of hope swells them. They are inside. Outside is the stable where the murder happens. A strange, unfathomable death.

Tyres on loose chip road.

Tom and James walking over into the dimness, night back down, cold again.

Behind the wheel in a figment of light is Daniel – the man – Daniel.

He gets out, looking around him. Small, confused. People who don't know they are part of something seem smaller and more vulnerable. Whoever he thinks he is looking for is not here.

Swoon

'Tom!' James says. He points at himself. I'm one man in the land-scape. I'm a bundle of papers. I'm an object going to the plastic heart of the wrecked ocean. It's everywhere and it's broken. My heart is full of love. My body is strong and young. His parents are dead. His voice is a gull rising up between us.

'Remember this?' I say, holding out a small soft thing. It's the toy. Mer-unicorn all bright white and glittering eyes. I take it, pass it one hand into another. James murmurs something in my ear.

'I can't make it play anything,' he says.

'Tom,' says Daniel, 'It's okay.'

There's a sea that I could just walk straight into. I am so ashamed. I don't even know why any more. I begin to walk, but Daniel holds me, just a moment, as I dissolve.

Sunk

The fire is crackling again when I wake up. Daniel smiles at me – a smile I've never seen before – and I try to get up off the boards to get away from it, and he is handing me a glass of water.

'Awake, at last,' he says.

My body won't let me do much, it's too weak. I go out of it. I wander across the brown grass. James says if I want, I can keep going, the cliff path, the point where it churns white below. There will be no gulls when I go, nothing at all to see. I shake at this. My throat pinches. Daniel's holding his phone. Watching me, but not trying to stop me, not trying to engage, but I can feel he wants to. I feel but maybe I don't feel correctly.

'Órla's being stubborn,' he says, 'she's coming up too, she set out a little bit after me. I couldn't get her to wait for you to come back. So, now we'll wait here. She's bringing some food, something to eat. Are you hungry? Do you want to wash your face? It's a bit dirty there.'

'I thought she was going to wait outside the house, holding the cat,' I say. I have my eyes closed because it asks less of me.

I hear Daniel laugh, gently. I listen to the crackling fire. Wind outside now. I think of the gully in the wind, cliffs like the cliffs I had run to in the city. I am called to go. I think I am called to go. This is no place, right here. I think, 'It's a matter of opening the door and bolting for the edge to go right off it. You can.' Then I think, 'Who wants you to do that?' And the question horrifies.

There's Daniel, knitting. No, not knitting. He's removing the back of his phone. He's removing pieces of paper from a book and folding them up into boats. He's surrounded by paper boats. The ends of his trousers are cuffed, and around his black firelit boots a fleet of boats are sailing. In his focus he looks so calm I sob. He looks up. I put my face back down under my head there is smooth fabric.

'My jacket,' he says. 'I used to go hiking, I used to go off and camp on my own all the time on the side of mountains. I haven't for ages and I don't know why.'

'Because a room swallowed you, and a machine. And the story you fed to the machine,' I said.

I expect him to ask me questions, but he doesn't. He only looks like he is thinking and returns to his phone. I want him to ask me questions about myself, but he doesn't. I sit, nothing to do. If he asked me a question, anything at all, it would prove – something. That I really existed. That was it. I want to exist so badly, and I only do if other people confirm it. Otherwise. Otherwise. Only I exist.

I hear a car. It's Órla. Surely Órla and Badr. And Mrs Boobs. I try or something in me tries to remember why I went. James. I, or something in me that is James, remembers James, standing holding a lantern. James' battered shoe. I remember also a shoe on a roadside. I stooped to pick it up. A piece of glass. Life scatters everywhere. I want to hold it together. Force it to make sense. But I am tired again, and what if it won't? What could happen to me. I don't think I care. I get up and go to the door.

But there is no car and I'm out on the cliff, cold and sweating. I've run. A scrap of a voice calls, but I can't tell what it is, if it has a body.

I want a time back that I never had. My throat pinches. I am looking at water if water is there, too dark, I can't even see my hands, I remember a knife, and horses stamping, and the smell of men, blood, horseshit, scorched wood. I am overlaid. I am too full. I go to my knees that get wet and I am like cold blood there, so fucking wretched that crying, tearing the grass a little, I find a small rough stone and hold it. Just an ordinary stone. I lean in and tell it things nobody knows about me.

Daniel Lightfoot

Rise

I'd never been that far north before and expected it would have a kind of epic quality to it, this place where the land gives out; it was less dramatic than I thought, even in the hardness of early November. Firstly came the hint of the sea, an ever-wholesome marine smell sucked in through the car's air vents, while a certain quality to the sky suggested that the moisture in it had come a long distance without the rule of soil. Dissolution, it said. The land that rolled past the car speaking with subtlety of its finality, with lower and lower hills, flattening out as if to make for the sea a welcoming landing spot – though in truth there are cliffs there, so I could feel safe that the sea would only rise to meet it after I was dead, when all the world's seas are coming in to lap up a portion of what our neglect has promised them.

I wasn't overly worried or thinking about anything beyond the practicalities of the journey until I parked up just off the main road and approached the bothy on foot along a winding gravel path. I wondered for a moment who might build something like this here. All I could see it being used for at that moment was bafflement and disorientation. It looked like an art installation, it didn't belong at all; crisp, bright pinewood, almost offensively yellow and new in the gloom. The windows were small slits in the façade, too small to allow an outsider to make out the whole of any scene inside it, though I noted there was light, which meant occupation, I hoped, still, by Tom. There was nothing on either side of this house – and I hesitate to call it that. Not house, nor dwelling, nor residence, nothing fits for a place so jarring. Stepping along on the crunching gravel I had a momentary, faint tilt into dizziness, a sense I could fall. There was no horizon because it was already too dark, and a dozen or so metres back over a few humps of earth was, I later discovered, the cliff. The cliff where Tom had been taking himself at intervals since he had arrived to stand in his temptation to give into the whispers of gravity.

I found Tom in the bothy, worse than I had expected, and about as bad as Órla had. He was filthy. He wore the same clothes he had gone to the party in, several days before, and in addition to not washing or removing the clothes he had been, it seemed, lying on the gritty strand or sitting in the smoke-filled bothy, not sleeping. His breath was awful. His greasy hair stuck up in wild patches, turned a dishwater grey. Purple halfmoons under his veiny eyes.

I couldn't tell you how we passed that first night. But in the morning, we took our walk to the beach, where I hoped he would feel refreshed at the water's edge (I don't now know why I could have thought that) and where he fainted. And I, in the weird mood I was in, tensed and almost expecting something like this to happen, just watched him slump down. I made no sound or rush to find help, deciding, quickly, that given how far out we were from the nearest village, help would not come before either Tom woke up of his own volition, or he slipped into a worse state. So I stayed still, down on my haunches looking at my friend's grey face on the pale sand, his hair blowing about. I reached a hand to his cheek and felt the cold there. I don't know why I wasn't more concerned, or agitated, at least. I stayed with him a while, taking in his face until its features lost all shape. Then I took in where we were.

The beach was a narrow shelf of sand ending in rocks, and the cliffs high and dramatic on either side of our small bodies. The sea storming in and out was murmuring and breathing, if considered in human terms, with every now and then a slap and fizz as a wave beached itself closer to us. And I thought, looking down at Tom, how much like a place of disaster this could be. If I listened to the enemy. If I made certain choices. The sky overhead was dark, even though it was morning; it was hard to tell where the sun was. Of course I considered this as metaphor. Wind getting up. If I knew this part of the country better, I could tell if a squall was coming in or not.

I searched my mind at last, digging, really, to see if I could overturn the bad feeling I felt should be within me; was I responsible, somehow, for all this coming to pass? I thought of our kiss with that familiar flare of griminess in my stomach. How drunk he'd been. I hissed through my teeth and remembered that this was something my mother had done, now and then, to herself, an anxious intake of breath in response to nothing. To picking up a pen and beginning to write a shopping list, for example. I hadn't thought of her in a long time. If the voices were hers too, then, that was something. I looked down at Tom. Should I put him into the recovery position? But I was wary of touching him. How drunk I'd been that night too. But had I done this, to him? Look at his face, it's pale and worn now, but then it was awake and healthy. I pinched a piece of grass seed from his hair, and wondered where the leaf had come from. I held the seed up to my face; it looked like wheat, ripe.

I decided I'd put that night down to antic happenings, not self-villainy. I'd been drunk, and so had Órla, and this was something else, and it was wrong of me to claim it as my doing, that was the thing; wrong to take credit for something, even if it's negative. I stared at his closed eyes, the wet spatters on his cheek. An inch of water would drown him, water gurgling down into his lungs. Things are not always your fault; that constant I must tell

327

myself. I crouched further and touched Tom's neck, taking his pulse, because I felt I should.

'Tom,' I said. 'Tom, you're all right.' Though who ever is? He woke shortly afterwards and I helped him back up the steep steps to the cliff top, I put him to rest on the bothy boards. Órla had texted, insisting we stay until she arrived, and I was thinking of all the food I should have brought with me. Then the image of spoonfeeding a pathetically weakened Tom stove-warmed soup floated into my mind, and I dwelled in torment and arousal for a while. Sometimes we spoke, Tom and I, sometimes he seemed to listen to voices and respond. I found myself listening to it, and thinking, perhaps. Perhaps some people need to stop living, if they are suffering. And that thought made me cold, and I shuddered, and fussed.

'There, Tom,' I said, 'we'll get help soon.'

Órla McLeod

Hind

I was excited, I'll admit it, to get to be on that ride. I had contacted my supervisor to let her know I was off on personal business and moved shifts at my work so I wouldn't lose any money this month. It meant a delay going up, but that was fine. Daniel was first response, I would be the one with the full kit. So I packed a bag for the rescue as if I'd practiced my whole life for this day. Warm clothes and towels and the like for the runaway, first aid, a camera, driving licence. I picked up the car and drove back to the house to see Badr one last time. In the end, it was him who was to play the worried wife.

'Take care on the roads at night, hey?' he said, and handed me a small fold of paper. Mark MacAshfall had dropped off a note or something of Tom's, thought it might help.

'Goodbye!' Badr said, and lifted Mrs Boobs and waved her white arm. She gave me a baleful glare.

I went through the city. A light went green, I indicated left. The streets were unfamiliar. Under surface thoughts of work – a conference was upcoming, my supervisor had not responded to my last two emails – a burn of worry in my guts, over Tom, and Daniel. I wondered if the two of them hadn't had some kind of repression-led showdown, and one or the other hadn't been killed. As much as the image struck me as interesting – a twist on a murder ballad, a good story for me to tell many years from now in beautiful knitwear, grey hair at my temples, sat at the head of table at a faculty dinner – I was fighting a frantic sense of doom.

It flared and sunk. There, a bus pulled out, and I saw a grave with Tom's name on it, and Daniel's, intertwined with ivy. A small child carrying a shopping bag waiting beside a bin: I'd been left. School – please drive slowly. And I'd miss it, the drama, I'd not be in time to stop whatever it was. Partly-demolished shopping centre. Another right, another right, doubling back. And Tom, I'd missed a sign, whatever had gone on between us three in the bedroom at the party, the rattling windows. The intense and beautiful activities in that huge bed. I went red. I swore, I took another right and got stuck behind a bus.

After at least an hour of steering and braking and breathing hard I veered off and sat parked awkwardly up by a supermarket and rubbed my head. I wasn't even heading the right direction for the motorway. A police car slowed to look in at me and I smiled and nodded, and it went on. I prodded the GPS. I brushed my hair which was in some state, and saw the bodies of Daniel and Tom sinking off black-shaded cliffs. Scrolling waves covering them, and the north wind as a cloud with an angel's face, blowing above it. I thought of old-woman-me, at a dinner table, several glasses into the wind, declaiming on the beautiful boys who had died because of me, because of love and trouble between them. I was a Tennessee Williams play, describing a tableau. I was playing up, no doubt. No more of that.

Hours later. Stopped in a turn-off to eat a sandwich in a roadside parking place, I hoped to push the panic down my throat. After I'd eaten I unfolded Tom's paper, or papers, rather – getting it buttery at the edge like some kind of heathen. I looked. Flipped the little sheets back and forth. Blank, creamy-coloured but raggedy with age. It occurred to me it must have come from the diary, but I could see no clue on it. Mark must have thought it had some meaning for Tom, so I wondered if there was lemon juice on it, or a hint of a message to be decoded, perhaps via creases, or faint scratches. The only comfort it seemed to offer was the kind I got from all old things long carried through the world in the protective casement of their books. I shook off a crumb and put the paper back in my bag.

It was November; I was somewhere parked by moorland, watching rain blowing in grey down the sweep of a hill, and I felt numb. Daniel had let me know Tom was alive but in some kind of state. I had no experience with madness, and so I thought then only two things: firstly how frightening and baffling it was to have grazed it a little with the tips of my fingers, the world of madness in which a completely unwritten-on piece of paper could sing just for you, that running off north out of your life was an acceptable thing to do; and secondly I felt resentment at the fact Daniel was there with him already. I remember rolling my shoulders, and the look of cars thundering past on both sides of the road, on home to loved ones, to lives. No one crossing this moor was going to work, unless they were postmen or van drivers. And there was me in a hired car with no one really wanting to see me at the other end of the interminable journey. I should have left it to Daniel and Tom to sort out. After all, I was the third wheel. I felt like I was nothing to them. Despite my involvement I felt I was almost a nothing, and felt in myself nothing but a little miserable. And how petty it was that I was this way, with all that was actually happening to Tom. I cracked my fingers and turned out back onto the road. It's true, Whitman, we contain multitudes; it's just that much of it is dross.

Later again, dusk. I still had a fair way to go yet. I had been startled out of my fog by a stag standing on a rock by the side of the motorway. Noble, as they always look. I left it behind and took it with me, imagining a monk drawing it in the margins of a book of hours, red and gold, a beast with eyes and lips like a man. I imagined it shot through with arrows, or like the famous tapestry of the captured unicorn, surrounded by deliberate plants, contained within its boundaries as if it was choosing to never step through them. As though to be trapped was to be thought of, to be beloved. It was already too late to do anything different but chase north, and to feel self-conscious in the chasing.

Daniel Lightfoot

Grip

I don't know at what time Órla drove in, but the distant lights of her car turning off the road triggered a panic in him. I looked over and saw his eyes open and his mouth, and heard him murmuring again a lot of senseless words. As I stared, he mouthed the sounds of the sea, and in my head I heard the door bang open, though when I looked up it was shut tight. Such a simple thing, precognition. I should have stroked his hair then, no matter how dirty. I should have been tender to him. At no point could I have really been said to be tender to anyone other than myself. I only sat aloof and talked back with Tom quietly, until, right as the car could be heard rolling over the gravel path to the bothy, Tom made a sudden run for the door, and out into the wind.

I swore and I stumbled, picked myself up and tried to guess at where he might be. Órla's lights blinded me, and I knocked on the driver's window as she was pulling on the brake.

'He's out there,' I babbled. 'Quick, come, have to get him – we have to go, quickly before he does something.'

At the cliffs I was overwhelmed by the smell of the air again in the dark, and the sense of infinite, not even uninterested stars above us. I was afraid, of course I was, then. Give me mortality, don't give me the inhuman gigantic nothing that is all around us. I shone my phone light over and picked out Tom, running, a slip, glowing in his white jacket. His shoes were off, we'd never find them. I held out an arm, only just stopping Órla from tumbling into one of the sea-cuts in the ground. I had moved to stop us falling without even thinking. So it often is that without thought I was all the safer. Tom was on the other side of a fissure, dark like everything else, but I could hear him ranting.

'Tom,' Órla said in a tight, positive voice, 'hey, it's me. Are you – you coming back in?'

And this was something I hadn't known, that the scene of an attempted suicide can feel so awkward and mundane. Tom paced about, waved, let his arm drop. The whites of this, unevenly moving, hurt to look at in the darkness, and also suggested a startling of some white bird that was trying to fly but could not, had forgotten how to rise.

'I'm fine,' he said, sounding hoarse. 'Umm, how are you, Órla?'

He paced. He shouted sometimes, though I could barely make out what he was saying. I thought: a poor, bare, forked animal, then of the constellation of the great bear, and the wind's bite and the yawning gap in front of us all, as metaphor, as hunger. I asked myself if I too wanted to fall in, and found no answer. And just like that, a calm feeling came. I counted myself safe, and that Tom was safe, because I was here to save him, I held Órla back from rushing round, in case, in the shock, he might have fallen. I heard her cry out nonsense. I felt, in that place, as I never had, burnished with purpose and the cold. I felt myself swell up with the sense that this was all awful, and we were all very much alive.

How? Above us the night sky spun, as did we, my fingers and toes lost all feeling, and I stamped from one foot to the other, and the sea breathed in and out, older than any living thing, smashing itself into fragments of sense. I sat on the ground – and I could have laughed at how little I was, and how uncertain, except on the matter that I was alive, and Órla, and Tom, here in the dark, as we had been in another dark, warm and gentle with each other. A tenderness could be brought on again, I thought, if I thought very carefully on how to enact it. I don't know how long we waited there, stuck in our places, filled with that sound of the sea making itself and making the shape of the rocks change. A heartbreaking scale of events. And I pulled up little handfuls of grass, and asked myself what friendship was and what desire was, and had no answers because I was small and stupid, and that was fine, thinking away and watching until there was a break in tensions, a moment when Tom decided he had had enough of confronting death, and sat down, and Órla, quicker to move than me as always, picked her way over and took him by the arm. It's as simple and mundane as that, in the end – the reason he didn't kill himself that night, was not even that we were there, nor that we did anything at all. It was him, or timing perhaps. A hesitation, or a clearing. That's it, that is sometimes enough, and is all that we have.

Órla McLeod

Meet

At the bothy by the cliffs we met again. Daniel and I ran about in the morning after our beautiful Tom, who ran in turn away from us through the whipwind and the dark in all different directions, nearly slipping, clambering over some rocks, nearly lost off the edges. Just like in a dream he was never any closer, or we were never any closer to him. There was too much land out here, and nothing of it. It had no shape in the dark, only little things to trip me. My own clumsy physicality got underfoot. I was tired, my body ached, I was tired of being the hunter, the active one. I was afraid too much so it made me sick and bored and sick again and nothing, nothing, nothing. We suddenly stopped, Daniel holding his arm out.

'What the fuck does Tom *want*,' I said, through the panic, thinking, where is he going, and why can't I catch up to him? We've lost him, I thought. I shuddered. Then Daniel picked him out with the light from his phone only a few metres away from us, across a gap. His eyes had a backshine to them. I turned to Daniel: 'Did you see that?' I said, 'humans don't reflect like that,' but he must not have heard me.

We stood at the break and I called out 'Are you all right?' and the part of Tom I could see in the light – a sliver of his face, showed a smile: recognition.

If we approached too close there was a risk he would take flight again, perhaps over one of the cliff edges that lay in every direction. After a time Daniel sat on the ground, while I kept yelling into the weather. Pleasantries, suggestions, as Tom stalked about and turned on himself answering for a while, then apparently talking to himself. I tried to engage with full sentences, until it seemed pointless. Half my words thrown back at me by the wind. Then I just tried, 'Hey Tom. Hey.' He turned his back and faced away.

I listened to only the wind. Tears started going down my cheeks. I wiped my face and then my hand on my clothes. My throat burned. So I stopped calling, so I stood, looking on, as Daniel had. I let my phone drop, its light finding out my shoes and jeans – I have a body, I thought, how strange I am not just a voice in the dark. The sky above us had come down hard, so it really seemed like existence was unlikely at all. I began plucking at a clump of salt-cropped spiky grass by my knees. It's oddly dull, I thought. And I'm cold now, as well as tired. But the chill at least was keeping the unwilling flesh of me alert.

Tom was also sitting down. He was only about five metres away, but the sea cut between us, down those cliffs. I thought, who is keeping him over there? And I blinked; it seemed to me that I saw in faint outline the impression of another person sitting down beside him, facing him. It moved oddly, as if parts of it were slipping away as it moved into non-existence.

As much as I wanted to believe in what I saw I'm no fool. I'd been driving for about eight hours, fractious and on little sleep, and it was so dark that I could barely make out much beyond the light I held up. Tom's head was low as if he was listening.

'Daniel?' I said, uncertain. 'Can you see something there?'

Daniel didn't answer. I turned the light at him and all he did was raise a hand against it. He was lying down, looking at nothing, scarf up to his nose and the hood of his jacket pulled up. He was exhausted too. 'Tom,' I called, and found myself asking: 'Who – who's your friend?'

'It's James,' Tom said, 'James.'

'James, Tom, why are you so far away?' I said, 'We're over here, if you want to come round?'

'I'm waiting – he wants – ' Tom said, almost inaudible.

'For what?'

'I don't like this,' he said, his voice with a crack in it.

'I'm coming over,' I told him. 'Wait for me. Just so I can hear you better, all right?'

Daniel and I looked at each other a moment and he nodded.

I hesitated. I was stuck between the sharpness of my thinking and the tactile mutability of what was going on. We should call someone; but who was there to call in all this world, who could help any of us? I thought, wiping my cold hand on my face again: I have no future. The terrible thoughts rushed over me. There's no one beside him. He's talking to no one. How awful – awful to go so mad. My cheeks burn from the wind and Tom's gone mad. So he has no future, no stability, even if we get him back. Anyway there is no future. It was like a flood of sadness, then. For all my careful study, I thought, all my enthusiasm for my subject, I'll die in poverty on this fucking coffin archipelago, there will never be a job in codicology waiting like a prize for someone like me. There will never be a secure old age from which I might tell stories of this time. In spite of this I was getting up, pushing myself, heavy in body and heart, sore arms and legs and frozen fingers – and so it was, otherwise how would I have written this? If we'd all just stayed. Or tipped one after another off the ledge for a lack of other options on how to live.

I went skirting round the gap, holding out my arms for balance. There was nothing below, no water visible, only the sound of it crashing and withdrawing and crashing. I got down next to Tom, and felt primeval there, hunched against the rages off the sea, like any ageless nameless number of people might have held down against the weather, waiting for the sea to give them an answer to some terrible equation.

'Are you going to come inside with us or what?' I asked. He twitched his hand, turned away still, and muttering, murmuring, though for the wind I could not make out one word. On the other side of him I glanced for the thing I had seen. And I sickened. There *was* something; a shape that moved when he did, that felt almost like a shadow he was casting, but on the dark air where it could not possibly be. But then again, now I write this, it could have been my eyes attempting to understand the gloom. We find patterns always where there are none. We make them, because we need there not to be nothing. I resolved to ignore the shape. If there was something, it wasn't mine. I took out the blank piece of paper and put it in Tom's hands. And he looked at it, and held it close. I talked softly to Tom, having him like a child to me, like a lost child who belongs to someone who is not there. It occurred to me I knew nothing about his childhood, not one thing.

'You're tired,' I said, 'come on up now, let's go in.' He looked at me and smiled. You can imagine in what way. Emboldened or desperate I took him by the wrist and stood up. That was enough. The wind shook out my hair and this man looked up at me. At some point as I was half-dragging him back he must have let the piece of paper go as I did not see it again.

I held Tom's wrist all the way back across the heath, never turning my head, trusting Daniel to follow. That journey, a few minutes only, was one of the longest of my life. I understood hardly any of the sounds I heard. I hesitate to write even approximations of them. But I had my Eurydice, my Tam Lin, my child, my burden, and I did not let him go, and I looked nowhere but the way to the light. Inside the bothy we would listen to the wind rage itself hoarse, until morning came.

Tom Mew

Find

There is no easy way to get back yourself. I hugged my body and the arms around me were this other man's, who was very cold and was also two shadows meeting. I felt sick and alive. What did James say to me on the cliff? Which James? Which cliff. Interior design cliff. Some beautiful image, they've made here, with the text underneath setting the tone of it all, cleverly so the consumer has to supply that little bit of hunger of their own. What time am I writing this from? You know I did not die. You think you know yourself and then. The ocean below a cliff at night's the fucking worst. It sings. Complete yourself with a final set of experiences: falling and drowning. If there's too many voices around you that are whispering and pulling, just pick definitively. The way down is the simplest and the quickest. I was thirsty, I was so tired. Have you ever been so tired, I wondered, looking at James. This James unravelled – loose – on a stone beside me, or sometimes nearer. He said: 'If you want to make gains, you should be eating more protein, ideally from a grass-fed source.' It seemed perfectly rational at the time. Daniel sat there, not looking at me. Did he know how far away I was? Black bubbles up my throat, the sting of it like there was already salt water flooding it. Pity is a kind of drowning. That feeling was the worst – that he had wanted me, and now I disgusted him, or something like that, so he wouldn't look to me. I knew I was in a state. I started touching my hair and feeling just sick – it was so greasy. I had done that. For some time I watched Minto or just my idea of Minto come creeping up behind Daniel, and I wanted to warn him he was going to be tossed downwards by the old menace. But I couldn't speak because I couldn't speak. The ties of Minto's dressing gown dragged along the ground – his old pale face was a hermit moon. He had thrown a man out of a window, right? Or furniture or something. Anyway his house was full of broken things; windows, musty books, men. If I was in charge of things I'd put him as a cartoon character, a sticker of a cartoon face, best for crisps or perhaps a start-up for a mystery book club.

With that actual bastard noise in my head the wind outside it was a comfort – actually some girl was away waving at me. Bitch, I thought, she wants something of me and I'm so tired. 'I don't want to help you. I'm exhausted,' I called. I'd been working in the stables all day and loving my master, who never looked at me, though James said, of course I did love you, in the way I could, which was not to look at you ever, to order you to saddle my horses and suck the splinters out my fingers and help me ditch the body. I disgusted myself with the sweat smell of horses which was me. How low I was in his eyes. He never wanted me, I realised. Someone did. I turned to see the woman again, across the darkness, a single light that hit me now on my arm, now on my face. I wondered at it – so precise and bright it couldn't be real. It couldn't be her that wanted me, could it? Had I failed her too? I was sure I must have. I failed her because I couldn't place her, at least not right then. I couldn't see that far. I was falling sick, I thought. I kicked out my foot to shake the pins and needles out of it, and a pinch of stones rolled off the edge of the world and I thought, dully, how simple it is to kick away even something so old and sturdy. Across the heath I saw figures in white – white gowns flapping, little white ruffles at the throats of the men, white cuffs, unbearably white – dancing to music that the wind swallowed. It was the turn of the year. I remembered it was November, and James had lived so far submerged in his unknowing that he would never see a real summer again – would have to invent it forever from these feeble materials. I saw my master dip his hand into my throat, through it, and hold there, as if warming his fingers in the stream of my living blood. Then I was really afraid. I put my head down and I cried, and a patch of light crept up my leg, small as a mouse. It seemed hopeful, then.

'Órla?' I said, licking salt off my lips, wiping my hair back off my head. 'What's going on?'

I looked around and saw I was sitting at the edge of a cliff. I got up and backed away. Órla came running towards me. Had she been here the whole time? Why had she let me just sit there? I was raw and cold right through to the bone. She gave me a piece of paper. I looked at it. I saw nothing on it. I saw words on it. Afraid of offending her, I gently let it go. It's for the best to be well rid of some things. To not take all that you're given. Just refuse to take it. Because you don't know how you'll take it, you don't know what you'll have to grow into to hold on to it. I shivered and she had me by the arm. She didn't seem to mind taking a piece of trash like me. We were going inside, back to the bothy. And I walked clumsily over the ground, thinking I'd left something behind. I kept turning to look. It was a man. He had my face, and he did not move. I felt so much love for him, and horror.

But inside there was the three of us. And the firelight expanded and throbbed through me, making me clean. Daniel washed my face with a cloth, and I let him, even when he was bad at it, and I wanted to adjust the pressure of it, to be more gentle with me. I let him go on until I was clean. Órla sprayed my hair and combed out the oils. I was theirs.

Us

How do we keep going?

We were going into the morning.

'I've been having such a hard time living lately,' Tom said.

'I know,' Daniel said.

'We know,' said Órla, helping Tom out of the blanket and into a second jumper.

Daniel held the copied toy by one of the narrow windows. Tom watched the curve of his back. Daniel was thinking, what shall we do with it?

'Let's bury it,' said Tom. The three went down to the shore. In weak, pearly daylight Tom knelt to dig a hole in the shallow sand. There wasn't enough to cover it.

'It'll never rot,' said Órla. We make a thing of lasting endurance, and then we try to forget it. But that is true of so much. Except of us, Daniel thought. After he was done, Tom straightened up and took Daniel's hand, and Órla's. The sea was low and still had the colour of night in it. The tide hadn't taken it out yet. Let us drop into one another like water. Let us go together for a while and make it home safe, Órla thought.

'You can't save anybody,' said Daniel, to himself, and to us.

'In the end, no,' thought Tom.

'No,' said Orla, 'but we will keep trying.'

Acknowledgements

This book would not have been possible without Douglas Dunbar, who means more to me than I can say. To all my friends and family who've kept me buoyed with their own works, recommendations and judicious comments. Particularly to my father, who is no longer here to read this one and call it 'good but strange'. Much of the sections on Codicology would not be possible without the colour and vibrancy brought to the discipline by Dr Johanna Green; thank you for speaking to me with such passion for your work. Thank you to Lucila Mantovani and Lourdina Rabieh of the Kaaysá Art Residency in Boiçucanga and Creative Scotland for supporting my writing. Immense thanks to my agent Jenny Brown, to Camilla Grudova for the books and friendship, and the wonderful Ali Smith for giving me a few encouraging words just when I needed them. Thank you to my editor Edward Crossan and the team at Polygon for keeping the book sailing on through difficult times.